THE BRASS
AND THE BLUE

**Center Point
Large Print**

**This Large Print Book carries the
Seal of Approval of N.A.V.H.**

THE BRASS AND THE BLUE

WILL COOK

CENTER POINT PUBLISHING
THORNDIKE, MAINE

Dedication: TO THEA—who makes life worth living

This Center Point Large Print edition
is published in the year 2004 by arrangement with
Golden West Literary Agency.

Copyright © 1956 by Will Cook.
Copyright © renewed 1984 by Theola G. Cook-Lewis.

All rights reserved.

The text of this Large Print edition is unabridged. In other
aspects, this book may vary from the original edition. Printed in
Thailand. Set in 16-point Times New Roman type.

ISBN 1-58547-507-6

Library of Congress Cataloging-in-Publication Data

Cook, Will.
    The brass and the blue / Will Cook.--Center Point large print ed.
        p. cm.
    ISBN 1-58547-507-6 (lib. bdg. : alk. paper)
    1. Large type books. I. Title.

PS3553.O5547B73 2004
813'.54--dc22

                                                                2004008724

. . . Time is drawing near so I write in haste, hoping you are well. Early this morning we marched to the depot five miles from the camp. It is now late afternoon; I think the waiting is the most difficult part of war. General Sheridan arrived on the early train. On the road behind the station the 9th Ohio are advancing with their machines of war. Great, black cannon; the rumble of caissons is deafening. Their dust obscures the sun. The corps commander keeps riding back and forth in front of the ranks. He is a small man, splendidly mounted, but one never notices that he is not tall; all of the officers seem tall after a while. There are two ranks, dear wife: the brass and the blue. . . .

1

FIRST LIEUTENANT TEMPLE JOCELYN REMOVED THE slender cigar from his lips to speak. "Mr. Schwabacker, inform Sergeant Finnegan that I wish to leave the post within the hour. I suggest double ammunition issue and rations for five days." Jocelyn's voice held the brittle twang of Vermont and the dogmatic surety of New England, characteristics which continually placed him at odds with men like Emil Schwabacker, who had not yet learned to conceal his uncertainties. Yet there was more to Jocelyn than this; Schwabacker felt it. Disappointment, perhaps, a forced withdrawal that left him misunderstood, apart from his fellow officers.

Jocelyn stood on the sutler's porch, his tall body inclined slightly, balanced against the gusty shove of the raw spring wind. He commanded a sweeping view of the frozen parade ground. A patch of snow lingered like a frosted doughnut around the flagpole, the thawing checked by a day-old cold snap.

Sentries stood in chilled discomfort along the palisade ramp, their cape-wrapped shoulders humped in silent protest against this unusual April weather.

"Do you anticipate action, sir?" Second Lieutenant Emil Schwabacker's manner was respectful, as it always was with Jocelyn, for the man did not invite familiarity; his very manner forbade it. Schwabacker was twenty-four, and two and a half years of frontier service had not seemed to dull his Academy riding-ring mannerisms.

7

Jocelyn said, "Mr. Schwabacker, again I impress upon you the necessity of preparedness. The duty here may be tedious and apparently without point, but I can assure you that our function is vital to the success of General Wessels' campaign at Fort Kearny." To preclude further discussion, he produced a hunting-case watch and glanced at it. "It's now a quarter after seven. You have less than an hour, Mr. Schwabacker."

"Yes, sir!" Lieutenant Emil Schwabacker wheeled and cut across the parade to the troop stables. Watching him, Jocelyn smiled, for there was an unmasked eagerness about Schwabacker that at times bordered on the amusing. Schwabacker had the habit of strutting when he walked, his body erect, arms stiff and swinging. Every time he said "yes, sir" he reminded Jocelyn of an affectionate puppy, insane with the desire to please.

When Schwabacker passed from sight, Jocelyn left the sutler's porch, crossing the southeast corner of the wind-scuffed parade toward the officers' picket quarters. He clutched his cape tightly and walked with his knees slightly bent. With his height, he was like a tree bending to the wind. Jocelyn was a spare man and as functional as an issue carbine. On his bony frame the cavalry uniform seemed almost dashing, for he had a manner of moving, a habit of immaculateness that lent charm to the brass and blue. His bones were hard foundations beneath a sun-darkened skin, and he gave the impression of a fine hunting dog who had been run too long. Jocelyn's eyes were gun-metal gray, containing a restrained humor, and an incalculable sadness.

In his own quarters he changed into uniform fatigues

and a pair of less polished but more comfortable boots. Dressed, he turned to his armament—pistol and repeating Spencer rifle with a leather case for spare magazine tubes. The pistol was a cap-and-ball Colt .44 Dragoon. Not as modern as his issue revolver, it was infinitely more ornate. Engraved from muzzle to backstrap, the pistol was the epitome of the gunmaker's art. Because of its size and weight, it required a special holster. Jocelyn held back the flap and slipped the revolver in place, but before he closed the leather over the bone handle, he tipped his head downward and read the engraved words on the backstrap: *God keep you . . . Evangeline.*

Jocelyn's expression softened, then he buttoned the flap and stepped out into the spring's blasting wind.

Sergeant Major Sean Finnegan was at the troop stables, a grizzled man with a fist-scarred face and a salute that bordered on the downright disrespectful. Fourteen years of mutual service lay between these men, and while Jocelyn's eyes conducted a brief inspection of the stable, Finnegan made a study of his commanding officer, for in this manner he learned much of Jocelyn's mood. Jocelyn had always given Finnegan the impression of grayness. He had dabs of gray at his temples and in his eyes, and perhaps some of it extended into the manner of his living, which no man questioned and which he explained to no one.

The matted clouds overhead chose to break then, and in a moment rain began to cascade from the roof extension over the stable archway. Finnegan swore beneath his breath. "Fine weather for a bottle of the sutler's best and a colleen, sor."

"I'd say the woman was extraneous, Finnegan." Jocelyn glanced through the stable and into the open yard beyond. Troopers pushed and cursed three pack mules into place and made a last-minute check of the equipment. After another glance at his watch, Jocelyn said, "Fifteen minutes, Sergeant."

"Aye, sor," Finnegan said in disgust. He was a square-faced man with an enormous mustache that dropped to his chin. His eyes were the shade of blue that reminded a man of some half-forgotten creek in boyhood, or the clarity of pond ice formed by a bone-cracking cold snap.

Second Lieutenant Emil Schwabacker came trotting across the parade, one hand gripping his saber to keep it from flailing his leg. He came up to Jocelyn as Finnegan went through the stable to form the troop.

Water dripped from Schwabacker's kepi visor and he brushed at the droplets clinging to his cape. "I'd give five years on the promotional roster to go on to Fort Kearny and Wessels' command," Schwabacker said.

Jocelyn smiled. "My first six years were served without action, Mr. Schwabacker."

"The galling part," Schwabacker said, "is to have history being made around you and yet be unable to participate in it."

"You are participating," Jocelyn said dryly. "Perhaps you are not mentioned in dispatches, or bleeding, but you have a job. See that you do it well, Mr. Schwabacker."

"Yes, sir."

Jocelyn then found several details that required his attention and went about his business with the same crisp efficiency that marked everything he did. Corporal Kykundahl's detail completed the ammunition drawing from the ordnance sergeant. Duty Sergeant McGruger finished battling the balky mules into line. Sergeant Major Finnegan's trained eye saw that every man was by his mount and ready.

He came forward with his report. "Ready, sor."

"Mount the troop informally," Jocelyn said and took the reins from the bugler. He stepped into the saddle and waited while his troop swung up. He turned and looked back at the double row of poncho-draped men. "Mr. Schwabacker, take the second section, please."

Another glance at his watch and he lifted his hand. The patrol left the stable yard, skirted the parade at a slow walk and at exactly eight o'clock passed through the gates to the dismal land beyond.

. . . *dismal land, dismal patrols* . . . This was Second Lieutenant Emil Schwabacker's thought. . . . *I've lost count during the past year. God, has it been that long? Another year of it and I'll be like the rest, not giving a damn. It has been a year since Colonel Henry B. Carrington came through with his seven hundred. A year of inaction. A year of waiting, a year of one dreary patrol after another. How many times have I promised myself I would transfer? A dozen?* . . . He looked at Temple Jocelyn at the column's head. *Two years of his infallible exactness, his cold reserve. How much can a man stand?* . . .

Through the rain-dulled morning the command

moved across rolling and densely brushed terrain. Patches of open ground appeared, running to tall grass bent by the pelting rain. The flatly swollen drops turned saddles soggy and drove the troopers from the knees of comfort to the very lap of misery.

During the noon stop, Lieutenant Jocelyn spoke to the bugler, a lad of sixteen. "Sound 'officers' call,' please."

The rain and vast reaches of this land swallowed up the bright tones of the "C" horn. Lieutenant Schwabacker came up from the second section at a gallop and flung off.

The expression on his face led Jocelyn to say, "I trust you'll excuse the unexpectedness of the horn, Mr. Schwabacker, and contrary to your present opinion, I haven't lost my senses. It seemed wise at the time to advertise our presence here." He pawed a bare hand across his face, brushing water to the point of his chin. "At this moment there is a company of infantry approaching Ryndlee's ranch buildings, so until dark we will proceed due east at the best possible rate of march. I'd like to swing south tomorrow morning. That will put me into Ryndlee's around supper time tomorrow night."

Sergeant Finnegan came up with a canteen of cold coffee and Temple Jocelyn had his drink, then handed the canteen back. Finnegan said, "Th' mail stage will be at Ryndlee's, sor."

"Yes," Jocelyn said softly. His glance lifted to Emil Schwabacker. "That should please you, Mister. I believe you have a fiancée back East."

"Yes, sir. Vermont, sir," said Schwabacker, surprised

12

at the introduction of a personal note into their hitherto formal relationship.

"Splendid," Jocelyn said. "I'm from Vermont."

Schwabacker waited a long moment while rain ran down his cheeks and into his collar. He had caught himself doing this before, waiting for Temple Jocelyn to speak, to add to the vast past he must have, but never revealed. Then Schwabacker realized that Jocelyn was not going to say more. He never would. "Sir," Schwabacker said, "if the bugler's call attracts the hostiles, do you mean to engage them?"

"Engage them, Mr. Schwabacker? I'd like nothing better, but my orders are firm: there will be no engagement unless we are attacked." He nodded slightly for Schwabacker to join him and walked a hundred yards in advance of the halted troop. His boots whispered as they brushed grass aside. Around them were many scuffs in the earth, and when Jocelyn pointed them out, Emil Schwabacker flayed himself for not noticing them. Somehow he felt that his lack of observation was a mark against him.

"Two shod ponies, Mr. Schwabacker. Do you attach any significance to that?"

"Army mounts, sir. Probably stolen."

Jocelyn waved his hand toward the distant smudge of land and sky. "They're out there, Mr. Schwabacker, and after a year of this cat-and-mouse game, I think I'd enjoy closing with them."

"We're only in troop strength, sir. There's no telling how large a force is out . . ."

"I'm familiar with the situation," Jocelyn interrupted.

"My orders are to patrol a given area and meet the infantry company when it arrives at Ryndlee's. If by coincidence I run into a hostile force and a fight is pressed upon me . . ."

"Oh, of course, sir! I didn't mean to imp . . ."

"I realize that," Jocelyn said and walked back to his horse. When he was in the saddle, he added, "And, Mr. Schwabacker, in the future, should the need arise to warp your commanding officer's orders slightly, do so in a manner that will preclude embarrassment." To Finnegan he said, "Mount the troop, Sergeant."

"Troop! Pre–pare to mount! MOUNT!"

Through the remainder of the day, Corporal Kykundahl rode at the point and Lieutenant Temple Jocelyn studied the drab land around him. He held the column to general march orders, halting fifteen minutes during each alternate hour to dismount and unbit for grazing. The pace was periodically altered to prevent bad posture and animal fatigue.

Late afternoon found them in land that was flattening with hock-deep grass. Corporal Kykundahl wheeled his horse and signaled. Jocelyn signaled Schwabacker forward and went to the point, the ever-present bugler following a pace behind. Kykundahl was dismounted and he opened his gloved hand, exposing a rattle made of buffalo toes. Jocelyn bent from the saddle and took it from him, turning it over several times. "What do you make of this, Corporal?"

"I'd say Kiowa, sir. I've seen plenty back home in Texas."

"Mr. Schwabacker?" Jocelyn handed it over.

. . . Another test? The damn man is always testing like a prunish schoolmaster . . . "Could be Comanche," Schwabacker said. "The Arapahoe, Cheyenne and Sioux make them too." He pointed to the carving on the rattle body. "That's Sioux work, sir."

"Sure looks like Kiowa to me," Kykundahl said again.

"Mr. Schwabacker has learned well, Corporal." Jocelyn took the rattle from Schwabacker and dropped it in his pocket. "Return to the point, Corporal, and keep your eyes open. We've been trailing a war party all afternoon and it would be uncomfortable if we got too close."

He wheeled his horse and rode back to the column with Schwabacker. Kykundahl went on, and when darkness began to close in, Jocelyn signaled a halt and they made a cold camp. To Sergeant Finnegan he said, "Picket, please, Sean, and I think a ground rope will do. Guard mounting in fifteen minutes and there'll be no squad fires."

Finnegan wheeled to his duties. Jocelyn spoke to Lieutenant Schwabacker. "I'd like to break camp around midnight, but before I go I want some brush fires started. If you dig up the dead stuff I believe it'll burn an hour. We'll need that much time."

"Time, sir?"

"Mr. Schwabacker, remember that when an officer finds himself outnumbered, he can do one of two things: retreat or call upon his originality." His smile softened his criticism. "Perhaps you observed me picking up objects this afternoon?"

. . . Another damned mark against me . . . "No, sir, I did not."

From beneath his poncho, Jocelyn produced a hardwood stick eight inches long. There were forty notches cut into two sides, and when he scraped it against his belt buckle it sounded like an alarmed rattler. "Rattlesnake stick," he said. "Cheyenne, and of the Elk Warrior society, if I'm not mistaken." He turned and called to Sergeant Finnegan. When he came up, Temple Jocelyn produced another trophy, the feathered end of a broken arrow. "Sean, you're a good man when it comes to Indians. Who does this belong to?"

Finnegan inspected the arrow, then said, "Sioux, sor."

"I picked that up less than a mile from the rattlesnake stick, and along the same line of march," Jocelyn said.

This caused a frown to corrugate Finnegan's forehead. "Cheyenne and Sioux together, sor?" He shrugged. "Possible, but up to now the Cheyenne's been stayin' out of Red Cloud's trouble."

Schwabacker stirred. "May I speak, sir?" Jocelyn nodded. "Sir, the tracks have been thinning out. The party we trail now is less than a quarter of the size it was this noon. I suspect a trick, sir."

"Ah," Jocelyn said. "Explain yourself, Mr. Schwabacker. I'm always interested in theories."

. . . *I ought to know better. He's done this to me enough times, pulled me in so he could show up my ignorance.* . . . "It's not the Indian's habit to leave such a defined trail, sir. I mean, the tracks, the rattlesnake stick, the arrow, the rattle. It's too plain, sir! Then there's the tracks thinning out. I'd say we were being circled, sir."

"Very commendable," Jocelyn said in a voice that told Schwabacker nothing. That was Jocelyn's way, to leave

16

a man wondering whether he was being laughed at or congratulated. Jocelyn looked around at the bivouac. Night was a blanket and the troopers were only vague shapes beneath their ponchos. "Perhaps this patrol will prove interesting after all. Now get some rest, Mr. Schwabacker. We have a long night ride ahead of us."

Schwabacker turned away. Corporal Kykundahl had his blankets and waterproof tarp spread and Schwabacker said, "I guess I'll never be able to tell whether he's laughing at me or not."

Kykundahl looked up quickly. "The lieutenant? He keeps his own council."

"It's his formality that gets me," Schwabacker said. "I'm an officer the same as he is, but he never calls me anything but 'mister.' He calls Finnegan by his first name, but I just can't get through to the man."

"Takes time, sir," Kykundahl said softly. "The lieutenant's got his problems, sir. Finnegan's been with him for years. That makes the difference."

"How long have you been with him, Corporal?"

"Five years, sir."

"God," Schwabacker said, "that's a long time to wait for a man to shake your hand."

"Aye, sir, but it's worth it where Lieutenant Jocelyn's concerned. He's a fine officer, sir."

"I know that," Schwabacker said, impatiently trying to make his point. "But I don't know him, Corporal. If someone asked me about him, what could I say?"

"That he's a fine officer," Kykundahl said. "That's all he wants you to say now, sir. A few years back it'd have been different, but not now."

"What do you know of him?"

Kykundahl shrugged. "That he was married. Had a son. His wife left him seven years ago."

"Why?"

"I wouldn't ask him, sir," Kykundahl said and went away, leaving Lieutenant Emil Schwabacker alone with his thoughts.

Jocelyn was rolled in his tarp and blanket, the poncho over his head. Schwabacker copied him, as he did in everything else, and lay there listening to the rain drum against his oilskins. He slept in fragments, waking often and at any slight sound. Finally he heard Jocelyn stir, and through a crack around the bottom of the tarp he saw a match flare as Jocelyn looked at his watch.

By the time Schwabacker got to his feet and rolled his blankets, Sergeant Finnegan had a crew gathering brush. The temperature had dropped and the rain carried a bone-numbing chill that made troopers flail their arms trying to induce circulation. Lieutenant Jocelyn was standing with his shoulders rounded in discomfort when Schwabacker joined him. This was a surprise, for Jocelyn was a man who showed nothing. Schwabacker had seen him drenched in a river fording, and then climb the bank on the other side impervious to the cold water. The sun could roast him and he would never raise his hand to mop away the sweat, and in this manner he created the distinct impression that he walked above the petty discomforts others endured under strong protest.

Finnegan was coming in with the brush detail. He had searched out the dead stuff, which was relatively dry. The piles grew as the two officers watched.

Schwabacker said, "That won't be much, sir."

"If it gives us an hour I'll be grateful," Jocelyn said. He motioned for Finnegan to come up. "Get the troop away from the area before mounting, Sean. Mr. Schwabacker and I will light the fires."

"Yes, sor," Finnegan said and began to form the troop.

"Still looking for action, Mr. Schwabacker?"

"Yes, sir. The sooner the better, sir."

"I think I can promise you that," Jocelyn said.

When Finnegan had the troop clear, Jocelyn and Schwabacker went around and ignited the four brush piles. As soon as the flare mounted they darted out of the circle of light and mounted their horses.

There were no more questions as Jocelyn led them east by southeast. Around three in the morning—Schwabacker had difficulty judging the time accurately—the rain slacked off a bit and the men rolled their ponchos. At five, Joceyn halted the troop and had them unbit for grazing. To Schwabacker he said, "We'll walk the rest of the way. I want every man alert."

And walk they did. The fresh sweet smell of rain gave way to the nitrogen of horses; the creak of leather and the rattle of carbine rings and bit chains laid a bold noise around the column.

Dawn rinsed away the night shortly after six and Jocelyn gave his close attention to the surrounding terrain. The promise of more rain was heavy; fat, swollen clouds made a gray curd of the sky and a spirited wind whipped them along.

Near seven, Schwabacker's alert ears picked up the muted pop of gunfire. A glance at Jocelyn assured him that he had heard it too. As a man, the troop lifted heads and eyes became widely alert.

Jocelyn spoke softly. "Mr. Schwabacker, it occurs to me that your suspicion of a trick is well founded. I'm going to mount the troop now and go into Ryndlee's at a gallop and under the horn. Pistols and sabers, Mr. Schwabacker. That's what you've been wanting; that's what you'll get. You'll command the second section and I want strict attention placed on the back trail. At the first sound of hostile pursuit, break away with twelve men and fight a delaying action."

"Yes, sir!"

"Curb your eagerness, Mr. Schwabacker. Please remember that this is not a maneuver on the Plain along the Hudson. They watched our camp last night, the sly devils, but I think our squad fires lured them into believing that we remained an hour longer than we did." He arched his back to relieve a stiffened muscle. "They intend to squeeze us, Mr. Schwabacker, and I intend to beat them at their own game."

A nod to Finnegan placed every man by his horse, ready to mount. Jocelyn put his foot in the stirrup. "I'm going straight through to Ryndlee's; no doubt the station is pinned down. As soon as my section breaks through, I'll sound 'recall.' Leave the holding action and come in at a gallop. We'll lay down a covering fire with the carbines."

"Very good, sir."

Jocelyn stripped off his gauntlets and offered his hand, the first direct overture of friendliness he had ever presented to Emil Schwabacker. In the distance a buffalo Sharps boomed and this was answered by a rattle of trade muskets. "The criterion of the cavalry is the charge, Mr. Schwabacker." He stepped into the saddle as another fusillade rattled in the distance. Jocelyn smiled as he added, "No doubt there will be a letter waiting from your fiancée, Mr. Schwabacker. Having once had a lady, I might urge you to discharge your duties most expediently, read her letter, then marry the girl and bring her to your post. Don't wait, Mr. Schwabacker. That's been fatal to many a man."

"Sir, I don't under . . ."

But Jocelyn had already turned to the young bugler, who sat his horse with the horn bell resting on his thigh. Finnegan had the troop mounted and waiting—forty-three hard-pratted regulars, fifty-cents-a-day dogface soldiers who listened to the struggle at Ryndlee's and knew what it meant.

Jocelyn spoke to the bugler. "Sound the 'charge' and put some spit into it. Mr. Schwabacker, strip romance from your mind and take command of your section, please."

2

LIEUTENANT EMIL SCHWABACKER WHEELED, BAWLING an order to Corporal Linahan, then the bugler split the vast silence with piercing notes and the command bolted into action. The road ranch was visible against the gray distance, a cluster of low sod buildings backed against the river. A mile separated them, yet every man saw the high shapes of the ambulance and the stage, the three abandoned escort wagons standing by the corral, and knew what that meant. Circling Ryndlee's, painted warriors strutted back and forth, occasionally shooting into the besieged buildings.

The column went in bent over the horses' necks, sabers and pistols drawn. Then Schwabacker saw the enemy coming up from the rear and suddenly wheeled to the right, turning about with his detail. Pistols cracked like brush fire and powder smoke was a drifting haze. Jocelyn pulled away, racing on with his men, while Schwabacker drove through in a plunging wedge, breaking the Cheyennes into milling segments. He led a daring charge that shocked the hostiles into momentary helplessness. This was not the way of the "long knives," to press an attack. Confusion came into their ranks and Schwabacker took advantage of it, going after them stirrup to stirrup, sabers whipping in the gray dawn light.

Close in now, Jocelyn could see clearly the hostiles that ringed Ryndlee's. There was no accurate way of judging the exact number; over fifty, he guessed. The bugler's blast had warned them and they wheeled to fight off Jocelyn's force. Trade muskets boomed, leaving puffs of dull smoke suspended for a moment before drifting with the wind.

The force closed to thirty yards, the new call of "commence firing" spilling from the bugle's bell. Jocelyn rode with dropped reins, saber poised, his engraved pistol recoiling against his palm. Powder smoke wafted back, rankly bitter, then the command was against the enemy, sabers drawn and drinking, pushing through, crushing the warriors who tried to block them. From Ryndlee's soddy a cheer floated up and the buffalo gun belched flame and smoke.

But Jocelyn did not make his charge without cost. A trooper rolled off his horse and went bouncing through the grass, a feathered ax imbedded in his back. Another reeled drunkenly, blood fountaining from his side. He fell forward to clutch the horse's neck. Trooper Gilcrest flung off his horse to be ground beneath trampling hooves.

Then they were in Ryndlee's yard, Jocelyn milling his troopers while the hostiles gathered themselves for a furious attack. "Dismount!" he shouted. "First squad! —Fire by volley! FIRE!"

This was his great fist, the heavy-caliber carbine, and he had been saving it for such a moment. Sergeant Finnegan's men were well trained, and while the hostiles poised for the thrust, the fire caught them, opening great gaps in the first ranks. At Jocelyn's command, the bugler blew "recall" for Schwabacker's benefit. Troopers rammed paper cartridges down the bores, seated lead bullets with wiping sticks, then capped their pieces while the second squad ripped into the Indians with volley fire.

A mile out on the flats, Second Lieutenant Emil Schwabacker was in the midst of a hot fight. When the bugle's clarion call ripped through the sounds of dying, he wheeled his section, gathered his wounded and began to race through, driving straight for the hostiles bunching again to storm Ryndlee's yard.

Jocelyn had three men down and he rallied the others.

When the Indians broke from flank attack to the circle, the troopers cut into them with individual fire, thinning the painted ranks again. Schwabacker was closing in now, shooting as he came on, and the hostiles were squeezed between the combined fires. Breaking through, Schwabacker wheeled his section to the rear of the soddy, cutting off a hostile flanking movement that had completely escaped Temple Jocelyn's attention.

Jocelyn's command had taken cover behind the stage and wagons and for a furious moment the battle teetered, then fell to the Army as the Indians backed out of range and waited.

"Cease fire" followed "recall," and Jocelyn went about the business of reorganizing his command. Four dead, six wounded; he had no accurate count of Schwabacker's losses. Jocelyn had the wounded carried into the road ranch.

Schwabacker came up, bleeding badly from an arm wound. He knew that he had performed gallantly, yet there was none of the braggart about him. His young face was darkened with powder residue and a splash of blood mottled one cheek. He saluted left-handedly and said, "A complete rout, sir."

"Not quite," Jocelyn said with customary dryness, "although I will certainly mention you in my dispatch for gallant action." He wiped his bloody saber in the dirt, then cleaned off what remained with gloved fingers before returning it to the scabbard. "Please observe, Mr. Schwabacker, that the hostiles remain in warlike numbers." He smiled thinly. "For the moment we've merely joined the besieged."

Sergeant McGruger and a detail hazed the horses into the stout corral behind the main building while Jocelyn walked around the yard, inspecting the shot-up stage and dead mules. From the position of the animals, he surmised that the Indians had killed them in harness while they stood in the yard. Both he and Schwabacker silently cursed the infantry commander for not caring for his mounts. This neglect had now reduced a heretofore clumsy force into complete immobility.

Near the wagons four infantry soldiers lay grotesquely postured in death. From their stiffness, Schwabacker guessed that they had died the night before. Schwabacker said, "Filthy mess here, sir." He had his blouse half off and was wrapping his neckerchief around his arm, tying it with his teeth and an awkward left hand.

"Help you there?"

"No, I've got it, sir." Schwabacker didn't have it but there was a core of pride in him that prevented him from admitting it.

Jocelyn summoned Sergeant Finnegan with a small hand motion. This always surprised Schwabacker and left him with the feeling that Finnegan must watch his commander like an obedient dog in order to catch these slight signals.

"Sergeant," Jocelyn was saying, "inspect the mail pouches. There may be a letter for me."

"Aye, sor." Finnegan wheeled away and a frown crossed Schwabacker's face like a shadow. How many times had he heard that? A hundred at least. Same tone, same buried hope beneath the flat twang of Jocelyn's voice. Did he actually expect a letter? From whom? His wife?

Finnegan came back. "Nothin', sor."

"Thank you, Sean. Perhaps on the next mail." He turned away and Finnegan handed Schwabacker a letter. As he took it he caught the lingering fragrance of sachet, and with it, a picture of candlelight, and soft music and gleaming shoulders. Schwabacker turned away and carefully opened the letter. Impatience urged him to rip apart the concealing paper, but remembrance of Henrietta Brubaker's innate gentility made such impetuousness seem improper.

He opened the note and read:

St. Albans, Vermont
April 9, 1867

My Dearest One:

Your wonderful letter of the 3rd instant is at hand and I hasten to reply. We enjoy good health here and the hard winter is leaving us. Dear Heart, we miss you and Pray for your speedy return. Last Wednesday your mother and sisters invited me to dinner. We had a pleasant time, talking about times past and about the time when you will return to stay. Please, do not think I fail to understand your choice of a military career instead of completing your medical studies. But you are so far away and your mother worries over your welfare, as I do.

Your father enjoys good health, although he approaches his sixtieth year, and I know he wants you to have his blessing, although he never men-

26

*tions your name, or allows it to be mentioned. It is
everyone's hope that time will soften his bitterness. . . .*

*I long to be with you, even in that Savage land.
Can you come back for me soon? It is my wish,
please believe me. We could be married in the
Grove Street Church. I miss you and think of you
constantly. God keep You and speed Your safe
return.*

Devotedly,

Henrietta

Schwabacker carefully folded the letter and slipped it
into his inner pocket. Jocelyn had strolled over to the
ambulance and was looking inside. Schwabacker joined
him and together they lifted a large leather trunk to the
ground. Jocelyn threw open the lid, then grunted in surprise when he discovered women's petticoats. Inspection of three other satchels revealed them filled with
women's clothes, and Jocelyn jerked his head around
when a feminine voice spoke from the door.

"Those are mine!"

They turned as one. Ryndlee appeared, a bear of a
man with dark, round eyes peering from beneath heavy
brows. He tried to take the woman's arm but she shook
him off and came toward the two officers. "I said those
things are mine. Please leave them alone."

She was a woman in her late thirties and beneath the
dirt on her face Emil Schwabacker detected the last ves-
tiges of beauty. She was tall, firm-bodied, and she gave
him a level look. Her eyes reminded him of a large

aquarium, a shimmering green, clear, yet fathomless. There was pain in her expression and a trace of fear pinched her lips. Blood had dried on one cheek and the bodice of her dress.

Temple Jocelyn bowed slightly; he had the height to do this gracefully. "My apologies, madam. Finding a woman here was a bit of a surprise. I'm Lieutenant Temple Jocelyn, commanding E Troop, 2nd United States Cavalry. May I present Mr. Schwabacker, my second in command."

Schwabacker swept off his kepi and bowed, his heels meeting like two blocks of wood. Even with his dirty face and wounded arm he was the epitome of gallantry, for in his manner there was a touch of Henry of Navarre at Ivry, Travis at the Alamo; the unconscious, forgivable swagger of men with unquestionable courage.

Sergeant Finnegan sidled up, eyeing the hostiles a few hundred yards away. "Shall I be movin' th' troop inside, sor?"

"Yes," Jocelyn said and took the woman by the arm. He turned her toward the door and she walked with the wooden steps of the nearly exhausted. Ryndlee closed the door after them, sliding the oak bar in place.

The main room was large, a combination dining room and bar. Along the base of the east wall, Jocelyn's wounded suffered in stubborn silence. Four more infantrymen lay with blankets covering them. "Died in th' night," Ryndlee said, stomping around, fretting like a woman who finds a strange dish in her cupboard.

From another part of the house a man moaned in a high, pain-pinched voice and the woman's eyes grew round and alarmed. She struck at Jocelyn's hand, then ran through a doorway. "Her husband," Ryndlee said. "Pretty bad off. He lost all his men."

Schwabacker looked around as a disheveled second lieutenant of Infantry appeared in the doorway letting out into the back. He was very young and, from his manner, very frightened. He saw Jocelyn and the solitary shoulder bar and came to a flaccid attention. "Lieutenant Eastwood, sir." He stopped talking and stared blankly.

Eastwood was tall, a little over six feet. His hair was a dirty blond, rumped now, for he had lost his kepi somewhere. His eyes were blue and watery and strain showed sharp and clear in the planes of his cheeks.

"How many men have you, Mr. Eastwood?" Jocelyn asked.

"No—none, sir."

Fires of temper and outrage flared in Jocelyn's eyes. "Mr. Eastwood, no officer ever loses all of his command!" Then he saw that Eastwood had, or someone had. "Mr. Schwabacker, see what you can do for the wounded officer." His hot glance condemned Eastwood. "Stay out of the way; that's an order!"

He had turned to Sergeant McGruger. "Man the openings with three squads; they'll come in after us. Finnegan, see what you can do for the wounded. There's laudanum in my saddlebag. Detail several men to fetch water and rations off the pack mules. We'll be here for a while."

The troopers took their places by the slots cut into the walls. They thrust the snouts of their carbines through and waited for the hostiles to close again. Out on the flats a wild singing awoke and Emil Schwabacker observed the celebration briefly through a window. He had been on the frontier long enough to recognize the sound and watched stone-faced as the hands and feet were hacked off the dead he had been forced to leave behind. The rising moan from the rear of the house, coupled with Lieutenant Eastwood's impatient presence, reminded Schwabacker of his duty and he went through the door and down a narrow hallway. In the end room a man lay on the bed, his eyes sunken and pain-dulled. His cheeks were without color and his right arm was swathed in bloody cloth, the elbow hopelessly shattered.

The woman whipped her head around as Schwabacker entered. She said, "God, can't you do something?"

The man was an officer, a captain of Infantry. Schwabacker peeled back the shredded sleeve and made a minute examination. The soft lead ball had done terrible damage, for the arm was half amputated.

He stood up and looked from the woman to Lieutenant Eastwood. "That arm has to come off," he said. "When did this happen?"

"Yesterday afternoon," Eastwood said. "A mile from here. Why did it have to happen? That's what I want to know—why?"

"For some things there are no answers," Schwabacker said and went to the door. "Corporal Linahan, on the double here!" He turned back to the woman. "Your husband, madam?"

She nodded. "This was his first assignment on the frontier. He wanted action so badly." Tears spilled over her bottom lids, rinsing streaks in the dirt on her cheeks.

Bending over the captain, Emil Schwabacker saw a semblance of recognition in his fever-glazed eyes. "Sir, can you hear me, sir?"

The man nodded weakly.

Linahan came in, a bandy-legged man with his hat tipped forward over his eyes. Schwabacker straightened and began to unbutton the captain's shirt. "Mike, I'll need all the clean cloth you can find. I'll have to suture; see what you can scrape up that's sinew."

"That fool Ryndlee's got a fiddle, sor."

"Bring me the strings and a pan of hot water to soak them in," Schwabacker said. "We'll need at least two buckets of hot water and a bucket of flour. Ask Lieutenant Jocelyn for some laudanum."

"Gone, sor. Th' last was given to Trooper Bush for his leg."

Schwabacker bit his lips. "We'll need something to smother the shock, Mike. Get a quart of Ryndlee's strongest whiskey and a straight razor."

"Aye, sor." Linahan turned away, stopping when Schwabacker spoke again.

"And, Mike, pick four strong lads to hold him." After Linahan went away, Schwabacker turned to the woman. "You'd better leave, madam."

"I don't want to leave."

"You can't stay," he said. "A woman shouldn't see this."

"I'm not afraid of what's to come," she said. She

looked squarely at Lieutenant Eastwood. "He's afraid."

Color darkened Eastwood's face and he clenched his jaws tightly to hold back hot words of protest. He spoke to Emil Schwabacker. "Can you amputate? Do you know how?"

"I know how."

Eastwood dredged up a cynical smile. "He wouldn't do it for you if he were in your place."

Jocelyn's sudden command to fire was a shock, followed by the rocking blast of twenty-five carbines. Schwabacker moved so he could see out the small window. The Indians were riding back and forth at a hundred yards, waving brightly colored lances and rifles, while a half-dozen riderless ponies trotted away. Corporal Linahan returned with four burly troopers and plenty of hot water.

The woman stopped weeping and stood there, brushing away tears with the back of her hand.

"I'm sorry," she said. "He's Captain Nathan Kincaid, in case he . . ."

Schwabacker spoke impatiently. "Mike, get her out of here!"

The corporal reached for her, but she whirled away, stopping flat against the wall. "Please, can't you see that I have to stay? I owe him that!"

He could make no sense of her words and did not try to fit meaning to them. He bent over Captain Kincaid and said, "Can you hear me, sir?"

A slight nod, a pale smile.

"The arm has to come off, sir."

Kincaid nodded again. "My . . . wife?" He lifted a

feeble hand and his wife was at his side, bending over him. With an effort he focused his attention on her. "Lydia, forgive me. The mistake was . . . mine."

"No, Nathan," she said quickly. "You'll recover; I know you will. We'll have a new start. I'll make it work out for us."

"A nice . . . dream. But then . . . all dreams are nice."

Schwabacker took her by the shoulders and pulled her away. She stood by the head of the pole bed, her knuckles white as she steadied herself. Folded sheets were made into a pad and slipped under the shattered arm. The slightest movement caused Kincaid unspeakable agony and his lips bled freely from the clamping force of his teeth. Lieutenant Eastwood pressed close, intent on helping, but Schwabacker's "Get out of the way!" sent him back against the wall. Corporal Linahan laid out the instruments, a razor-sharp knife, Ryndlee's straight razor, a curved harness needle, the bucket of flour and the pan containing the violin strings.

"I need a light in here," Schwabacker said and one of the troopers left, returning with a lighted lamp. Schwabacker's arm was giving him pain and he began to lose his grip. He massaged it above the wound and hoped it would last until this job was done. Handing the lamp to Mrs. Kincaid, he thought for a moment that she was not going to take it. Then she gripped the glass base with both hands and held it without trembling.

While Schwabacker made final preparations, the troopers poured whiskey into the captain. He had a capacity for it and nearly a half-hour passed before he began to get drunk. By continually sponging the wound,

Schwabacker could make his last examination. He drew Corporal Linahan close. "You can see where the wall of the artery is nearly burst through. When I ligature that after removal of the arm, the pressure is liable to break through there. I want you to apply pressure under his arm to close off the worst of the bleeding so I can suture. Do you understand, Mike?"

"Aye, sor. You're the doctor."

At Schwabacker's nod the four troopers seized the captain by the shoulders and legs. With the razor, Schwabacker made his incision deep and quick. In spite of the whiskey and the weight holding Kincaid's body, it bent into a bow and his scream filled the room. It soaked into the walls like a stain and lingered after he had fainted.

Blood fountained, soaking Schwabacker's arms to the elbows. Some struck the hot lamp chimney and shattered it. The flame flickered and then began to smoke, but Mrs. Kincaid stood there holding it, unaware that it had broken. Eastwood turned away, vomiting, while Schwabacker's nimble fingers made his first closure.

The shattered bones saved sawing, and when the artery burst, Linahan threw a strangling grip on the pressure point. For fifteen minutes Emil Schwabacker dredged up his training, cauterized, made his closing flap, sutured and fabricated a drain out of a celluloid collar. He completed his bandage and then stood up, sweat dripping off his nose. The lamp broke as it struck the floor and he turned in time to catch Lydia Kincaid before she slid after it. The spreading coal oil burst into flame, but the troopers doused it with water and flour.

At his nod, one of the troopers took her while he plunged his arms in a water bucket, rinsing away the blood. By the wall, Eastwood stood pale-faced, ashamed of his weakness.

Schwabacker found Ryndlee in the hallway, his face anxious. Without speaking, Schwabacker turned back into the captain's room, took Mrs. Kincaid from the trooper's arms and carried her down the hall to another room. Ryndlee followed with his prattling voice. "Don't put her in there! That's my room. God, you wreck a man's fiddle, ruin his razor . . ."

"Shut up and get out," Schwabacker said without heat, without care. He placed Lydia on the bed, and when Ryndlee's face grew stubborn, Schwabacker propelled him into the hall with a shove, closing the door after him. Returning to Captain Kincaid's room, he found the man's breathing labored and his face ashen. One of the troopers had the amputated arm wrapped in a rag. He took it out of the room.

"Better get this cleaned up," Schwabacker said, pointing to the blood-splattered floor. He looked at Eastwood and said, "What good are you anyway, Mister?"

"I . . . I don't have to take that, sir," Eastwood said.

"Then do something about it," Schwabacker said. He looked and felt like a man ready to fight. His arm was a flaming fury and the last hour had been a severe drain on him, not so much physically as mentally, dragging up all the things he was in the army to forget. Schwabacker could see that Lieutenant Eastwood was not going to do anything. He said, "If you can shoot a rifle, then get out there with the other soldiers."

Eastwood left, his face stiffly angry. Schwabacker turned to the door as Sergeant Major Finnegan came up. "Can you step out here a minute, sor?" Finnegan's forehead was worry-wrinkled, his voice gravelly with worry. Schwabacker stepped into the hallway. "Sor, Lieutenant Jocelyn caught a bad one that last round."

Command! Command at last . . . The inner voice was a shout, a whoop of immense joy. Long afterward Emil Schwabacker would feel shame for this thought, but in that moment he could not help himself. He was alone at last, in command of a troop and a desperate situation. If there was anything in him, it was bound to come out, good or bad, and a man had to know. He could not live without knowing.

He found voice. "Bad? How bad?"

"I don't know, sor," Finnegan said. "Mike speaks like you was a doctor, sor, judgin' from th' way you worked on th' captain. It's in his chest, sor. High, but he's blowin' blood with every breath."

"Jesus God!" Schwabacker said. He pushed past Finnegan and went into the main room. A gathering of troopers around Temple Jocelyn parted when he knelt down. Jocelyn was conscious, but in deep pain.

He said, "You're in . . . command, Mister. Now we find . . . out what you . . . are. A soldier or a . . . parade-ground dandy."

Linahan was there. He said, "You got to do somethin', sor!"

"Keep him in a sitting position," Schwabacker said. "Strip off his shirt." Jocelyn made feeble protest, but

36

Schwabacker would have none of it. He examined the wound carefully, noting that there was no exit hole. The lead was still in him. There was a fragment of torn metal in the wound and Schwabacker removed this. In Jocelyn's shirt pocket he found the cause, a daguerreotype of a young woman holding an infant in her arms. The bullet had passed through it, bending it badly.

Schwabacker stood up. "Mike, I'll need a stout wire with a hook bent into the end. Sharpen it if you can, and bring another lamp here. We'll have to sterilize it in the flame."

"Aye, sor."

While Linahan went about his business, Schwabacker saw to a dozen details of defense. All the while Temple Jocelyn watched him with pain-dimmed eyes, like an exacting schoolmaster, mentally tabulating his errors for some future accounting.

Schwabacker's arm was a bough of pain and he walked with it cradled against his stomach. The warrior's knife had sliced the length of the forearm. He could recall the feel of the knife point raking bone; this was his only distinct impression of the whole fight. The rest was a mud-gray haze in the inner recesses of his mind.

To get away from his own misery, he thought of Lydia Kincaid. Being a man who had lived a genteel existence, he believed that no woman should be subjected to this kind of life; he considered the captain seven kinds of a fool for bringing her along.

Linahan came back with his homemade probe. Schwabacker looked at it, then flashed this rough

Irishman a quick smile of appreciation. "More water, cloth. You know what, Mike."

"Aye, sor."

Temple Jocelyn had the question in his eyes when Emil Schwabacker knelt again. "Are you a . . . surgeon now, Mr. Schwabacker?"

"I would have been," Schwabacker said bluntly. "I had seven months to go before graduation."

"A man of . . . hidden talents." Jocelyn panted heavily and sweat bathed his face.

The man's indifference galled Schwabacker. He said, "It seems that we're all hiding something, sir."

Jocelyn did not take whiskey to ease the pain. He made few sounds, save the agonized sawing of his breath. Sweat came out of every pore, and when Schwabacker dropped the lead ball into the pan of pink water, Jocelyn was too weak to open his eyes.

Leaving the bandaging to Corporal Linahan, Schwabacker drew Sergeant Finnegan to one side. "You've been his sergeant fourteen years, isn't that right?"

"Aye, sor."

"Then you know a lot about him."

"That's right, sor. All there is to know."

Schwabacker drew a deep breath because he felt slightly dizzy. The pain in his arm was numbing. "Sergeant, I'll give it to you straight. You heard what I said to the lieutenant; I was once nearly a doctor, so I know what I'm talking about. He may die. So I want to know about him." He took the battered tintype from his pocket. "I want to know about her."

"The lieutenant keeps that to himself, sor."

"You're lying," Schwabacker said flatly. "Sergeant, don't you think she'd want to know?"

Finnegan pawed his face out of shape. "I guess, sor." He glanced at Jocelyn, who sat propped between two troopers, his head tipped forward on his chest. "They met before th' war, sor. A real Southern beauty. Proud she was. One of the Fawnstock women from Richmond." He smiled, finding remembering pleasant. "He was different in them days, sor. Always laughin' he was. When the states began to secede, th' feelin' was a bit high, sor. Like I said, she was a real Southern aristocrat. Th' war broke 'em both apart, sor, but I think they could have forgot that exceptin' for her brother. The lieutenant caught him one night past th' Union picket lines, sor. Cap'n Fawnstock was in civilian clothes."

Schwabacker's shock was intense. "You mean—?"

"Aye, sor. Th' lieutenant commanded th' firin' squad."

"God! What a thing for a man to carry."

"What I've said is for you alone, sor," Finnegan said. "If he lives and I ever hear you speak of it, I'd have to kill you, sor." He spoke without heat, a flat, positive statement that rang true.

Somehow Emil Schwabacker was not offended. He touched Finnegan on the shoulder briefly. "I understand, Sergeant. Is that why he watches the mail? Because he thinks she'll write?"

"Aye, sor. The lieutenant's written every week for seven years an' never got an answer, sor. If he lives, he'll write every week until he dies, or until he gets an answer."

"Thank you, Sergeant." Schwabacker turned away and met Sergeant McGruger coming up.

"It's possible to go outside, sir. Cassidy and a couple of the others have been doin' some long-range sniping and they've shoved the Indians out to about four hundred yards."

"Excellent. Get a five-man detail together and tend to the mounts." He turned, composed, in complete command of himself. The pain in his body was a detached pain and he found he could endure it. He looked at Lieutenant Jocelyn and found the tall officer conscious.

Sergeant McGruger said, "How long are we staying, sir?"

"I think we'll take our chances late this evening," Schwabacker said. He caught sight of Lieutenant Eastwood in the hallway leading to Lydia Kincaid's room. The man's idleness, his apparent indecision irked Schwabacker. "Sergeant, take the lieutenant with you outside, but he is not in command."

"I understand, sir."

As McGruger moved away, Lydia Kincaid came to the doorway. "I think I can be of some use," she said. She was running on nerve alone, he decided. . . . *What the hell, so am I. . . .*

"Do what you want," he said.

She moved past him and dropped to her knees beside trooper Hotchkiss, who bled from a thigh wound. Like most men who live for a time in a womanless world, Hotchkiss was embarrassed by this attention.

Corporal Mike Linahan, who had been with Schwabacker since his frontier assignment, hovered like a fretting hen. "Can I tend to that arm, sor?"

He wanted to let him, but he could feel Temple Jocelyn's judging eyes boring into his back, measuring him now as he had always measured him. Lieutenant Schwabacker said, "Forget it, Corporal. Go see what you can do for the lieutenant."

He felt a little silly after he said it.

3

AT NOON JACK RYNDLEE WENT INTO THE KITCHEN AND made ten gallons of stew, which was ladled into mess kits. Schwabacker had been alternating his time between Captain Kincaid and an observation post he had established in Ryndlee's attic. Plainly the hostiles were settling down for a siege; a fire was visible and they were gathering around it, eating, gesturing often toward the road ranch.

Under Schwabacker's guidance, Corporal Linahan proved his value as a surgeon's assistant when he sutured Schwabacker's arm and bandaged it. With the laudanum used up, Schwabacker could only sit back with his pain and put up with it. He lessened it by telling himself that Jocelyn and Captain Kincaid had suffered infinitely more. Corporal Linahan left the attic to get Schwabacker a plate of stew. He came back and the young lieutenant balanced it on his knees.

While Schwabacker ate, Linahan looked out at the hostiles. Finally he turned back and said, "Damned near two years now they've been content to watch us. Now they attack. You got any idea why, sor?"

"We're at war with them," Schwabacker said. He shook his head. "I'm not a general, Mike. I don't know the answers. Things have a way of passing me up. The important things, anyway."

Linahan leaned back against the wall. His voice was softly slurred. "I been at Laramie nearly ten years, sor. Seen a heap of Injuns there; Cheyennes, Arapahoe, Kiowa; you name 'em, I've seen 'em. This is Spotted Tail's bunch, sor. Up to now he's been a peaceful Cheyenne. It don't figure, him startin' trouble this far east on the Bozeman Road, sor. Not with Laramie only a day's march west."

"Figure or not, you've got trouble now," Schwabacker said.

Steps on the ladder brought their attention around and Lydia Kincaid settled in the loft. She smoothed her dirt-spotted dress over her legs and sat down across from Emil Schwabacker, her head bent to one side to clear the roof joists. Corporal Linahan excused himself, and when he had gone, she said, "I want to thank you for what you did for Nathan."

"We'll get him out of here tonight," Schwabacker said.

"Is that possible?"

He shrugged. "Both your husband and Lieutenant Jocelyn need hospitalization. The nearest is a good day's march from here. So it becomes not a matter of can I move them; I must move them, and soon."

"My husband's suffering terribly from shock. Will he die?"

"Not if I can get him to Laramie," Schwabacker said.

42

"If is a big word, Lieutenant. I've heard it enough to know."

He sighed. "Corporal Linahan will rig a litter in the ambulance." He studied her. She was holding herself in; she had the will and courage to do it, too. But then he received the distinct impression that this was a long habit with her, that her disappointments had been many. Impulsively he touched her hand. "Mrs. Kincaid, the army takes good care of its soldiers. We'll get him to the post safely."

"Yes," she said softly, "I believe you will. I saw your holding action, Mr. Schwabacker. Very impetuous and very brave."

"Desperate is the word," he said, revealing to her a fragment of his uncertainties, his doubts. He wondered if all command was this heavy on a man's shoulders, and if it was, where he would get the strength to bear up under thirty-five years of it.

Late in the afternoon the rain began again, one of those languorous rains with no wind behind it, so that the droplets seemed to float down, turning the horizon to a slate-gray smudge. Lieutenant Schwabacker studied the Indians through the downstairs window. Actually he had a better position of observation in the attic, but he felt a pressing need to show Lieutenant Jocelyn that he was not hiding. Jocelyn still sat against the wall, a bloody bandage binding his chest. His eyes followed Schwabacker's every move. Schwabacker could remember distinctly how his father would watch him like that, even when he was a child, as though he

43

expected some heretofore hidden flaw to appear suddenly and was afraid he would miss it.

Schwabacker brought himself up with a start, for never before had he consciously noticed the similarity between Temple Jocelyn's eyes and those of his father. To get away he turned and went into Captain Kincaid's room for a look. In spite of the whiskey-induced stupor, Kincaid was suffering terrible agony. His pulse was rapid, his breathing shallow and he perspired freely, although shaking as though he had chills. Schwabacker stood there, recognizing the symptoms of shock, yet unable to help the man. If he only had some laudanum . . .

Lieutenant Matthew Eastwood came in. He said, "He looks bad." Eastwood had found water and washed his face. His hair was still damp from the recent slicking and his mustache was neatly arranged. For a reason beyond his understanding, Schwabacker could find offense in Eastwood.

"Mr. Eastwood, how long have you been in the army?"

"One dismal year, give or take a few months."

Schwabacker brought out his black book; it was his now that Jocelyn was unable to command. Schwabacker wrote that down. "Now, Mr. Eastwood, I would like the particulars of Captain Kincaid's engagement with Spotted Tail's Cheyennes."

Eastwood shrugged. "They caught us on open ground and opened fire before he could deploy. The captain decided to make a run for it." He cocked his head to one side. "Did you ever see infantry run from a mounted force?"

44

"I'll make the necessary inquiries," Schwabacker said flatly. "Mr. Eastwood, please recount any constructive action you displayed during this engagement."

"I wasn't in command," Eastwood said. "I'll say that at Captain Kincaid's court-martial. I take orders just like you do." He fished a cigar out of his blouse pocket and put a match to it. "Stop acting like the important man with me. When the time comes to command, I'll command, not show my tail." He turned to the door. "It'll be interesting to see whether you can get us out of here or not. Personally, I don't think you cavalry boys are as good as you think you are."

For several minutes after Eastwood went out, Schwabacker concentrated on controlling his temper. Finally he returned to the main room and spoke to Sergeant Finnegan. "I believe it's time to trick Spotted Tail, Sergeant. Take three men in the yard and hitch the mounts to the stage and wagons."

"Yes, sor," Finnegan said, turning. He took two steps before halting and turning back. "Hitch them, sor? They won't take harness, sor."

"Nonsense," Schwabacker said, smiling slightly. "You have a way with animals, Finnegan."

"If you say so, sor." He glanced at Jocelyn as if in apology, then went out.

Sergeant McGruger was crouched against the south wall and Schwabacker motioned for him to come over. "We'll have to have a hanging litter for the captain, Sergeant. Lieutenant Jocelyn can be tied to his horse." At McGruger's frown, Schwabacker explained: "I believe I know the lieutenant's pride; he'd have to be

45

dead before he'd permit himself to be hauled in a wagon."

"Yes, sir."

"After you rig the litter, I want the troop moved into the yard and into the wagons one at a time. It is important that the Indians do not see you. This can be accomplished by placing the wagons in a tight row, thereby hiding your movements."

"I understand, sir," McGruger said. "You want to move out while they think we remain in force."

"Precisely," Schwabacker said. "They'll no doubt attack the wagons, thinking they're empty, but I believe a surprise raking with volley fire will discourage them."

After McGruger left, Schwabacker opened the side door and stood there, watching the four men in the yard. He saw that Jocelyn's head was turned, his eyes still intent on him. On impulse he knelt and asked, "How are you, sir?"

"Better than . . . I expected to be. You're a good . . . doctor, Mr. Schwabacker." He found strength for a smile. "I couldn't help . . . overhearing. A bold plan. If they want . . . to crush you, a volley . . . won't stop them."

"That's a chance I have to take," Schwabacker said. "Do you approve, sir?"

"Your decision . . . Mr. Schwabacker." Jocelyn paused to saw for wind. "When you command . . . seek advice from . . . no man. Command is an . . . island. A lonely . . . island."

For a moment Second Lieutenant Emil Schwabacker could not understand this man, then he did, fully.

Temple Jocelyn would not offer advice. He was forcing Schwabacker to stand alone or fall, and if he fell, Jocelyn was the kind who would let him lie. A hard school, Schwabacker decided, but no harder than that of his father, who neither understood nor tolerated weakness in anything.

Jake Ryndlee came up, his face wrinkled with worry. "What's goin' to happen to me?"

"I'd advise you to come along."

"They'll burn my place," Ryndlee said. "Never had trouble with th' Injuns 'til th' army started messin' around th' Bozeman Road." He jerked his thumb toward Kincaid's room. "That sojer boy thought he'd march right through 'em. Look at him now."

"How is it that you're alone here?"

"Injuns ran off my horses a day or two back. My help went after 'em." He paused to scratch his whiskered face. "That damn General Wessels at Fort Kearny's been keepin' Red Cloud stirred up. They get all riled and folks like me's got to pay for it."

"There are eleven dead soldiers here who paid for it," Schwabacker said. "Get your valuables together and get into one of the wagons with the others."

"I could take my chances here," Ryndlee said stoutly. "I don't like for th' army to order me around."

"Mr. Ryndlee," Schwabacker said crisply, "if you're asking to be knocked down and carried out, that can be arranged with very little trouble." . . . *Good God, I even sound like Jocelyn now.* The honesty of the thought was a shock, but he let none of it carry through to his expression. In that moment he could see how much originality

47

he lacked; how much he copied those he admired. First his father, and now Temple Jocelyn.

The two men stared at each other, then Ryndlee said, "I guess I'd better throw together my possibles." He turned and went into the back rooms.

With the litter rigged, one escort wagon was pushed to the barn, where hay was strewn on the floor for the wounded enlisted men. Lieutenant Schwabacker went out to help the troopers fight the insulted horses into harness. Schwabacker's arm bothered him considerably and he swore at the handicap. Finally the teams were waiting and a strong trooper stood at each horse's head, talking in low tones to calm it.

The Indians paraded back and forth, savage and patient, watching every move that was made in the yard. They had come in on foot and had taken away their dead. Tonight the Cheyennes would be erecting burial scaffolds where prying eyes could not see them.

Darkness was an hour away when Sergeant Finnegan said, "Ready, sor. Th' wounded's aboard, 'ceptin' th' capt'n and his missus."

"Well done, Sergeant. Have Lieutenant Jocelyn brought out and tied to his horse."

This was a pain-infested interlude for Jocelyn and when the troopers finished knotting the ropes around his ankles he leaned forward on the horse's neck, breathless from pain. Schwabacker said, "Get McGruger and we'll take Captain Kincaid to the ambulance." He went into the back room the captain shared with his agony.

Mrs. Kincaid raised her head when he entered. Darkness was like thick smoke in the room. She said, "Mr.

Schwabacker, I'm frightened for him."

McGruger came in with Finnegan. "I think we can carry him in th' blanket, sor," Finnegan said. "Be careful, Mac. Don't bang that arm now."

When they lifted Kincaid, pain ate through the whiskey stupor and engraved lines in his face. He cried out in a loud voice. Gently they carried him to the waiting ambulance. The troopers hiding inside helped lift him to the sling litter suspended from the top cross members. Ryndlee came out last, a sack on one shoulder and a Henry repeating rifle sagging in the crook of his arm.

There was a flurry of activity out on the flats as the hostiles gathered to engage Schwabacker's wagons. Schwabacker urged Mrs. Kincaid into the ambulance, then mounted his horse, which the bugler led from the barn. Jocelyn was still tipped forward in the saddle, his head resting on the horse's mane. The command mounted—those who had been chosen to be in sight— and Schwabacker gave the hand signal to move out. Without haste they vacated Ryndlee's yard, and although he set this slack pace, Schwabacker found it drawing his nerves as tight as a dulcimer string.

The Indians broke away from their former position and one segment cut around to the rear of the moving column, finally drawing up in a line a hundred yards to the left. The remaining hostiles paralleled the troop on the right, keeping the same distance.

After a nerve-smashing mile of this, Schwabacker said, "Why don't they come in and get it over with?" He had a button on his blouse undone and rode with

49

his hand tucked into the opening.

Sergeant Finnegan, riding close on Schwabacker's right, said, "They haven't figured it out yet, sor. Be dark in another twenty minutes. If they're goin' to close, they'll do it before then. They don't like to fight at night without special medicine."

Swinging around in the saddle, Emil Schwabacker looked back at the closely bunched wagons. Troopers drove with their carbines across their knees, splitting their attention between team handling and the pacing Indians. The bulk of the command was in the wagons, completely hidden.

An officer, Schwabacker reminded himself, was supposed to draw conclusions, and he put his mind to this task. After a year of constant patrol in this area he had observed many things, most particularly the Indians, who always seemed to be moving about, but had never before been actively hostile. This attack on Ryndlee's was not a spur-of-the-moment result of some medicine man's preaching; careful planning was evident in the running off of Ryndlee's spare horses, which in turn drew the help away from the road ranch. And then there was the matter of organized intelligence; the Cheyenne had known an infantry company was marching toward Fort Laramie. And they had stopped it completely.

The conclusion was not hard to reach: Red Cloud had at last succeeded in uniting the Cheyenne and the Sioux for the all-out push against General Wessels and Fort Phil Kearny along the Bozeman Road. The winter sniping offensive was over now. Colonel Henry B. Carrington had been relieved of his Kearny command and

50

the bungled campaign solidified by Wessels' genius for command. Red Cloud would understand that the time was here to rise or fall. Closing off Wessels' supply line woud be the first logical step.

Sergeant Finnegan must have been thinking the same thing, for he said, "Sor, General Wessels's goin' to be in for a divvil of a time if this road is closed off." He gnawed off a chew of plug tobacco. "Wessels must be pressin' Red Cloud pretty hard at Kearny, sor. We're feelin' th' pinch two hundred miles away."

"I'm not concerned about our feeling it, Sergeant. Think of what'll happen to Wessels' command if the Bozeman Road *is* closed off."

"Aye," Finnegan said. "Them poor divvils at Kearny, sor." He paused to chew his tobacco and look around. The hostiles still paced the moving wagons—same distance, same threat. "Aye, sor, things'll be bad along th' Bozeman, but right now they're bad for us, sor."

Schwabacker didn't want to talk about it; he was trying not to think too much about it, for the next few minutes could hold death for the contingent. "Better see how Lieutenant Jocelyn's coming along, Sergeant."

"Aye, sor," Finnegan wheeled his horse and reined inside the lead rope held by the bugler.

Schwabacker tried to relax to the motion of the horse, ticking off the passing minutes in his mind. He moved his wounded arm to a more comfortable position, and when he did, his fingers brushed Henrietta Brubaker's letter, making a fresh, crisp sound.

Her beauty was something he could never quite get over, that and the fact that she loved him. At times, when he examined himself critically, he could not understand how this could be. She had a heart-shaped face framed in dark hair and she was looking down the path. When she saw him, she smiled, but the change was greater than that. It always seemed to him—and he was sure that he imagined it—that her life suddenly took on purpose at the sight of him. An animation came into her eyes and her manner was yearning, reaching out to him with her mind and her love. He heard the letter wrinkle in his pocket and was sure she heard it. They kissed, her lips speaking silently to him. Then he stepped away and said, "Henrietta, I have something to tell you."

She did not seem surprised, but unerringly placed her hand flat against his chest, covering the letter. "I think I know, Emil. This changes nothing."

"How could you know?" he asked. He withdrew the letter. "Do you want to read it? I've been appointed to the Military Academy at West Point."

She shook her head and her ringlets stirred. "Is it so important that you get away from him?"

"Yes," he said. "As long as I'm near him, I'll never know whether I'm a man or not. Every decision I've made has to be approved by him. I'm twenty, Henrietta. Just twenty, nothing more."

He had been listening for the back door to open and close, and when it did he looked past her to see his father coming down the path. Big, almost looming in the evening shadows. About him were the flavors of his cigars and medicines. He spoke with a soft, deeply base voice, a voice filled with more than parental authority. His voice held the absolution of God.

"Your voice carries, Emil. What is it you've made up your mind about? . . ."

Sergeant McGruger unexpectedly edged close and said, "Looks like they've made up their minds, sir!" He pointed to the left flank as the Indians swung abreast and then broke into a wild run toward them, rifles snapping, wild cries breaking the silence.

Schwabacker's raised hand halted the wagons. A wild cheering rippled through the hostile ranks, for this was the way they liked their enemy, stationary, drawn into a defense on open ground. Schwabacker's first impulse was to shout his command to the bugler, but he did not. He thought of Temple Jocelyn and this stayed him, for the habit of pleasing someone else was strong.

Allowing the range to close to sixty yards, Schwabacker spoke calmly to the bugler. "Sound 'commence firing,' if you please, Malloy."

The brassy-voiced command broke over the wagons like water spilling down rocks and carbines appeared along the top sideboards like steel bristles. Schwabacker unflapped his holster and drew his pistol, extending his arm to aim. The troop fired in volley, the first and third squads, and at this range, from a stationary rest, their aim was devastating. The scythe of Schwabacker's fire swept the charging line and ponies went down thrashing. Men were flung off to lie motionless. Then the Cheyennes were no longer charging, but milling in angry surprise, for they had expected only a few and had found many.

The second section, now commanded by Corporal Linahan, shattered them completely with fifteen carbines.

Hurriedly, almost panic-stricken, the hostiles fled the field, leaving their dead and dying behind. Riderless ponies following them until they disappeared into the increasing grayness of night.

"Sound 'cease fire,'" Schwabacker said, and the bugler's notes brought silence, deep and engulfing. Schwabacker sat his horse, the fine film of sweat a dry nettle-stinging on his face. "Sergeant Finnegan," he said, "ascertain the number of casualties sustained on this attack." He looked around and found Jocelyn with his head raised, the ice-gray eyes boring into him.

. . . *The expert handling of a scalpel, the equally expert attention to duty; what did it matter? The result was always the same: a sense of inferiority. Was that cool enough, damn you? Was it?* . . .

While he waited for Finnegan he awkwardly held his revolver under his leg and crushed paper cartridges into the cylinder, then capped the Colt before returning it to his holster.

A moment later, Finnegan returned. "Trooper Gallagher's dead, sor. I put Lopez on the reins."

"Very well. Take the point, Sergeant."

He knee-reined the horse aside and sat there while the wagons lumbered into motion. Letting them file past, he swung alongside the ambulance. The six troopers who had been crowded in with the captain and Mrs. Kincaid dismounted and walked ahead. Sergeant McGruger came back, bending from the saddle to unhook each axle lantern. He lighted the lanterns, rehung them and returned to the column's head.

Schwabacker left the saddle and entered the ambulance, tying his horse to the end gate. He found a storm lantern beneath the seat and managed to light it, then suspended it by the bail on the litter ring. The sides of the ambulance were up, and through the falling rain the yellow light was like suspended fragments of glass.

He knelt beside Captain Kincaid and studied the man's waxen face. The bandage around the arm stump was a soggy red, but the bleeding had stopped. Shock was the demon here, eating at Kincaid's feeble strength, robbing him of life.

Lydia Kincaid said, "He's dying, isn't he?"

"Shall I lie to you, ma'am?"

"I don't think you could do it well enough to convince me." She looked long at her husband. "I'm sorry that he's dying. Not sorry for me, but for him. He wanted to live so badly."

"We all want that."

"I suppose," she said. "How's your lieutenant?"

"As well as can be expected," Schwabaker said. "He'd never let on otherwise. Not him."

"You don't like him?"

He shook his head. "You could say that he's the nearest thing to God I know. Him and my father." He paused to sort his thoughts. "I hated him at first. He's always right, and always catching me when I am wrong. I've broken my back trying to be as good as he is, but I never will be. He outweighs me, that's all. Most men do."

"You wouldn't have liked my husband," she said. "He wasn't successful. He wanted to be, Mr. Schwabacker. That's why I want him to live, so he can try again." She looked at Kincaid and the light struck her face, unflattering, harsh. Schwabacker read sadness there, regret, but this was for Nathan Kincaid, not herself. "He had a great, unsurmountable fault, Mr. Schwabacker: a complete lack of talent—no ability to rise above the prosaic."

"That's harsh judgment," he said.

"It's true and he knew it. The other day, when the Indians attacked, I was afraid for him and what I knew would happen. You get to know what a person will do after fifteen years, even if he's never done it before. He wanted to rout the Indians; this was his first combat. But he didn't. He lost nine men during the first charge, and forty-six on the second. After that it was run and die all the way." She extended her hand and stroked his brow. "The shame of it was that he knew beforehand how it would turn out. He's felt this inadequacy so hard and fought it for so long."

"A man can fight too hard," Schwabacker said. "I know."

"If he doesn't die," she said, "there'll be retirement at half pay, or perhaps they'll keep him on as quartermaster at some arsenal." She shook her head. "He's forty-three, Mr. Schwabacker. Fifteen years to make captain."

"I'm sorry," Schwabacker said and climbed over the back of the ambulance. Once mounted he turned toward the head of the column, the horses' legs splashing through puddles of light thrown by the axle lanterns. Lieutenant Eastwood was riding in the lead wagon, but he did not speak to Schwabacker, who made a mental note to investigate more thoroughly the questionable conduct of this officer.

Finnegan gave him a glance when he pulled alongside, but said nothing. Jocelyn was a loose sack tied to his horse and he would have fallen off long ago if he had not been securely fastened. But he was conscious. Occasionally he raised his head, and when he did his eyes swung to Emil Schwabacker, who rode with the full weight of command on his shoulders.

Hunched in the saddle, Schwabacker kept his hat tipped forward so the rain funneled off the crease. The felt campaign hat was not regulation for second lieutenants, but he had picked one up from Ryndlee's yard.

To hell with regulations. He was in command now and would do as he damned well pleased.

4

SECOND LIEUTENANT EMIL SCHWABACKER MAINTAINED an unvarying three miles an hour throughout the night, halting only for housekeeping stops and to graze the horses. During these times he stayed with Lieutenant Jocelyn, who seemed to live only because a core of disciplined flame in his brain forbade dying. Jocelyn was a relaxed lump on his horse, too weak to raise his head off the animal's neck, but he looked at Schwabacker with unwavering eyes.

Once he spoke: "My . . . congratulations. Perhaps in . . . time you may grasp . . . the fundamentals of . . . command."

There was no more talk. Schwabacker ordered the

troop on. When the wet and miserable dawn broke, Captain Nathan Kincaid released a final sigh and Lydia's sharp call brought Schwabacker to the rear at a trot. He entered the ambulance and found there was nothing he could say to this woman. She sat with her back braced against the side boards, her hands folded calmly in her lap. Stamped indelibly were the hard years she had spent with this man. Years of hope without end, now turned to years of emptiness.

In this woman's face he could see something of Henrietta Brubaker; she always repeated her wish to join him, to share his life. But such a thing was impossible; Schwabacker had long ago decided this. A man's death on the frontier placed a woman in too perilous a position, left her too alone. Dying wasn't the same back East. Living wasn't the same either.

. . . I'll write her and tell her about dying here. How different it is. . . .

But he knew he wouldn't. He wouldn't tell her about that or about his own engagement with the Indians. The strange thing about a fight was that a man never remembered much of it afterward, the important things anyway, the feel of it, the emotion of it. These things never occurred when a man had the leisure to observe them, and when the battle died, a curtain drew closed over the mind, blocking out everything except the brass taste of fear left in the mouth. No, he wouldn't tell her anything about it. He'd write the same things over again, asking her to wait for his return even when he suspected most strongly that he never would.

He inventoried the captain's possessions before making the entry into Sergeant Finnegan's record book: *Kincaid, Nathan B., Captain, United States Infantry, unassigned. Died of wounds sustained April 20, 1867.*

There were other entries, all enlisted men, all familiar faces and voices that he would never see or hear again. Fifty-cents-a-day heroes, unsung, unknown save for some woman who would cry and fondle a man's watch or a packet of his letters. Then the crying would stop and the mementoes would go into the bureau drawer, and a sergeant at Jefferson Barracks would look at his roster sheet and say, "E Troop of the 2nd needs another replacement, sir." Then wheels turned and another man off the street worked his way along the system's rails and eventually came into the troop to complete the cycle.

Emil Schwabacker failed to see the logic of such a life, yet he had chosen it and now would have no other.

Nathan Kincaid's accumulations were minute, almost insignificant when held up to the light of forty-three years of living. The cash Schwabacker turned over to his wife. There would be the stage ticket to buy. Always a stage ticket, for the East sent out their best and had them returned dead.

The clothing was packed, along with Kincaid's pistol, dress sword, binoculars and watch. These would be returned to her after the commanding officer at Fort Laramie signed the necessary papers.

He realized that Lydia wanted to be left alone and departed as soon as possible. Throughout the day he continued the march and at three o'clock he saw a band of Indians on the horizon, but they did not approach too close.

Finnegan said, "Spotted Tail, sor. You beat him twice, sor. He'll never forget it."

"He isn't supposed to," Schwabacker said. Later, with Fort Laramie in sight, he looked at his watch: five o'clock exactly.

The gates swung wide for him and he drew the command into formation on the parade edge. Schwabacker dismounted with great weariness. He spoke to Finnegan. "Sergeant, dismiss the troop and offer them my compliments. Have Sergeant McGruger fetch the contract surgeon on the double." When this was done, Schwabacker stripped off his gauntlets and stood with the rain coursing down his cheeks.

Mrs. Kincaid dismounted from the ambulance, and when she saw him standing there she came up. The officer of the day trotted across the gumbo parade and led Mrs. Kincaid to the duck boards and the sanctuary of dreary quarters near Suds Row.

On the headquarters porch the commanding officer appeared, a round little man with the infallible instincts of the natural-born military man. He took one look at the troop and knew what kind of fight they had been in. He read victory in their scars, for there was nothing tail-between-the-legs in their manner. The contract surgeons came on the run, followed by four orderlies and two ambulances. Jocelyn was lowered to a tarp spread on the parade and almost immediately transferred to a waiting ambulance.

With the important details of his command and the

wounded attended to, Schwabaker could turn to his report. He straightened and with considerable effort walked to headquarters porch, where Brevet Colonel Nelson Ashford waited.

"Come inside, man," Ashford said. He glanced at Schwabacker's tenderly cradled arm. "Is that serious, Mr. Schwabacker?"

"No, sir. Merely a flesh wound."

"You're a poor liar," Ashford said, closing his office door. "You're as white as a curd. How bad off is Jocelyn?"

"Through a lung, sir." The stove was hot and Schwabacker stripped off his poncho, backing up so that he could steam the seat of his pants dry. He made his report, briefly but completely. His statements concerning Lieutenant Eastwood were honest, uncolored and hardly flattering. Colonel Ashford dispatched an orderly to fetch Eastwood.

While they waited, Ashford produced a bottle and a glass. He poured a stiff one and offered it to Schwabacker, who tossed it off with a great deal of choking.

The orderly admitted Lieutenant Eastwood, who came to attention and saluted. "You wished to see me, sir?"

Ashford's frown was like the gathering of thunder clouds. The wrinkling of his forehead pulled his short-cropped hair forward until his whole countenance was menacing. "Mr. Eastwood, perhaps you can account satisfactorily for this impossible report of Captain Kincaid's losing his entire command."

"Indeed I can, sir."

"And I'm also interested," Ashford said, "in your personal actions during this engagement."

"I was inactive, sir," Eastwood said. "When the Indians attacked, I disputed Captain Kincaid's orders. He ordered me into the wagon under arrest. His wife will verify that, sir."

"Thank you," Ashford said. "That will be all."

Eastwood went out, closing the door softly behind him. Ashford waited a moment before speaking. "You fought a brilliant action, Mr. Schwabacker. I'll see that it's included in my dispatch to General Cooke." He stood up and offered his hand. "You've done us a service, Mr. Schwabacker. Spotted Tail and his Cheyennes have been hanging around for a year, ever since Carrington first marched through with the 18th Infantry. None of us ever knew what he was waiting for, and we all disliked the idea of a hostile force hanging out there. Now I believe we know where we stand. Red Cloud means to use the Cheyennes to close off Wessels' supply route. That can only mean a bitter summer campaign at Kearny. Now that we're forewarned, we can be forearmed." His glance touched Schwabacker's wound. "Get over to Cove Butler's office and have that dressed. That's an order."

"Yes, sir," Schwabacker said and left immediately. He paused on the porch, feeling a little ill, a combination of the whiskey and his wound, he supposed. Sergeant Finnegan was near the troop barracks across the parade; the last of the troop was just entering the near door. A detail from the farrier's shed had taken the escort wagons and the stage to the equipment yard and a group of recruits gathered to see first hand the bullet holes, the arrows protruding from the side boards. The ambulance bearing Kincaid was now at the infirmary's side entrance and two corpsmen carried the dead man in. Schwabacker stepped off the porch into the rain and walked along the duck boards, reaching the infirmary as the ambulance was being wheeled away.

He found Cove Butler in the laboratory. Butler's two assistants, Kisdeen and Maxwell Owen, were both tending the wounded enlisted men. Schwabacker could hear their voices through the thin wall. Captain Kincaid was on a leather-topped table, a sheet covering him. When Schwabacker closed the door, Butler turned from the sink where he had been washing his hands. The bloody bandage that had covered Kincaid's arm now lay in a bucket beneath the sink.

"Rough patrol," Butler said. He leaned his shoulders against the wall as he toweled his hands dry. He looked carefully at Emil Schwabacker, as though he too measured him, but with a newly formed opinion. Schwabacker had one of those young faces that women instinctively trust, especially with their marriageable daughters. His eyes were brown, almost matching his hair. He wore his sideburns halfway to the jaw hinge and with a razor-cultivated flair at the base. His mustache reminded Butler of a duck's first down and the young man kept it meticulously clipped, still hoping that someday maturity would give it character.

"I was glad it happened," Schwabacker said.

Butler nodded understandingly. "That looked like

your parade awhile ago. From where I sat, Temple Jocelyn was just holding down his horse." Butler was a man of forty, dry-skinned and dry-humored. He seemed to regard the entire military system with a cynical amusement.

"How is he?"

"Resting," Butler said. He motioned for Schwabacker to sit down and took the bandage off the forearm. He examined Linahan's needlework, and rebandaged it. "You leave me in a hole, Emil. I don't know whether to call you lieutenant or doctor."

"I'm not a doctor," Schwabacker said. "Jocelyn doesn't think I'm much of an officer either."

Butler's glance was amused. "A doctor amputated Kincaid's arm. And a doctor probed for the bullet in Jocelyn. What did you use?"

"A bent piece of wire," Schwabacker said.

"And a better job than I could have done, in either case." He turned away for his pipe. "You don't think you're much of an officer. Did Temple ever say so?"

"He doesn't have to say. He has a way of looking at a man that says enough." Schwabacker made a sweeping motion with his hand. "Go ahead, draw your damn conclusions!"

"Is that what I'm doing?" Butler packed and lighted his pipe. "Emil, you don't have to copy Temple Jocelyn."

"I didn't think it was that obvious," Schwabacker said. "Understand me, sir; I don't want to copy any man. It's just that he has a way about him that makes a man feel inferior. I . . . I know that feeling, sir, from

64

a lifetime of living with it."

"Where did you get your medical training?"

"Colby."

Butler grunted. "Good school. I learned most of mine holding the doctor's horse." He puffed on his pipe for a moment. "What bothers you, Emil? Are you afraid of making a mistake Temple Jocelyn wouldn't have made? Something he'll hold against you?"

Before Schwabacker could answer the connecting door opened and Dr. Kisdeen came in. His celluloid sleeve protectors were bloody. There was a smattering of blood on his smock. He said, "I've completed an examination of Jocelyn. The breast bone deflected the bullet to one side and only a portion of the lung was touched. Just enough to cause respiratory bleeding."

"Can I see him now?" Schwabacker asked.

Kisdeen pursed his lips. "Not too long."

"Thanks," Schwabacker said and went through the connecting door. Jocelyn's face was pale and wan against the white pillowcase. He dredged his strength and found a small smile.

"Congratulations . . . Mr. Schwabacker. It's your . . . troop."

The young lieutenant shook his head slowly. "It'll never be my troop, sir. Every order I'll ever give, they'll question and wonder if that's the way you'd give it."

"You're a . . . fool," Jocelyn said with surprising bitterness. "Get out. You're not . . . the man I . . . thought you were."

Schwabacker colored deeply, then whirled and hurried across the parade to his own quarters, his cheeks still burning. He could have taken Jocelyn's remark had not it been based upon a lifetime of remarks just like it. The chill wind blew against him and he remembered . . .

The spring had been unusually raw and windswept. His term hadn't started yet and two weeks with his family had seemed like a wonderful holiday, but it was spent in a buggy making the rounds with his father. Early one morning they had visited the Cady farm west of St. Albans. Cady was in traction with a badly mangled leg, the result of carelessness with an overanxious mule and a newly sharpened John Deere plow. As always, his father had insisted upon standing back, "So my son can demonstrate all those things he's learned in college," but he was never allowed to complete a task. There was always something, a bad dressing, some clumsy suturing, something that proved displeasing and he would be shoved aside, the job taken over by his father.

Later, in the buggy, going on to another call, his father would say, "You're not quite the doctor I thought you were, Emil. These things take time, my boy. Experience."

His quarters were cold and damp and he spent fifteen minutes stoking up the fire to heat water for his bath and shave. Afterward he changed into clean, dry clothes. His back ached and a pounding commenced at the base of his skull. Rain made sad, sagging patterns on the windows as the daylight faded. Finally he heard the regimental bugler blow "mess call," but he did not go out, although he was ravenously hungry.

Instead he sat at his desk and, taking Henrietta's letter

from his pocket, read it again before attempting to answer it. For nearly an hour his pen scratched monotonously in the silence. To read his letter over he had to light the lamp.

Fort Laramie, Wyo. Terr.
April 22, 1867

My Darling Henrietta:
   By God's good chance I was a member of the patrol that met the mail stage a day's march east of the post, and thereby read your wonderful letter a day sooner. To view the matter in retrospect, I see now that if I had not been on this patrol, I might never have received it, as the stage station was under hostile attack upon our arrival. One pauses to think at these times about how tenuous is the thread between loved ones during these uncertain times. I hasten to add that there was no danger involved for me, for the real campaign is many miles to the west, at Fort Phil Kearny, and it has always been my lot to be in the backwater of great events, rather than participating in them.
   During the brief encounter, my commanding officer, whom I admire and revere as much as my father, was sorely wounded and I was compelled by necessity to dredge up my half-forgotten and ill-learned skills as a surgeon to save him. God was with me and the contract surgeon here assures me that he will make a speedy and noble recovery.
   I have written to you before of this man, how like he is to my father, whom I worship, as you know, in

spite of his great disappointment in me. There was
great pain in my heart when I was forced to render
surgical aid, for somehow it seemed that the pain I
caused him was a pain against my father. They have
the same eyes, you know, and many of the same
mannerisms and attitudes. He is a great man, my
commander. One feels small and insignificant
beside him.

Know that I miss you, my dearest, and wish to be
with you, save that this duty binds me here. One fin-
ishes a job one starts; at least I've always wanted to
do that, just to see if I could. This land is not genteel
enough for a man's wife, but it soon will be. Then we
will be together; it is my fondest wish, for I love you
dearly.

Bless my mother and dear sisters. Kiss them for
me and give them my love. If you can, speak to my
father and tell him that I am well.

Your most devoted,
Emil

An hour later the rain stopped. He opened the door and stood there while he scanned the dark parade ground. The eaves drained moisture from the roofs in uneven drips. Every window in regimental headquarters was bright with light, and across the parade, Dr. Cove Butler moved before the window, his shadow clearly discernible across the interval.

A runner passed on his way to headquarters and Schwabacker halted him. "Trooper, would you see that this letter goes out on the first courier east?"

"Yes, sir. There's one leaving tonight, sir." He took the letter and trotted away.

Schwabacker's idleness induced him to take up hat and cape. He crossed the muddy parade to the hospital and scraped his boots before entering Cove Butler's office. Butler was brewing a pot of coffee in a glass beaker. He turned his head quickly, then said, "You can stand some, can't you?"

"Thanks, yes," Schwabacker said and toed a chair around.

Butler poured into glass measuring cups and they drank the coffee without sugar or cream. "You've got a fine pair of hands there," Butler said dryly. "Take care of them. Better yet, give up the damned army and finish your medical studies."

"I like the damned army," Schwabacker said.

"Sure, sure," Butler said. "Emil, look at me. Do you think I'm here because I want to be? Man, you've got the touch, the magic I'll never have. I examined Kincaid thoroughly. You did work with kitchen tools I couldn't duplicate here on the operating table. Are you going to throw that away?"

"Is this going to be a lecture, Cove?"

Butler finished his coffee. "Forget it. I'm a nosy man who doesn't know when to let up."

Knuckles gently rattled Butler's door and he opened it. An orderly stepped in, saw Schwabacker and said, "The colonel's compliments, sir. He'd like to see you right away."

"Very well." He answered the trooper's salute, emptied his coffee cup, said his good night to Butler and

69

went out. In the outer headquarters office the regimental clerk popped to attention and hastily ushered him into the colonel's chambers, closing the door behind him.

Colonel Nelson Ashford fanned a pall of cigar smoke away from his face and said, "Sit down, Mr. Schwabacker. How's the arm?"

"Fine, sir." Schwabacker looked at the other officer, who was seated on Ashford's right. Major D'Arcy Davis was the regimental adjutant and acted like one, very prim, very definite, and occasionally very hard to get along with. He had the pugnaciousness usually associated with small men.

"Mr. Davis and I have been combining reports," Ashford said, "and our conclusions are indeed dismal. First, I'd like an opinion, Mr. Schwabacker. Do you believe we've seen the last of Spotted Tail's Cheyennes?"

"No, sir. He took a licking, but I doubt he'll be inclined to forget it."

"Ah," Ashford said, as though immensely pleased. "How do you feel about being live bait, Mr. Schwabacker?"

"Do you want me to engage him again, sir?"

"Well, you had such smashing success," Ashford said, "I was wondering if you could do it again. Mr. Schwabacker, my command is mainly one of supply. That and keeping the Bozeman Road open to Wessels and his fight at Kearny and Fort C. F. Smith. Quite obviously the hostiles mean to close this line by force. I have to take action, and not in the abominable manner of Captain Kincaid, a matter, incidentally, that I'm investigating to the fullest." He paused to shroud his face in

70

cigar smoke again. "Mr. Schwabacker, I have an opening for an able first lieutenant of cavalry. To confirm this promotion only requires my signature. It's in my mind to recommend you for this rank. However, it will necessitate a change in assignment for you. If Spotted Tail is bothering the movement of reinforcements—and that's obviously it, for he never molests a dispatch rider—then I want you to take command of E Troop and march to Fort Kearny. Wessels needs that troop desperately, but more specifically, I need someone to give Spotted Tail another licking."

"I . . . I don't know what to say, sir," Schwabacker said. "My seniority, sir; I haven't any!"

"But you have originality," Ashford said. "You've proved that to me and Major Davis."

"This is quite sudden, sir. Jocelyn . . ."

"Jocelyn's in the infirmary," Ashford snapped. "All right, Lieutenant, he took the news a bit ungracefully, but Jocelyn is not in command. I am." He got up from his desk and unrolled a large wall map. "At eight o'clock tomorrow morning you will pass through the palisade gates with your troop and march at the most expedient rate to Wessels' command. The quartermaster is now readying a civilian wagon train. Thirty wagons, Lieutenant, and I want them to get there."

"Yes, sir."

"A courier came through from Kearny after this evening's mess. He'll return with you and act as scout. Any questions?"

"No, sir. The orders are quite clear, sir."

Ashford offered his hand, shaking gently because of

71

Schwabacker's wound. "You're sure that doesn't bother you?"

"It's fine, sir."

"Carry on, then. And remember, I want Spotted Tail engaged and drubbed good. Another licking at the hands of a much smaller force will soon turn his medicine against him."

"I understand, sir," Schwabacker said and went out.

First Lieutenant Emil Schwabacker. An officer with a silver bar in his shoulder box. Never again would he be called "mister."

He went to his quarters and there dispatched a runner for Sergeant Sean Finnegan, who appeared ten minutes later, out of uniform and sleep-rumpled.

"Sit down," Schwabacker said. "The colonel has promoted me to first lieutenant and in command of E Troop, Sergeant."

This was a belly kick to Finnegan, but nothing showed on his face. The elasticity of his skin turned to an expressionless clay mask. He said, "Congratulations, sor."

"Let's start off right," Schwabacker said. "I'm not Temple Jocelyn, Sergeant. There's no greatness in me. I'm afraid at times, and I make mistakes. But I mean to run a tight troop, Sergeant. I either have your word now, your support, or I'll transfer you out. I'll not have my commands questioned or held up to the light of Temple Jocelyn, like an egg being candled. What's it going to be, Finnegan? Are you my soldier or Jocelyn's?"

For a moment, Finnegan mulled this over. "Twenty-three years, sor; that's a long time for a man to sojer." He smiled then. "I don't want to leave th' troop, sor. And I'll not be thinkin' back either. There'll be no talk from me about you to th' troop, and I'll stand for none of them buckin' you either, if you understand what I mean."

"I do, Sergeant." Emil Schwabacker turned away, vastly relieved. He was not an old soldier, but he had been in brass and blue long enough to know what kind of a relationship had to exist between an officer and his sergeants. They had to be with him to the man, all the way, without question. If they were not, then nothing was any good. Every command would be silently questioned and half-heartedly performed, passively resisted until the officer broke under the weight or killed them all like Kincaid had, by his stupid uncertainties.

Schwabacker explained the march orders in detail and, like a good officer, left the details to the sergeant, who knew what to do and would do it without fail.

After Finnegan left, Schwabacker turned out the lamp and crawled between scratchy blankets, thinking of tomorrow, and all the tomorrows to follow. Never since he had left the quiet house on Grove Street to enter the Academy had he felt so complete, so satisfied. A second lieutenant was neither fish nor fowl; all that was now changed with Brevet Colonel Nelson Ashford's scratchy pen upon a document.

Now he was truly "brass," with a bar in his shoulder box. Behind him tomorrow would be his command, the fifty-cents-a-day "blue." The brass and the blue, a dream for which some officers waited fourteen years.

Now he had to live with dignity and he wondered if he could.

5

First Lieutenant Emil Schwabacker's troop passed through the palisade gates an hour after daybreak and was waiting on the flats north of the post when the massive supply train of Beal and Hughes, sutlers, began to trickle into position. From the side gate the spare horse herd was driven out and bunched. Schwabacker gave the hand signal to move and the command proceeded west at a slow walk.

The day was dull and low clouds moved across the sky like bulky cotton while the threat of rain lingered on the perky wind. Schwabacker had his scouts out, his flankers in position, and before the command could settle into the routine of march, hostile Indians were reported flanking them to the north.

Schwabacker kept this bit of intelligence to himself but thereafter he maintained constant communication between his command position and the scouts. There was little need, he believed, to alarm his command now. When the first feathered warrior made his ominous appearance on some hill crest, then a soldier could steady down and earn his money.

Schwabacker conducted the march according to the manual—halt, rest, walk—although this was difficult in the rain-soft ground. That evening he drew the command into bivouac on the bank of a small creek. To their rear, massive rocks loomed skyward and a short mountain range built up in jagged rises. He put the sutler's wagons in the center; cavalry squad fires burned in a

74

circle around them. As commander, Schwabacker found a dozen pressing tasks to occupy him. He saw that the horse herds were picketed and proper guards posted. By the time he completed his rounds, the cook fires had gone out and the wagons were silent. Sergeant Finnegan had saved him a mess kit full of rations and his water-proof ground cloth was spread. Emil Schwabacker ate in silence, then settled down for the night.

He was up before daybreak, had his coffee and bacon and was taking his horse from the picket line when the bugler blew reveille. When the ringing echoes of that call died, Schwabacker instructed the bugler to saddle-bag his horn until the command reached Fort Kearny. He had no immediate wish to call the hostiles down on him like Gabriel at the walls of Jericho.

The march continued, a regulation four miles an hour when accompanying wagons. From the prairielike river bottom the Platte suddenly swung left through cliffs a hundred feet high, fortress-like walls of sheer rock with cedar-covered, conical summits. His scouts continued to report hostile sign and Schwabacker bunched his command to a closer interval until this section was passed and the land again became prairie.

Late in the afternoon another misting rain com-menced, stayed with them for an hour, then left, leaving a chill and wet blankets to make the night miserable. Fires sputtered, half refusing to burn. Finnegan was waiting after the evening rounds, his face concerned. "Them Cheyennes is studyin' us all th' time, sor. I don't like it."

"Neither do I," Schwabacker said. "Any suggestions?"

"You're in command, sor."

That's the way it was in the army; Schwabacker considered it ironical. While an officer was second in command, a section officer, a noncom would advise. But when an officer assumed command, the complexion changed. A commander was supposed to know the answers for himself.

So Schwabacker said, "I think he wants to pick his own ground, Sergeant. Maybe we can beat him to it."

"Aye, sor, that's likely. But it makes a man jumpy nevertheless."

The meal Finnegan provided was cold and he offered no apology for it. Overhead the clouds were breaking and a silver sliver of moonlight appeared. There was the promise of fair weather in the morning, for a strong wind was coming up, dissipating the storm. The horse herd stirred on the pickets, and beyond that guards moved back and forth, speaking softly to the animals.

"It's quiet, sor," Finnegan said. He lay back on his ground cloth, hands laced behind his head.

"Merely the illusion," Schwabacker said. "I wonder what's going on in Spotted Tail's camp, Sergeant. A little medicine?"

"Aye, and he'll be needin' that. You gave him a fair lickin', sor. He'll not be forgettin' that."

"And he'll not be so careless the next time," Schwabacker said. "I fooled him once, which was easy, but this time I wonder if he'll fall again."

He turned over and pulled his blankets tighter. Finnegan said no more. One by one the squad fires died to ashes and the command rested.

The weather in the morning held, and during the next five days the sun and strong winds firmed up the trail until the march rate could be increased to six miles an hour. Daily reports assured Schwabacker that Spotted Tail's warriors still clung to the outfringes of the hills, waiting for a time dictated by Cheyenne medicine.

After they passed Fort Connor without stopping, the weather turned freakish. The sky became an inverted blue dome, startlingly clear, and the wind died to nothing. The heat began to mount steadily and all day the sun stood molten. Emil Schwabacker had never seen such a sky. The days came in a burst of orange, spreading as though the edge of the world were on fire. The first blue of day turned to a pale purple and the sun's color was brightly polished copper.

The green of chemise and soapwood turned to gray beneath this thick heat. Temperatures hovered near a hundred in the afternoon. Dust rose in choking quantities and the insects came in clouds: buffalo gnats, flies and mosquitoes. Men and animals suffered constantly and many horses went temporarily blind because the mosquitoes seemed partial to the soft flesh under the eyes. Even the wagons were not immune to the heat and dust. Moisture fled from the wheel spokes and they were loosened, causing frequent halts while the teamsters made repairs. Dust sifted into everything—the food, the weave of clothing—to become a flesh-eating abrasive.

That night the scout reported medicine being made in the hills. Schwabacker felt the first rat-gnaw of suspicion, and when it would not crystallize, it turned to worry. Each day he studied his troopers, cheeks reddened by sun and dust, bloated by insect bites. Their clothing was stiff with ground-in dirt. He looked at them and they looked back with dull stares. He was the commander.

Finnegan was a rock in this sea of discomfort. Over the evening meal, Schwabacker said, "Sergeant, I can't do anything about the weather. Why don't they blame it on the damned Cheyennes' medic . . ." He stopped talking and sat that way, his mouth a round O, his food dribbling off his fork.

"What is it, sor?" Finnegan's voice was concerned.

Schwabacker put his plate aside. "Bugler!" he shouted, and the youth came up on the run. "Bugler, from now on I want all garrison calls sounded properly and on the minute."

"All, sir?" He was inclined to think his commander had gone mad; his expression said so anyway.

"Yes," Schwabacker said, smiling. "'Mess call,' 'work call,' 'fatigue'; the whole thing."

"Yes, sir," the bugler said and walked away to get his horn.

For a moment Sergeant Finnegan said nothing. Finally, "Sor, if he toots that damn horn th' Injuns will flock to it like Bible readers to a meetin' house."

"More than likely," Schwabacker said. He was no longer worried; there was no trace of it in his face or voice. "Sergeant, you said once that Spotted Tail would want to pick his ground. Well, I don't think I'll let him. I'm going to pick it for him and make him come to me."

"Jasus, sor . . ."

"Patience, Sergeant. Look at this weather; unusual as hell. That's what we call it, but it dawns on me that Spotted Tail's taking credit for bringing it on with his medicine. If that's so, he must think the time's right to fight, but if we stay here, he'll have to come to us. We'll be ready for him."

The first call blown was "retreat," just before dark. By the time the first bell tones died, the entire command were on their feet, trying to figure it out. Schwabacker watched and waited, and just before the gray shades of night gave way to black, there was a rising smudge of smoke on a distant bluff.

Finnegan saw it; every man saw it. Rutledge Hughes, the chief sutler, didn't like it and came immediately to Schwabacker's fire. "What the hell are you doing, blowing that damned bugle?"

"Calling Indians," Schwabacker said. "It's too hot for whist." He smiled at Hughes's glowering displeasure. "It's an army sound; I like it."

Ollie Beal came up then. He was Hughes's partner, the money man who had always been content to let Hughes talk, but fright made him bold. "Goddamn it, you'll call every Cheyenne within twenty miles! The heat got you, or something?"

"No," Schwabacker said evenly. "Twenty miles, you say? I had no idea a bugle carried that far."

"Agh!" Hughes said. "He's crazy!" He turned to leave, but halted when Schwabacker spoke.

"Tight wagons now, Mr. Hughes. Have your men keep their rifles at hand. We'll remain here several days."

Hughes had more to say but he choked on it. In blind anger he stomped out of the camp with his partner. Sergeant Finnegan shifted his weight first on one foot then the other. "Sor, I surely hope you know what you're doin'."

"Don't you know, Sergeant?"

Finnegan shook his head. "I take orders good, sor, but I'm poorly at makin' 'em up."

With a doubled guard walking the perimeter, Schwabacker rolled into his blankets and slept well and in the morning was up before the sun. The bugler blew reveille on time, "mess call" forty minutes later, then followed it with "inspection," "work" and "fatigue." By ten o'clock the brass voice was playing to more than Schwabacker's command.

The hills began to bristle with mounted Cheyenne.

By noon the temperature rose to staggering heights, but not a man in the command paid the slightest attention. There was a more annoying enemy to think about now. Meanwhile, First Lieutenant Schwabacker went about, making quiet preparations, odd though they seemed.

Contrary to usual rules of defense, he had the wagons abandoned and the horse herd moved frequently. Using the animal herd for cover, he instructed the first and third squads to dig pits large enough to hold four men, two soldiers and two civilians to the pit. His survey revealed that a good many of the civilians were armed with the new Henry repeating rifle, or the seven-shot Spencer. He arrayed them in the dug positions according to fire-power potential.

Finnegan kept his mouth shut, and at times this was difficult. Lieutenant Schwabacker had somewhere lost the "book," for he violated every concept of General Philip St. George Cooke's new dictates.

Spotted Tail must have thought the white commander completely crazy, or so indecisive he couldn't make up his mind where to picket the horses; they were moved eight times in the space of three hours. But each time they moved, troopers and civilians stayed behind, secreted in their trenches. Schwabacker took care to see that these positions were adequately covered with brush and that the men stayed out of sight. He had his look at the completed job, and ten yards away they were completely invisible.

By four o'clock the camp was strangely quiet, yet the bugler continued to sound off the calls. Schwabacker drew Sergeant Finnegan aside for his final instructions. "The waiting will be hardest."

"Aye, sor, it can eat a man."

"I want you to command the forward position, Sergeant. It's my guess that Spotted Tail will try one big one before the sun goes down. They'll be after the supplies in the wagons. Don't fire until you hear the command."

"Aye, sor."

"Get on with it, then," Schwabacker said and went around the camp for a final look. He had thirty men near the wagons, all civilians and armed with Henry repeaters. Rutledge Hughes was in charge and Schwabacker repeated previous instructions. "In no event fire until they break past the second ring. This is

81

for record. I want a man down every time a trigger is squeezed."

"It's crazy," Hughes grumbled, "just asking for it this way."

"I have my orders; you have yours."

The second ring of entrenched riflemen was seventy yards out, about the most effective range of the Henrys. The men in the second set of trenches were armed with Spencers, more powerful, longer ranged. Seven powerful volleys without reloading. Ollie Beal was in command there, supported by the experience of Sergeant McGruger. The first and outer ring was cavalry to the man, a hundred and seventy-five yards from the wagon hub of the camp. Carbines in this position, single shot, but in capable hands a tremendous weapon of range and accuracy.

Schwabacker moved around the camp as though he had all the time in the world and he exercised his control to the limit to keep from appearing more nervous than he was.

This was the apex of command every officer sooner or later reached, the crowning moment when his orders would or would not be executed to the satisfaction of the higher echelon. "Give Spotted Tail another licking"—no orders had ever been more clearly given. Now he was on the periphery of success or failure; that made waiting difficult.

But he did not have time to worry long about it. From a far slope a line of mounted braves breasted the crest and started down at an easy gallop. At a range of five hundred yards they increased their speed, shards of yelling preceding them.

The bugler was by Schwabacker's side, nervously sucking his mouthpiece. Schwabacker unflapped his holster and drew his pistol, holding it at arm's length along his leg. He watched the Cheyenne come on; he udged there were several hundred. And when they approached his first position, perspiration beaded his forehead. His thought was that some of the ponies were bound to step into the trenches, and because of this, he said, "Sound 'commence firing.'"

The command came at the right moment, for the first rank of racing Cheyennes was almost upon the concealed trenches. The ground trembled with the tattooing of hoofbeats, then suddenly gray brush became alive, presenting a wall of fire that turned the charging mass into chaos. Hurt, surprised, enraged, the Indians wheeled once, then came on, intending to crush this brave handful, but as they drove to the attack, the second section released their fire, repeating fire that blinded, caused the proud Cheyenne to stumble and finally reel back, mortally wounded.

Two dozen warriors were down and others followed with a stumbling, crippled gait. The Indians raced away from the Spencers, but by that time the first section had reloaded and followed them an additional hundred yards with well-aimed lead.

Instinctively Emil Schwabacker sensed that this was not the end. To Hughes he shouted, "Forward! To the second position!"

Under cover of Indian dust, Hughes and his men ran out and went into the prepared trenches. Now the

83

Spencers were reinforced with Henry rifles.

A thousand yards out the Cheyenne were shouting, turning for another assault. Schwabacker let them come on; he could guess their strategy, and when they were fifty yards from the first line of defense, his nod sent a bugle command outward. The first bars brought carbine fire.

Spotted Tail lost men, but he was prepared to do that now. He had to close and there was a price to be paid, and he paid it with fifteen downed men. His next obstacle was the Spencer rifles; he had to crush that force. Driving past the first entrenchments, he met a suddenly increased fire as the Henry rifles entered the fight. This was a numbing shock; Schwabacker could see the hostile mass shudder like a wounded beast.

Dust rose in blinding clouds and gunfire rattled like dice in a wooden box. Then with a yell of bitter defeat, the Cheyennes withdrew from the field. A few braves remained behind to carry away the dead and wounded.

"Sound 'recall,'" Schwabacker said and stood there while the "C" horn gathered his forces. He knew that he had lost men. Knew he would before the fight opened, but Finnegan's report still jarred him.

"Eleven dead and nine wounded, sor."

"How did the civilians fare, Sergeant?"

"They're missin' a few too, sor."

"Re-form the command and see that the wounded are placed in wagons," Schwabacker said, replacing his unfired pistol.

He knew a feeling of satisfaction, for now he could report his mission accomplished. At least half of it was, giving Spotted Tail another licking. Schwabacker waited while his command assembled. Waited for their verdict, positive that one would be rendered by his men. He had invited this attack and men had been killed. They could blame him. Never forgive him. From Rutledge Hughes's expression Schwabacker saw that here was one man who never would. But he didn't give a damn about Hughes.

He watched the faces of his men as they came in.

A group of troopers stopped nearby, purposely idle. Sergeant Finnegan returned and just stood there, not saying anything. Finally one of the troopers said, "That was a damn good fight, sir."

. . . Now ask it! Ask it now or forever go on wondering. . . . "As good as Lieutenant Jocelyn would have made, Cassidy?"

Trooper Cassidy grinned and squeezed a bullet-pierced forearm. "To hell with Lieutenant Jocelyn, sir. We're with you."

Now he knew what he had hoped to know, all the time believing that he never would. Schwabacker turned to his own camp and Sergeant Finnegan followed. Finally he said, "I'm just a dumb Irishman who takes orders, but by God, sor, you give 'em and this troop'll follow 'em." He grinned. Schwabacker had seen him grin before, but this was different, for it went beyond pleasure. It was the grin one man gives another when he's just glad to be a friend. "Looks like you got a bucko command, sor."

"That's the kind of command I like," Schwabacker said. "Can you fix a pot of coffee, Sean?"

"Aye, an' th' best you ever drank, sor."

6

WHATEVER BONDS OF LOYALTY AND RESPECT LIEUTENANT Emil Schwabacker welded between himself and his men, he lost with the civilian personnel. Four dead men, according to their way of thinking, was too much to pay. A soldier was paid to stand and bleed, but not a civilian.

Rutledge Hughes made this plain when he came to Schwabacker's fire and stood there, legs wide spread, anger splashed across his face. "I want some talk and I want it now, Lieutenant."

Finnegan and Schwabacker both looked up from their coffee. "Sit down," Schwabacker invited.

"I'll say my say standing," Hughes said. "This little stunt you pulled don't set good with me."

"Sorry to hear that," Schwabacker said. "From a military standpoint, the engagement was a success. That entirely settles the matter for me."

"But not for me," Hughes argued. "We don't think there would have been any fight if you hadn't invited them. When we get to Kearny, there's going to be something done about it." He hitched up his pants and snorted through his nose. "My men aren't going to have their lives imperiled because some snot-nose officer is glory-hunting."

Schwabacker started to rise, but Sean Finnegan put out his hand. "You got a bad arm, sor. Let me."

"Permission granted," Schwabacker said as Hughes looked from one to the other. His attention centered on Finnegan when the sergeant stepped around the fire, his eyes belligerent. The instant Hughes correctly read Finnegan's intent, he bellowed and charged, arms swinging. Finnegan struck out, catching Hughes flush on the mouth. The sutler staggered back, blood welling from split lips. Finnegan hit him again.

From a prone position, Hughes looked up, but the fight was over. Schwabacker said, "Return to your camp, and if there is any more of this you'll ride to Kearny in one of your wagons, trussed up like a chicken."

"I fight my own fights," Hughes said and got to his feet, hands flailing dust from his clothes. He glared once more at Schwabacker then went to his own camp.

Schwabacker said, "I'm in your debt, Sergeant."

"Ah, sor, it was a pleasure."

The morning dawned bright and yellow and the day turned stifling hot before they had traveled fifteen miles. That evening they reached Dry Creek, but at this time of the year there was water in it. Schwabacker allowed bathing privileges, enlisted men first. For this Rutledge Hughes put another mark against him.

By noon the next day they reached Crazy Woman's Fork and on the day after raised the log palisade of Fort Phil Kearny. Drawing his troop into precise formation, Schwabacker led them the final mile to the gate. He entered first, wheeling aside with his command so the wagons could skirt the parade and go on to the quarter-master yard. Sergeant McGruger was placed in charge of the burying detail, for Schwabacker had the dead in two wagons. The wounded were taken to the infirmary while Sergeant Finnegan dismissed the command and made arrangements for billets and stable space.

Lieutenant Schwabacker was impressed with the fort. In spite of the derogatory tales he had heard about Carrington, he decided that the man had done a good job of construction. The stockade was heavy pine trunks, eleven feet tall, hewn to a touching surface, pointed and looped for firing positions. Blockhouses sat on the two diagonal corners and the massive gates had small wickets and huge locks. Three frame warehouses, the hospital and four company quarters were each eighty-four feet long, the largest billets Schwabacker had ever seen on the frontier.

The flagstaff was in the center of the parade, surrounded by an octagonal bandstand upon which Carrington had nightly concerts. Diverging walks, each twelve feet wide, passed to each street. The powder magazine was in one of the squares thus formed.

The commanding officer's quarters were along the southwest wall, and after turning his horse over to the bugler, Schwabacker went there to make his report. An orderly admitted him and he came to attention before a graying general of Infantry.

"Lieutenant Emil Schwabacker, sir. Commanding E Troop, 3rd United States Cavalry."

"Welcome to Fort Kearny, Lieutenant." He waved Schwabacker into a chair. Brevet Brigadier General H. W. Wessels was a blunt-bodied man, slow moving, but with a keen intelligence in his eyes. His fingers were short and thick and he had the habit of drumming them on the edge of his desk, or his belt buckle. "I'll be frank,

Lieutenant; I expected to see Temple Jocelyn at the head of that column."

"He's been wounded, sir." Schwabacker recounted the fight at Ryndlee's road ranch. He then made his complete report, covering the invited attack, Spotted Tail's defeat, and Rutledge Hughes's objections.

This impressed General Wessels. He said, "The duty here is rough, Lieutenant, but you show promise. The Fetterman massacre is still Red Cloud's strong medicine. Couple that with Carrington's bungling tactics and this Sioux believes he is invincible." His fingers continued to drum. "I must say that it is heartening to know that Red Cloud's allies can take a licking. I'll see that you receive proper credit in my weekly dispatch."

"Thank you, sir."

"I like written reports, Lieutenant. In great detail. Word of mouth is easily misunderstood or distorted. See that such a report is placed on my desk by work call tomorrow."

"Yes, sir." Schwabacker saluted and went out, where he found the officer of the day waiting. His quarters turned out to be a small room near the end of a long row of identical rooms. After the formality of signing for the spare furniture, the O.D. left and Emil Schwabacker waited for his orderly to fetch his few belongings.

But Sergeant Finnegan brought them, along with the report that the wounded were being cared for and that none was likely to die. Finnegan, for some reason known only to himself, felt an inclination to remain while Schwabacker unpacked and hung his uniforms.

Finally the sergeant said, "Sor, can I ask a question?"

Schwabacker looked at him. "Yes. Forget the rank in this room, Sean."

"Ah, that's th' way it should be, sor."

"Was it that way with Jocelyn?"

Finnegan frowned. "You're always bringin' that up, sor? He's out of th' troop, sor. You're in command of E now."

"What did you want to ask me, Sean?"

"Just that, sor. How come you got to work so hard, as though you was tryin' to outdo him all th' time."

"Maybe I am," Schwabacker said. He peeled off his shirt and poured a basin of water. "I've lived a lifetime in the shadow of a man who was so big I just knew I could never be as good as he was. So I went to the Academy to be on my own." He paused to splash water over his face. He talked through the towel. "The gods are against me, Sean. The war was over by the time I was commissioned, my assignment to Fort Laramie was one of inaction, and on top of that I got Temple Jocelyn for a commanding officer, another man like my father, only more kind, even greater than my father."

Finnegan rolled this around in his mind before speaking. "You've been workin' mighty hard these last two years, sor. I've sort of watched from time to time. Beggin' your pardon, sor, but that's fool's business, tryin' to top another man."

"Some things we can't help," Schwabacker said. "But it's my troop now. I mean to command it to the best of my ability."

"Ah, that you will, sor. The lads all know it too."

"Thank you, Sean. Now if you'll excuse me, I have a

lengthy report to write for the general."

Finnegan smiled and went outside. Schwabacker changed into a clean uniform and scraped the chair up to the small pine desk. He labored for several hours over the report, and because he had been under the influence of perfectionists so long, he recopied it so that there were no errors.

He finished in time to answer mess call and during the meal answered numerous questions, most of which he felt incapable of answering authoritatively. The other officers, however, viewed the matter differently. After all, he had been at Laramie, and they expected him to view the entire campaign objectively. They failed to understand his insignificant part and he was glad to return to his quarters where there would be no more questions.

With moments of idleness confronting him, he drew paper and pen toward him again, this time to write to Henrietta Brubaker.

An hour later, Schwabacker left his quarters and walked to the guardhouse, where he posted the letter with the officer of the day, who would see that it went out by the next courier. After that he returned to his quarters and lay down on his bunk. He listened to the sounds of the post until tattoo, then blew out his lamp and undressed.

Sleep came easy for him, and when reveille woke him he bathed, dressed and went outside, frogging his saber. He met Sergeant Finnegan, who had the troop in dismounted formation. After receiving the sergeant's report, Schwabacker dismissed them and went to headquarters, fully expecting some assignment. Instead, the officer of the day informed him that the troop was inactive for the rest of the week.

Because he had been taught that idleness was a sin, Schwabacker used his credit at the sutler's store and bought a few things—a large brush and a bucket of calcimine with which to improve the interior appearance of his quarters.

Sergeant Finnegan came around frequently—twice during the first day—always knocking discreetly, but once inside settling himself with complete disregard for rank. He seemed to glean the gossip from the post and quite volubly related it, bit by bit, until Emil Schwabacker felt fully informed as to the disposition of General Wessels' command, and the current pregnancy of the major's favorite mare.

During his relief from duty, Emil Schwabacker went over his troop with an exacting eye until he could find no flaw, however minute.

On the fifth day a dispatch rider arrived from Fort Laramie with the mail and the regimental clerk brought Schwabacker his letter, which he took to his quarters before opening. The bulkiness of it gave him an odd feeling, a foreboding of trouble.

He read:

St. Albans, Vermont
April 21, 1867

My Dearest Son:
It has been nearly a year since this mother's heart has been lightened by word from you, save what

Dear Henrietta gives me in your letters to her. And this is always in secret so as not to anger your father, who has never forgiven your entering the military life.

Dearest Son, I implore you to make your peace with him. . . . Each night I pray for your safe return and that you might resign your commission. I know, Dear Son, that this is wrong, . . . Your father would condemn you for resigning even more than he condemned you for giving up medicine, but he is a good man, Emil, and he loves you; I swear this. His only wish in life was that you follow his footsteps, and his disappointment was sharp when you did not. Forgive him, if it is in your heart.

God Speed you home.

Your Loving,
Mother

The other letters, from his sisters, Gretchen and Carrie, were repetitions of his mother's plea. Go back? He couldn't. People, he decided, were always making plans for someone else. And that someone was always doing something to make the plans go wrong. His remembrance of his father's anger when he chose the Academy instead of medicine was still sharp and clear. There had been the moment when his father had simply stared, too stunned by this Judas act to speak. Then there were phrases. "After all I've done for you." "This is the reward I get." But he had expected to hear that. After the shock wore off, violent words, fury. Talk, his father had said. "Let's talk it over, son."

How? he wondered. How could you explain to a wonderful man that it was impossible to live with him because his only fault was being too wonderful?

So there were no explanations. Long into the night their voices rose from a conversational tone to shouted warnings, and instead of wishing him success his father prophesied failure. There was something terrible, Schwabacker decided, about being ejected from one's own home. A door closes, but it is more than a door. More like a wall.

Sergeant Finnegan's knock pulled Schwabacker out of the bog of his thoughts. The sergeant stepped inside and closed the door. "Letter from home, sor?"

"Yes," Schwabacker said, and folded it before tucking it in his pocket. "What is it, Sergeant?"

"Th' general just got word that there's a regiment of infantry approachin', sor. A couple days out yet, but Captain Jocelyn's commandin' th' cavalry escort."

"Captain?"

"Aye, sor. He got a promotion." Finnegan sat down on Schwabacker's bunk and put his shoulders against the wall. "I heard that ol' Jim Bridger's been in th' hills scoutin' with th' Crows. He's due in in th' mornin'. Looks like this Gener'l Wessels's goin' to make a push against Red Cloud, bringin' in another regiment an' all."

"Jim Bridger," Schwabacker said softly. "I've heard of him since I was a small boy." He thought of Temple Jocelyn then, and a cloud came into his eyes. "Jocelyn hardly seems well enough to sit a horse, Sergeant. You're sure of this information?"

"Aye, it's gospel, sor. Jocelyn sent a rider ahead."

Finnegan paused before adding, "Likely he's goin' to want th' old troop in th' regiment, sor."

"Yes," Schwabacker said bitterly. "I thought for a time that I was his equal at last."

"Bein' equal ain't important, sor."

Schwabacker opened his mouth to explain, then closed it, knowing he would never be able to explain. What could he explain? About being on the fringe of everything and never in the center? Even now he was on the outside. He was at last stationed at Kearny, but somehow the fight had moved on, to Fort C. F. Smith, or to somewhere, but certainly not here, where he could be a part of it.

Finnegan said, "Th' troop's ready, sor. We can move in an hour. Jocelyn liked it that way, sor."

Angrily Schwabacker whirled on him. "Damn you, you're under my command, not Temple Jocelyn's!"

This straightened Finnegan. "Well, sor, I didn't . . ."

"You're dismissed!" Schwabacker said crisply and the sergeant went out, and after he had gone, Schwabacker stood alone with his shame.

An orderly knocked ten minutes later and Schwabacker gathered his hat and cape to report at headquarters. The clerk admitted him to General Wessels' office, where he came to attention, then, "at ease," which was Wessels' command.

The room was choking with Wessels' cigar smoke and the general's manner was impatient. "Lieutenant, I have received a message from Dr. Cove Butler. He has asked for you to meet Jocelyn's command on Crazy Woman's Fork. This request is unusual, and normally I would disregard it, but Jocelyn is out there with one troop of cavalry, which I understand is mainly recruits, to ride security patrol over a regiment of infantry. You can see how difficult his position would be if he were attacked, and I can assure you, Lieutenant, that those hills are swarming with Red Cloud's Sioux."

"Yes, sir. My troop can move in an hour."

"Then you are so ordered to move," General Wessels said. "Stay alert out there, Lieutenant. Red Cloud's had a good winter to gather his army. I expect him to strike at any time and a large force of slow-moving infantry would be a temptation."

"I understand, sir."

Wessels rose from his chair and pulled down a cloth wall map. "Bridger has been out these past weeks on a scout to the west. Red Cloud is in force north of Lodge Trail Ridge, which is hardly a good cannon shot from the palisade wall. I expect the attack to come from there; all the sniping has issued from that locality. However, it's possible that he has forces to the east. Those Cheyennes you engaged were a part of that force." He faced Lieutenant Schwabacker. "Bring that regiment of infantry to this command; that's an order. I need them badly."

Schwabacker left the general and went directly to the troop barracks. A word to the bugler turned them out, and he was at the stable saddling his horse when Sergeant Finnegan arrived with the other troop sergeants.

Schwabacker searched for an opportunity to speak to Finnegan, to apologize for his behavior, but there were too many details to attend to. Finally the troop was mounted and Schwabacker led them around the parade and out the main gate. With them strung out behind him in a double column, he could then wave Finnegan forward.

The sergeant offered a strict neutrality until Schwabacker said, "My conduct toward you was inexcusable, Sean. I'm sorry for it."

"Ah, sor," Finnegan said, his smile flashing, "I knew you was troubled, sor. Be thinkin' no more about it."

"Thank you," Schwabacker said. "Take charge of the second section until further advised."

"Aye, sor." Finnegan wheeled and trotted back to his position.

E Troop of the 3rd settled down to a fast march.

7

As HE HAD MISSED EVERY LONG-DESIRED THING IN HIS life, Lieutenant Emil Schwabacker missed the arrival of Jim Bridger by better than eight hours. Some men lived to become legend, some men witnessed legends, while others merely had legends pass them by, close, but pass nevertheless. Schwabacker was beating east through the night when Bridger came off Lodge Trail Ridge, an old man, humped in the shoulders and dressed in a dirty canvas coat. But he had the softness of forest winds in his voice and eyes that were accustomed to gazing at inscrutable distances. Ancient now, Bridger had tobacco-stained whiskers and deep wrinkles in the goiter beneath his chin, which had earned him the Sioux name, Big Throat. Mountain man, trapper, horse thief, squaw man many times over. He was everything a man could be, and more, and the post watched as he came through the gates, going directly to headquarters, the buttonless coat flapping as he walked. About him were the wild, nameless flavors of years past. He was the living link to the Bents, to St. Vrain and Hugh Glass, all gone now in the shadows of the great fur trade. He was a link to the dead years and the smoke of a thousand lodge fires and of the rendezvous at Pierre's Hole. All this the men felt who watched Jim Bridger, his old body bent to the wind.

The orderly woke General Wessels, who had slept the night at his desk. Bridger took a chair while the general splashed water over his face. He turned with a towel, his words slightly muffled through it. "What's going on out there, Jim?" He threw the towel aside and rummaged around for a cigar.

Bridger slumped in the chair, studying his gnarled fingers with their broken nails. "Been a hard winter fer th' Sioux, Gener'l. They fussed around until it was too late to hunt much. Been livin' off their moccasins an' that's poor fixin's."

"What's their strength? They've united with the Cheyenne."

"Heap much," Bridger said. "I seen a heap o' Cheyenne lodges, wimmen, kids an' all." He raised his head then. "You want some advice, Gener'l?"

"I'm not Carrington, Jim. I'll take all I can get."

"They sot fer a whoop-up," Bridger said softly. "Th' medicine's right, th' weather's right. Was I you I'd send all th' sojers I could spare to Fort Smith. When Red Cloud hits, he'll hit there first."

"Any reason to think this?"

Bridger's shoulders rose and fell. "Hunch. Th' smell in th' wind. I've been sniffin' it all m' life. I here'n now get th' feelin', that's all."

Wessels ran his fingers through his thick mustache, worry building furrows in the flesh of his forehead. "I'm under strength and General Cooke is pretty tight with his replacements. Carrington lost a lot of men and there'll be a stink raised about it before the campaign's over. I've a regiment of infantry on the way. I'll have to make do with that, Jim."

"Ain't hard to figure Red Cloud's strategy," Bridger said. "For nigh onto a year now he's been snipin' away, a man at a time. Guess Carrington lost a heap of sojers that way, one at a time. That fool Fetterman killed nigh onto eighty at one whack; that was Red Cloud's big day, yessiree. You want an ol' beaver's opinion, Gener'l? You pull them sojers out of Fort Smith and let th' Injuns have it. What is it they call it in lawyer talk? Sue fer peace; that's it!"

"And after I pull them out, what? Have them killed while marching here?"

"Wal now, that ain't too likely," Bridger said. "Red Cloud just wants you folks outa his huntin' grounds. He's said so afore, but no one wanted to believe him. Was I to make a guess, I'd say he'd just watch while them sojers marched south."

"Then I'd have to make my stand here," Wessels said flatly. "Jim, I have orders to follow."

"Dang-fool orders they be too," Bridger said and moved toward the door. He stopped when Wessels spoke again.

"Jim, I've never asked, but what's in this for you, besides the pay?"

"Nothin'," Bridger said. "I'm old. M' kids is growed an' things is changin' so's a man can't keep up with 'em no more. I keep sniffin' th' wind like an old dog, hopin' there's somethin' out there. But there ain't nothin'; this nigger's seen it all. But a man's a fool who don't know when to quit." He shook his head sadly. "There was a time when I'd ask a man for nothin'. I can recollect th' day I'd ride into rendezvous with m' hosses sway-backed with plews. Now I ain't got a good rifle."

For a moment Brevet Brigadier General H. W. Wessels was held motionless by the honesty of Bridger's words. Then he said, "I believe we're all near the end of something. You. Me. Red Cloud. This is the great year, Jim. We've made our threats and shaken our fists. Now this is the year for dying. I think you're right; you can feel it in the air."

After Jim Bridger left, Wessels sat down behind his desk and placed his blocky forearms flat, considering the great Indian campaign of 1867. He had never known Colonel Henry B. Carrington personally, yet the man's deeds, and misdeeds, were already legend in the small, intimate corps of officers. How easy it was to sit back now and, using hindsight for ammunition, pucker full of holes the tactics of another man. General Wessels could not bring himself to do this.

Yet he felt he understood Carrington, and the others

too: Captain Fetterman and Lieutenant Grummond. All had been on the threshold of new and important things, like that new lieutenant, Schwabacker. This was the sort of campaign an officer dreamed of, a campaign that could bring him fame, the chance to excel, to rise above the dull mill of peacetime promotion. And a chance to die, as Fetterman had died; as Grummond and others had. But it would be a hero's death, a death to inspire prose.

The thought left General Wessels unmoved. There was little romanticism in war; a belly-full at Seminary Ridge had convinced him. So ambition wasn't the compelling force. Every man wanted something, including himself. He supposed in a way he was the instrument of destiny, and as the instrument of such power, could act dishonorably and gain absolution. The military relationship with the Sioux could hardly be regarded as honorable.

Yes, he decided, that was it. He had sensed it in his staff, an attitude of the completely righteous. Now he possessed that attitude and he wondered for a moment where it would lead him.

Finally he went to the door and summoned his orderly. "Corporal, see if Portugee Phillips is in his barracks. Have him report here on the double."

When the orderly dashed away, Wessels closed his office door. "Maybe Bridger is right; I ought to let Red Cloud have Fort C. F. Smith. I could withdraw the troops and give it to him. If I can't fight and win a summer of peace for Fort Kearny, then maybe I can buy it."

He waited patiently for the courier.

First Lieutenant Emil Schwabacker sighted the infantry camp on the north bank of Crazy Woman's Fork. He drew his column into a gallop and went in under the horn and guidon, heading for the cavalry detachment's command tent. Schwabacker turned the troop over to Sergeant Finnegan for dismounting and bivouac.

Captain Temple Jocelyn was seated on a folding camp chair, and Emil Schwabacker was shocked to find him so drawn and pale. Cove Butler was there, just completing a dressing on Jocelyn's wound. He smiled and toed another chair around. Butler's face was long and narrow, and since his eyebrows bent down at the ends, he wore a perpetually sad expression. He said, "Glad to see you, Emil. Maybe you can talk some sense into this man. He has the bad habit of unraveling my sutures by riding instead of lounging in the ambulance."

Butler snapped his bag shut and Schwabacker drew his chair close to Jocelyn's. On Jocelyn's forehead sweat slickened the skin like oil. He was in pain, for his lips were pinched and the corners of his eyes drew into small wrinkles. Schwabacker said, "Sir, with your permission I'll lead the command into Fort Kearny."

"Denied," Jocelyn said, eyeing Schwabacker's shoulder boxes, where the solitary lieutenant's bar stood out fresh and new.

"You're a stubborn jackass," Butler said bluntly. From his duster pocket he withdrew a bottle of whiskey and uncorked it. After his drink, which left him gasping and wiping tears from his eyes, Butler said, "Blisters, bullets and hemorrhoids—truly a prosaic existence for a man of science. What wouldn't I give for a quiet place in the country, a small laboratory and a cage of mice all infected with tubercle bacillus." He had another pull at the bottle. "To become famous and rich I would simply effect a cure that sold for no more than a dollar a bottle."

"You talk too much," Jocelyn said. "It's your only failing." He was seized with a fit of coughing, and put his handkerchief quickly to his lips. When he drew it away there was a smear of pink phlegm on it. Schwabacker forgot all about being an officer and became a doctor. He shot Butler a worried glance, but Butler only shook his head. "Cove," Jocelyn said, "if you had a country place you'd turn it into a billiard parlor."

"You're right," Butler admitted. "I'm too restless. The army holds me down." His smile was deep and genuine. "Care for some advice, Temple?"

"If it's cheap."

"Let Schwabacker take the command in. Get in the ambulance and stay there." He saw by Jocelyn's inflexible expression that his advice was unheeded. "Oh, well," he added. "Had I been anything but a fool I might be doctoring the governor's prize mare now and reaping a handsome fee instead of talking to fool captains."

He turned away, but before he did he managed to catch Emil Schwabacker's eye. A moment after Butler walked away, Schwabacker said, "Will you excuse me, sir?" and followed the doctor to his slab-sided wagon.

Butler finished the bottle and cast it against the wagon hub, shattering it. "You saw him. What do you think?"

"Are you asking for a medical opinion?"

Cove Butler nodded.

"Then he's putting one foot in the grave," Schwabacker said.

"Try and tell him that," Butler said. "I can't save a man who doesn't want to be saved, Emil. No doctor can."

"If I could give him that will to go on," Schwabacker said, "would you help me?"

"Help you what?"

"Relieve him of his command."

Butler let his breath whistle through his teeth. "That will get you court-martialed, son. But quick."

"I know that," Schwabacker said. "Doctor, Jocelyn is the kind of a man who'll go as far as his legs will carry him, then he'll travel a little farther on guts, but there has to be an end. I give him six weeks at the outside if he doesn't get to bed and stay there."

Cove Butler shook his head. "I don't owe Jocelyn a damn thing, Emil. He can make up his own mind; I've told him the truth, what would happen if he didn't rest. You be smart and keep out of it."

Schwabacker looked around the camp. The infantry were lounging in the army's manner of systematic disorder. The cavalry were dismounted, but still waiting on the flanks. "Who picked this bivouac, Cove?"

"The captain. To tell you the truth, he couldn't go any farther and didn't want to admit it. Pretty poor, isn't it?"

"From a military standpoint," Schwabacker said, "it's terrible."

"There are hostiles around here too," Butler said

softly. "More than I care to think about. They've been pacing us all the way from Fort Laramie."

"Cheyennes?"

"Sioux too," Butler said. "Between you and me, I think Jocelyn means to make a last-man stand here."

Schwabacker shook his head. "Not with one troop of fresh cavalry recruits and a regiment of infantry too fat to run."

"Two troops of cavalry," Butler contradicted. "He's got yours now, boy." He paused to scan the bracketing hills for several minutes. "I saw smoke up there all afternoon. Jesus, but I wish they'd drop the other shoe. It nearly kills a man to know they're out there and have to wait for them."

"Who's in command of the infantry?"

"Captain Blaine. This is his first tour in Indian country." Butler smiled. "That young second lieutenant you rescued, Eastwood, he's here too."

"He's worthless," Schwabacker said coldly.

"Well, that was sudden judgment," Butler said, and Emil Schwabacker went back to his own bivouac, where he found Sergeant Finnegan inspecting the surrounding terrain and not liking a bit of it. No one had to tell this troop of hard-bitten fifty-cent regulars that hostiles were out there or what they were there for.

Finnegan said, "How's th' capt'n, sor?"

"Very poorly," Schwabacker said. "Well, Sergeant, what would you say our chances were here?"

Finnegan took off his kepi and made a mess of his hair with probing fingers. "Well, sor, it surely is hard to say now. Them duck-footed infantry men is mighty temptin' to a mounted Sioux. Then again, there's somethin' holdin' 'em back or they'd have attacked already. Meanin' no disrespect, sor, but it sure ain't th' capt'n's cavalry. I'd say medicine, sor. Them heathens is sure funny when it comes to their medicine."

"In short, Sergeant, you don't know any more than I do."

"Aye, sor," Finnegan said, grinning, "but I was sort of hopin' you wouldn't find that out." He scuffed dust into a small pile, then kicked it into a cloud. "I just don't like this goddamn country here, sor."

He was justified, Schwabacker decided. To the east lay a nearly sterile sage desert that at this point began to change, to climb into timbered mountains with pines crawling down the rocky slopes. Even the relatively open spots were choked with young balsam and hemlock.

Crazy Woman's Fork was a rough, muddy stream, at this time of the year bloated with run-off water and the snow's last melt. Jocelyn's camp was in the only open stretch of land for the next fifteen miles. The stream, just at the crossing, made a sharp turn, creating two separate forks. The entrance bank on the east slope was steep, but across the water the land rose more slowly, tapering gently to a small divide a few miles beyond. Jocelyn had his picket line formed in the grove near the bend of the stream. A circular bivouac could be formed here, but Schwabacker struck the possibility out of his mind. The only answer was to move, with or without Captain Temple Jocelyn's consent.

"Sergeant," Schwabacker said, "what are the possibilities of making a night march?"

"Poorly, sor. It's all right for the cavalry, sor, but them poor foot sojers'll stumble all over themselves."

"They'll have to get along the best they can," Schwabacker said with finality. "Sergeant, you took me into your confidence once concerning Captain Jocelyn's past. I want you to go a step further and give me his wife's address."

"I couldn't do that, sor."

"Finnegan, I don't mean to pull rank on you, but I haven't time or inclination to explain at this time. I simply want his wife's address. If the man insists on dying, then I think she has the right to choose between being with him at the end or not."

"Jasus, sor, is it that serious?"

"I'm afraid so," Schwabacker said. "Now, will you give me her address?"

"Yes, sor. Sexton's Junction, Virginia, sor." He paused to wipe a hand across his mustached mouth. "I sure hope this is right, sor."

"If you can save a man's life it's right," Schwabacker said. "He's been waiting for a letter from her. Maybe I can get what he wants." He touched Finnegan on the arm. "Fetch my dispatch case and select a man who can ride. I want this letter taken to Laramie in time to catch the Wednesday stage."

"Yes, sor," Finnegan said and turned away. The bugler brought the leather case and Schwabacker sat with his legs crossed to write:

Fort Kearny, Dakota Territory
May 8, 1867

Dear Madam:

Forgive me for writing to you in this manner, but I feel a most urgent necessity. For the two years past, it has been my honor and privilege to serve under your husband, Captain Temple Jocelyn. However, it saddens me to report, that he is now grievously wounded, and apparently has little purpose in carrying on the fight toward recovery. I am aware that he has written to you, and has constantly searched for a reply. Knowing little of the circumstances, I feel that great tragedy must have befallen both of you to cause this painful separation.

Madam, I implore you to search your heart and forgive, if you can, this man who has suffered unendurably for whatever wrong he caused you. You have my word that I will do all in my power to sustain his life as long as possible, in the hope that a message will arrive from your hand to cheer his last hours.

He has carried your picture constantly, the missile so wounding him, having passed through it.

I have the honor to be, very respectfully, your most obedient servant,

                    Emil C. Schwabacker
                    1st Lieut, 3rd U. S. Cavalry

With the letter sealed and in the hands of Trooper Johnson, Schwabacker walked over to Captain Jocelyn's tent. Jocelyn was still sitting in the camp chair, his head thrown back, his eyes closed. He heard the trooper ride out and his eyes followed him until he passed from sight. Then they focused on Lieutenant Schwabacker and in their depths was a shine like the reflection of light from a polished gun barrel. "Lieutenant, I authorized no one to leave this bivouac."

"He left on my authorization, sir," Schwabacker said firmly. "I'm sorry to disturb you, sir, but I would like a word concerning the disposition of the troops."

"As you can see, they are in bivouac," Jocelyn said flatly. "Lieutenant, I suggest that you unite your troop with mine."

"Under your command, sir?"

Jocelyn's eyebrow went up. "Do you find that so odious, sir? You served under me for two years."

"That's not what I meant, Captain," Schwabacker said. "Do you relieve me of my command?"

"No, no, of course not," Jocelyn said with a trace of irritability. "I'm only suggesting a solidification of command for safety and maximum security."

"Sir," Schwabacker said bluntly, "I believe that this bivouac violates every concept of field security. It's unwise to remain here."

The look Temple Jocelyn gave Schwabacker was a shock to the young officer, for something of Schwabacker's father came into Jocelyn's eyes and the stony cast of his cheeks. Sergeant Finnegan chose that time to come over. He stood to Schwabacker's left, near Jocelyn, but the captain did not even favor him with a glance. "Lieutenant, are you pitting your picayune experience against my years of service?" He waved his hand. "You've served me; you know I'm not a martinet! But I believe I'm the best judge in this case."

"I have no intention of debating . . ."

"Neither have I, Lieutenant! As your senior officer I might remind you that your conduct is bordering on the disrespectful. I'm not going to be tied to a saddle again, do you understand? As long as I have voice to command, command I will!"

For a moment Schwabacker could only stare in stunned disbelief. Even Sergeant Finnegan, with his long relationship, could not quite hide his shock. At first, Schwabacker was unable to understand Jocelyn's meaning, but the pieces fell into place like a difficult puzzle. All along, he had mistakenly believed Jocelyn was grateful for having been saved at Ryndlee's. But Temple Jocelyn was not! Instead of uniting them, Schwabacker's action had only pushed them further apart. Jocelyn, like Schwabacker's father, felt shame, not gratitude, when a weakness was exposed. With this new knowledge, Schwabacker was certain that the only thing that would ever right this would be a time when he was weak and Jocelyn could bestow his strength. In that moment he learned a startling truth about Temple Jocelyn, and his own father: how perverse was the attitude of the weak toward those who help them. Generosity became oppression. A man did not win the weak by sharing strength. They were won only by sharing weakness.

Lieutenant Emil Schwabacker said slowly, "Captain, I'm sorry, but I deem it inadvisable to remain here. I'm ordering the command to move in one hour."

"In that event," Jocelyn said evenly, "I will see that you face a general court-martial." He coughed and flecks of blood came to his lips. Quickly he covered his mouth with his handkerchief.

"Sergeant Finnegan," Schwabacker said, "ask Dr. Butler to come here. I want the captain removed to the ambulance."

Finnegan started to turn, but stopped when Temple Jocelyn unflapped his pistol holster and drew his gun. The cocking hammer was a series of snapping sticks, then the bore settled on Emil Schwabacker's belt buckle.

"Your saber, sir. I'm placing you under arrest."

8

COVE BUTLER CAME OUT OF HIS WAGON AND GLANCED toward Captain Jocelyn's tent in time to see him flourish his pistol at Lieutenant Schwabacker. Butler cursed beneath his breath and hurried toward them, his yellow duster flapping as he ran.

Jocelyn heard him approach and did not turn his head. Butler's voice was loud and outraged. "What the hell do you think you're doing, Captain? Put that gun away!"

"This is a military matter, Doctor," Jocelyn said. "Please refrain from any impetuousness that might lead to the termination of your army contract."

He was holding himself in, one arm braced heavily against the arm of the chair. The wrist of his pistol hand rested on the other arm, for he was almost too weak to point it. Schwabacker watched Jocelyn with unwavering attention, and Sergeant Sean Finnegan watched Schwabacker; the young man's thoughts were clearly written on his face. Schwabacker was on the fatal edge of a great military mistake: jumping his commanding officer.

Jocelyn said, "That was a command, Lieutenant. Your saber and pistol, please." A fit of coughing racked his bony frame, and when he clapped the handkerchief over his lips, Sergeant Finnegan stepped forward and clubbed the pistol to the ground with his heavy forearm.

Cove Butler picked it up and held it at arm's length.

The eyes Jocelyn turned toward Finnegan were pained, stunned by this betrayal. "You, Sergeant?"

"Aye, sor," Finnegan said flatly, knowing full well the consequences of his act. "Th' lieutenant's right, sor. You'd best ride in th' ambulance."

Jocelyn would have had more to say, but his strength fled and he would have pitched forward on his face had not Emil Schwabacker caught him. Butler yelled for several of his corpsmen and a moment later they bore Jocelyn away on a litter.

To Sergeant Finnegan, Schwabacker said, "Send Sergeant McGruger to the infantry commander's camp and inform him that we are marching in one half-hour."

"Aye, sor."

After he trotted away, Butler said, "You're in trouble, Emil. So's Finnegan."

"Yes, but I was right, Cove."

Butler shrugged. "You *think* you're right. So does Jocelyn." He turned to go back to his wagon, then stopped. "What made you do it, Emil? Up until a moment ago you worshiped him."

"I suddenly found out he isn't God," Schwabacker said.

Butler grunted. "That must have been quite a revelation," he said in his dry voice, then he went on to his ambulance.

The details of readying the cavalry troops were left to Sergeant Finnegan, who handled them as efficiently as any officer would have. Lieutenant Schwabacker walked over to the infantry commander's tent, which was being struck, and found Captain Blaine in conference with his junior officers.

Lieutenant Eastwood was there, and he and Schwabacker exchanged chilled civilities. Captain Blaine turned, a desk-fat man placed in a situation not at all to his liking. "Lieutenant," he said, "I make this plain before witnesses: you accept full responsibility."

"I've already done that," Schwabacker said crisply. "Captain, my request may sound unusual, but I want your infantrymen to march six abreast."

"My God," Eastwood said, "that kind of a formation isn't even in the manual!"

"Nevertheless we'll march that way," Schwabacker insisted. "I have no intention of trying to supply flankers to a line a mile long. Bear in mind, gentlemen, that if the head of the column is attacked, fully twenty minutes will be required for a foot soldier to advance forward to the point's aid." He looked at each of them, and in that moment his eyes were like Temple Jocelyn's, like the muzzle of a double-barreled shotgun. "Six abreast, gentlemen. And in the event we come under hostile attack, which is more than likely in the morning, the men will fight in ranks. The outside file in the prone, the second kneeling, the third standing. The infantry will defend itself, back to back, covering their own flanks while my mounted troops deploy!"

"Now he's teaching infantry tactics! Von Steuben's at that!"

"Be quiet," Blaine said sharply. He looked keenly at Emil Schwabacker. "You're a military theorist, Lieutenant. Only time will decide whether you're a good one or not."

"I won't insult you by asking you the discipline of your troops," Schwabacker said firmly. "But I promise you this: If they bolt under fire, my men will have orders to shoot them." He glanced at his bull's-eye watch. "We move in exactly twenty-one minutes."

This was a short time and they all knew it. When the hands finally moved around Schwabacker's watch face, he found Sergeant Finnegan waiting. Schwabacker took his horse from the holder and stepped into the saddle. "Mount the troop, Sergeant."

"Trooooopppppp! Pre—pare to mount! MOUNT!"

The infantry shook itself into formation on the fife and drum commands, six abreast as Schwabacker had ordered.

"Take the point, Sergeant," Schwabacker said, and Finnegan wheeled his horse, entering the water a moment later. The cavalry went across first, then dismounted to cover the infantry's crossing. The water was high and cold and there was considerable floundering, but at last they were over, miserable and dripping. Schwabacker remounted his command, then strung them in a row fifty yards to each side of the marching troops.

The shadows of evening began to stretch long and he kept his pace even. Behind him the drum beat cadence, and at the column's rear Butler and his ambulance section trailed along, guarded by a squad commanded by Corporal Linahan.

He ordered a rest stop shortly after dark, and ten minutes later moved on. A hundred and fifty pairs of infantry shoes tore up the trail, and the dust began to rise in strangling proportions. This, coupled with the darkness, made the march torture, but Schwabacker ignored the troop's discomfort.

Twice the infantry commander hastened a runner forward with pleas to slow the pace, but Schwabacker refused to obey. By midnight he knew that he was not making the time he had hoped for, but each weary step drew them nearer the dubious protection of Fort Phil Kearny. Each mile lessened the possibility of attack; or did it amplify it? He couldn't decide. He did know that the Indians would be cursing now, not daring to attack in the darkness. But dawn would come, and with light, hostiles in howling waves. He had a few brief hours remaining to select ground of his own choosing on which to make his stand. And it could be his last.

At three o'clock the decision crystallized and First Lieutenant Emil Schwabacker altered his march path, leading them north and away from the trail. Sergeant Finnegan had the question in his eyes, but he never voiced it. A fresh chew of tobacco satisfied him and he exercised his jaws on that.

The infantrymen were wearing out—Schwabacker could tell from the tempo of their marching—but Captain Blaine did not send the runner forward again. Schwabacker supposed it was Blaine's pride which prevented additional complaint, but he was grateful for it; he had no ear at this time for petty annoyances.

He figured the dawn at six o'clock, or perhaps a few minutes later. At five he halted the column, and then Sergeant Finnegan knew what he had in mind. They all knew, for in the pale night light they could see Lake De Smet. The north shore was rugged and backed by red lava hills and jumbled boulders. The southeast shore, where they now halted, was hilly, but less rocky. A few hundred yards out, timber began, held away from shoreline by the severely alkaline water.

Schwabacker said, "Dismount the troop, Sergeant. Bugler, 'officers' call,' please." He stripped off his gauntlets while the call blared in the silence. His eyes burned from lack of sleep and there was a weary soreness in his wounded arm, although it was healing nicely.

The infantry officers assembled. Blaine was a weary man and he dragged his feet when he walked. "Gentlemen," Schwabacker said, "it is an hour until dawn. You have that time in which to position your companies with their backs to the lake."

"I don't want to make a damn stand!" Blaine said testily.

"You have little choice," Schwabacker said. "Had you remained at Crazy Woman's Fork, you would most

116

surely be fighting now on unsuitable ground." He waved his hand toward the timber. "The Sioux will come from there, although they have a deathly fear of timber." He swung around to face the lake. "The Sioux have two tactics, the circle and the frontal assault, in waves. Since our position against the lake prevents their circling, nothing remains but a frontal assault, and even that is extremely limited. It is their habit to ride through the enemy, regroup on the other side and ride back. As you can see, the lake makes this impossible. Hence our defense is ideal. They will have to slow their attack at fifty yards or ride into the lake. At best they can only engage us in hand-to-hand fighting, and at great cost to their numbers."

Blaine grumbled under his breath, but if Schwabacker's plan was not written up in the manual, it was at least sound. He went away with his officers and placed his infantry companies along the lake shore. Shovels bit into the dirt and entrenchments grew. Finnegan waited, for the cavalry would have to be dispersed.

Drawing him to one side, Schwabacker said, "Sergeant, pick eight good men and leave immediately for Fort Kearny. By hard riding you should raise the gates in an hour. Advise General Wessels of our position and tell him that we are sitting in the middle of the Sioux nation. I don't think it's necessary for me to point out our precarious position. It's my firm belief that we will soon be under severe attack, and I think we can hold for three hours, certainly no more than that." He offered his hand. "Good luck, Sergeant, and get going."

"I'll bring th' whole damn post back, sor," Finnegan said and made his selection of men quickly. When they mounted and rode out, Captain Blaine hurried up, his manner anxious.

"Lieutenant, where are those men going?"

"To Fort Kearny, sir. It's an hour's ride from here."

"Jesus God!" Blaine stormed. "If it's that close, why don't we march on in?"

"Because I don't believe we'd make it, sir," Schwabacker said calmly. "The Sioux would cut us to pieces while we were moving."

"What's to stop them from cutting up your sergeant and his detail? Cavalry superiority?"

Schwabacker refused to rise to the bait. "Sergeant Finnegan knows Indians, sir. He'll stay to the thickest woods, where the Sioux hate to go. We'll make our stand here, Captain."

"This is all your doing," Blaine snapped. "Unfortunately I allowed my inexperience to sway my judgment, subjecting my command to the whim of a glory-hunting yellow-leg."

"Are you finished, sir?"

"Yes," Blaine said, a little shamefaced. "But I'll make a full report of this, you can rely on it."

"Captain, let me inform you of a few facts. The Sioux were ringing your bivouac last night, and they meant then to give you a licking. The Fetterman massacre is fresh in their minds, strong medicine. I don't propose to add to it by getting myself killed. *This* is the ground upon which *I* will fight."

"Get something straight, Lieutenant! I didn't come

out here to lose half of my command!" Blaine slapped his thigh impatiently and studied the dark out-fringe of timber.

"I have never believed," Schwabacker said, "that it was a soldier's duty to die for his cause, but to make sure the enemy soldier died for his. Now if you will excuse me, Captain, there are many details that require my attention."

Blaine's expression froze, for no man, especially a superior, likes to be pushed out. And yet he was, and he knew it and felt completely helpless to counteract it. There was superiority in Emil Schwabacker, in manner, in grasp of command, that left Captain Blaine feeling incompetent, and a little foolish. He whirled on his heel and rejoined his own command.

Schwabacker then walked over to Cove Butler's ambulance, which had been pushed to the lake edge where the rocks all but hid it. Butler was sitting on the dropped tongue.

"How's Captain Jocelyn, Cove?"

"I gave him some laudanum to quiet him," Butler said. He found a cigar, pared off the end with a scalpel, then popped the smoke into his mouth and touched a match to it. "Nice place you have here. Better than Jocelyn would have picked. He really meant to make a fight of it at Crazy Woman's Fork. It's hell when a man gets to the point where he can't go any farther, and yet's so proud he won't listen to anyone else."

"Don't run him down," Schwabacker said. "He taught me everything I know about Indian fighting."

Butler pursed his lips. "You seem original enough,

Emil. Don't sell yourself short." He looked to the east where a grayness was beginning to thin the black night sky. "In another half-hour you may be either living or dead, Emil, but either way, you'll be a hero."

Schwabacker laughed at this. "Did you just finish a bottle?"

"What are you laughing at? I'm serious."

"I was thinking of what my father would have said had you told him that." Schwabacker shook his head. "Heroes are born, Doctor."

"That may be your opinion," Butler said. "But this is the third time you've challenged the hostiles to come and get you. You puzzle me, Emil. Is there something personal between you and Red Cloud?"

"Red Cloud?" Schwabacker laughed again, softly. "Cove, I'll never see Red Cloud."

"That's a pretty positive statement to make," Butler said.

"Not for me," Schwabacker said. "You want the story of my life, Doctor? It's the things that happen when I'm not there. When I was young my father took me to see General Andy Jackson. We stood on the depot platform for three hours waiting for the train. Then I had to go to the toilet. When I came back, the train had come and gone." He smiled ironically. "That's it, Doctor. I wanted to go with Carrington and build Kearny, but I missed out by a week. Then I hoped for a transfer, but I missed that too. You know, Jim Bridger was supposed to come back to the post, but I had already left with this patrol and I missed seeing him. Doctor, I'm going to miss the whole goddamn thing! That's the way things go with me."

"What does it take to convince you?" Butler asked. "It could be that you're doing more than your share of fighting."

"Ryndlee's?" He snorted. "A piddling backwash engagement. It'll never be mentioned against the Fetterman massacre."

"All right, let that one go," Butler said. "But you picked your ground and fought Red Cloud's Cheyenne friends to a halt. Hell, we heard about the licking Spotted Tail took clear back at Laramie! That was big, son!"

"Big? Doctor, I tricked Spotted Tail. In a stirrup-to-stirrup fight he'd have slaughtered my entire command." Schwabacker paused. "No, Red Cloud's after Fort Kearny and C. F. Smith, not me."

"Now you're all set to pick another fight," Butler pointed out. "Emil, if you're not careful, Red Cloud's going to get fed up with you cutting up his bucks and come after your hair personally."

"The invitation's open," Schwabacker said. "Unless I settle down to business, the campaign will be over before I can get into it."

"Man, you're into it now! Up to your ears!"

"Not quite," Schwabacker said softly. "But I will be when the sun comes up." He looked east, where the day was being born.

9

SERGEANT SEAN FINNEGAN MADE HIS RIDE THROUGH the dawn and the Sioux allowed him to pass with his detail through their tightening lines. He knew they were there, but he saw and heard nothing. He supposed it was the complete stillness that convinced him of their presence, and he wondered why no bullet came, no bowstring twanged. The detail followed him in single file, looking often at their back trail, studying carefully the deep shadows of the rocks and trees. All of them had the wire-drawn tightness of men who feel something is wrong and cannot define it.

He cut onto the Bozeman Road as the first light bloomed and pushed the detail into a trot, raising the palisade walls as the regimental bugler blew reveille. A guard challenged them, then the gates opened and Finnegan flung off to speak to the officer of the guard.

Brevet Brigadier General H. W. Wessels was immediately summoned and came from his quarters, pulling up his suspenders as he trotted toward headquarters. He answered Finnegan's salute, and because he knew old soldiers, poured him a water tumbler full of whiskey before asking any questions. First things first with these Irishmen.

Finnegan made his report. "Lieutenant Schwabacker met th' command, sor. He relieved Captain Jocelyn and placed him in th' ambulance."

"With Jocelyn's permission, Sergeant?"

"Na, sor." Finnegan explained the circumstances, and

his part in disarming a superior officer. This drew a deep frown from Wessels, but did not blunt his curiosity. "Lieutenant Schwabacker's taken a defense position near Lake De Smet, sor. He's askin' for reinforcements. Like as not he won't be able to hold th' hostiles off, sor, 'cause they got him fair surrounded. Comin' in it felt like we was ridin' through th' whole Sioux nation, sor."

"Can you show me his position on the map, Sergeant?"

"Aye, sor. To the dot." He went to the wall map and pointed to Schwabacker's exact position.

General Wessels pursed his lips and thought for a moment. "He chose good ground anyway. Better than Crazy Woman's Fork would have been. Did you have any trouble getting through, Sergeant?"

"Na, sor, and it surely puzzles me, sor. It ain't like them to let a patrol through."

"You could have been wrong, imagining there were Sioux about."

Finnegan shook his head. "Sor, I've been in Injun country a long time. There was hostiles all around us, sor. Th' men'll back me, sor."

"All right," Wessels said. "We'll assume you're right, that Red Cloud's bucks are thick as ticks. Ever since Carrington built this mouse trap there's been one sniping after another. That's been Red Cloud's way of fighting, up until Fetterman made his foolish mistakes. One man a day; two if he's lucky and someone gets careless. He's always been out there, so why shouldn't he be now? However, this goes against Red Cloud's grain, closing with a strong force."

"Not this time, sor," Finnegan said. "Th' lieutenant's probably in th' thick of it now, sor."

"Yes," Wessels said. "But I can't help thinking how strange it is that the Sioux let you through, Sergeant." He gnawed his lip. "Red Cloud's a capable general, Sergeant. Oh, there's no swagger stick and mustache wax about him, but he's clever, and smart. He's used to Carrington and his impulsiveness. Carrington would dash out with his command to the rescue and get half of them killed." Wessels left his chair to pace the floor. He rambled on, talking more to himself than to Finnegan. "Suppose by letting you through with a message, Red Cloud figured I'd come with reinforcements. That might be what he wants, all the long knives in one nice package."

"I'd say that was good figurin', but what about th' lieutenant, sor?"

"If I've guessed right, I could be walking into a trap, couldn't I?"

"Aye, sor," Finnegan said in a worried voice. "An' if you don't, th' lieutenant's liable to get hisself killed, along with th' command, sor!"

"He's young, Sergeant, but he's not a William Fetterman." He shook his head. "I'm sorry, Sergeant, but Lieutenant Schwabacker has to get out of this the best way he can."

"Aye, sor. Do I have your permission to rejoin him?"

Wessels looked long at Sean Finnegan. He had seen this before, this kind of man, this kind of loyalty to an officer, and by this he measured his officer's ability, for a man who commanded this commanded greatly. Wessels said, regretfully, "You do not. You're dismissed, Sergeant."

"Aye, sor," Finnegan said, anger a flame border around his mind, and in his voice.

General Wessels understood. "Hate me if it'll help, Sergeant."

Finnegan opened his mouth to speak, then waved his hand futilely and stomped out without saluting. General Wessels let him go, deciding that an angry man deserved this liberty—and perhaps more.

Dawn came and all the night shadows vanished. Schwabacker stood along the rocky lake shore, his eyes turned to the only possible lane of attack, the fringe of trees several hundred yards away. Every man in his command had his eyes fixed on this target.

The sun's hot shape looked over the shoulders of the hills, bathing the lake in fire. The troopers began to look around nervously, seeking an answer as to why there was no attack. Trouble, Schwabacker reflected, had a habit of growing worse when it failed to materialize when expected. There was no movement at all in the trees, save the vague stirrings at the tops where the morning breeze fanned the uppermost branches. The land was silent and the men were silent. Even the horses picketed by the water's edge were quiet.

Emil Schwabacker's first thought was that he had again made some terrible, unforgivable mistake in judgment and his glance whipped around to the ends of the lake, but there was no evidence of a hostile flanking movement. A glance showed him the impossibility of such a maneuver.

No, the attack had to come from the front. There was no other way.

No other way. Why? Because he thought so? How many times had he thought that, only to discover that there *had* been another way, a better way? How many times had he had his nose rubbed in his own mistakes . . . ?

"Do you have the time, sir?" This was the apple-cheeked bugler speaking.

"Huh?" Schwabacker was startled, like a man coming out of a deep sleep.

"The time, sir?"

"Oh!" He bared his bull's-eye watch. "Ten after seven, Malloy."

"Thank you, sir." The bugler passed the time along the row of dirty-shirt blue.

The infantry were beginning to show signs of restlessness and Schwabacker could not blame them. Nothing in the manual covered this. The hours on the drill field faded to insignificance and a man was left doubting himself, his weapons and his officers. At least until the first whoop split the silence, or the first bullet made a man down the line thrash in agony. Then there was no more doubt. Then a flame dropped down and seared away from a man all but the core inside, which burned on until the last breath.

Lieutenant Schwabacker left his command position and went rearward to where Captain Jocelyn lay in the ambulance, his engraved pistol firmly grasped in a steady hand. He watched Schwabacker approach and when he stopped, said, "Doubts, Lieutenant?"

"Yes," Schwabacker said. He turned his head for another look at his breastwork lined with rifles. "I can't make it out, sir."

"You're in command," Jocelyn said. "Figure it out, sir."

The resentment in Jocelyn's voice caused Schwabacker to look at him sharply. He said, "Captain, I'm trying to understand you, but somehow you've always managed to make it difficult. I think you enjoy being an enigma. I believe you'd wither and die if you had to be like other men. You're a martyr, Captain, and you're enjoying every minute of it." He saw flames of anger in Jocelyn's eyes and knew that he had at last struck upon the truth. "Captain, I've written to your wife. Do you understand me, sir? I've written her, advising her of your wound."

He was prepared for anger, but Jocelyn's action surprised him, caught him completely unaware. The pistol arced even as Schwabacker ducked, but the barrel caught the young man on the shoulder with numbing force. Schwabacker clawed out for Jocelyn's hand, seized the wrist and bent the arm against the joint until the pistol fell from lax fingers.

Jocelyn's breathing was raspy and sweat beaded his forehead. "I'll kill you for that," Jocelyn said. "Meddling pup!"

"No, sir," Schwabacker said. "You won't kill me, Captain." Butler had heard the raised voices and came back to see what was going on. Schwabacker said, "This is private, if you don't mind, Doctor."

"All right," Butler said and turned and went back to the lines.

Schwabacker looked into Jocelyn's chilling eyes and found that the chill had vanished. "Captain, I think I understand much about you. Can it be that for years now you've been secretly joyed because your wife has never communicated with you? Can it be that you discovered how martyrdom made you stand out importantly, brought you the notice and talk that otherwise you might not have ever received? There's nothing like a secret past, is there, Captain? Nothing like speculation to keep up interest, is there?" Schwabacker stepped back as if there were something untouchable about Temple Jocelyn. He tossed the ornamented pistol into the ambulance with great contempt. "I'm sorry that I wrote to your wife, Captain. Sorry, because I don't think she had much of a man to start with."

When he turned on his heel, Jocelyn said, "Wait!"

Schwabacker turned back, for he was the kind of a man who could never refuse another. "What is it, Captain?"

"I . . . I have a good deal to apologize for. Will you allow me?"

"To me, sir?" Emil Schwabacker shook his head. "Don't apologize to me. For two years I waited for a word, sir, your approval. Now I don't need it. I never needed it; suddenly I realize it."

He returned to his command position and found everything the same, the wind in the trees, the silence of the woods and the sun's mounting heat. His small hand motion drew Sergeant McGruger close and they

128

huddled down for a conference.

Schwabacker said, "What do you make of it, Sergeant?"

"I'm wondering why I ain't dead, sir. I ought to be."

"You think the Sioux are still there, Sergeant?"

McGruger laughed softly, ironically. "Listen, what do you hear out there?"

"Nothing. Absolutely nothing."

"That's just it," McGruger said. "Birds is always singing, sir. There's always noise in the woods, but now there's nothing. Everything shuts up when Indians is around, sir."

Schwabacker listened as McGruger had been listening, if a man can listen to silence. Somehow the vacuum of sound was almost deafening; after a moment of intense concentration, Schwabacker found his ears almost aching.

"Why are they waiting, Sergeant?"

McGruger shrugged. "Detail's my line, sir. Strategy I leave to officers and gentlemen."

Did Finnegan get through? Did he? How can a man tell? Would they boast if they had caught him and his detail? Likely. They had their hacking party at Ryndlee's. The Sioux were even more vain than the Cheyennes. There was no boasting, no riding out in sight with blood-dripping scalps. Assumption one: Finnegan and his detail made it . . .

Schwabacker began to perspire freely.

One mistake, that's all it'll take. Assumption two: Finnegan got through and General Wessels is on his way with the command. Wait! Wrong! Why haven't they attacked? What are they waiting for? Go back! Assumption number one: Finnegan got through. Assumption number two: The Sioux let him get through, but for a reason. Reason . . . everybody has a reason—Jocelyn, Father, Henrietta . . . Wait! Fetterman; what did he do? What was it about Fetterman to remember? Sure! He was decoyed into making a mistake. Red Cloud tricked him into an ambush by pinning down a small force. Wait! Decoy! Assumption number . . . No! Fact number one: Finnegan got through. Number two: They wanted him to get through! Fact number three: They want the general to come into a trap! . . .

He paused to mop his face again and look at his watch: five after eight.

Wessels has to be stopped! But how? Two and a half hours from Kearny by forced march; he can't force infantry too hard and still keep them fresh enough to fight. Eight o'clock now. If Wessels is coming, and we have to assume he is, he'll get here around ten. No, closer to eleven. . . . Diagnosis completed! Prognosis? God, how much weight can a man stand? Prognosis! Yes, the prognosis. Death? Another Fetterman massacre? Another feather in the brilliant bonnet of General Red Cloud? Prognosis . . .

He spoke to Sergeant McGruger. "Convey my compliments to Captain Blaine and his officers. Ask them to report here."

McGruger moved away to the infantry positions on both flanks. The officers gathered one by one, first Lieutenant Eastwood, then Blaine and the other two commanders. Captain Blaine wore a heavy frown of displeasure. He was sweating freely and not entirely from the heat.

"Gentlemen," Schwabacker said, "I have come to the conclusion that help will not arrive from Fort Phil Kearny."

"That's ridiculous!" Eastwood said. "Do you mean to imply that the general is abandoning us?"

"Nothing of the kind," Schwabacker said firmly. "I am merely convinced that the Sioux are using us as bait for a trap. And I have no intention of becoming a piece of cheese, even figuratively." He glanced at his watch. "At exactly ten o'clock, Captain Blaine, I want a frontal assault directed at the woods. I will split my cavalry forces and create a diversion by a flanking maneuver. The object is to break through the Sioux and get onto the Bozeman Road again."

"We never should have left it in the first place," Blaine snapped, "and I'll be most happy to testify to that at your court-martial."

Schwabacker found that he too could spear a man with his eyes. He held Blaine in this manner, like a medical student examining a small specimen on the end of a scalpel. "Do you wish to assume command, Captain? Do you want my saber, sir?"

Blaine waved his hand, vastly annoyed. "Good God, man!" This was all Blaine had to say.

"If there are no more questions?" Schwabacker saw that there were none. No questions, just the mad desire to vacate this ominous place and gain the dubious security of four palisade walls, which Red Cloud could come over quite easily any time he so desired.

The infantry officers went back to their flock and Schwabacker gave McGruger his orders. "Split the cavalry evenly, Sergeant. Have every man by his horse by ten. Mount on my hand signal and we'll try to flank the woods."

The impossibility of this was written in McGruger's blunt face. "Who'll command Jocelyn's green bunch, sir? He didn't bring a second officer."

"You will," Schwabacker said. "Have you ever wanted to be an officer, Sergeant?"

"Not enough to get killed for it."

But he would be, Schwabacker was sure of it. And he would do his best, which was all that any man could ask. There was nothing left now but waiting, and that was always the most difficult part of war. He tried not to look around, to see these men, but looking at them was something he could not help. Looking at them as men alive, but seeing them as men dead. McGruger. There was that night in Platte junction when McGruger tried to whip his way through a cow outfit. He'd always remember McGruger that way, getting knocked down and getting up, always getting up. And Malloy, the bugler. Fourteen when he joined the troop. Sixteen now. The age when a fellow should kiss a girl or sit on some porch swing with the moonlight drifting down through oak leaves like silver dust. But Malloy wouldn't know those things now. It was as if suddenly Schwabacker possessed divine perception, as if he could reach out his hand and touch those marked for dying.

He pulled his glance away from his men and studied an ant crawling across the breastwork, trying if he

132

could, to find meaning in this lowly form of life.

Nine o'clock came with silent marching steps. The waiting became intense and unendurable, yet each man dredged his courage and found some strength heretofore unknown to him. At a quarter to ten, Schwabacker left the breastwork and assembled his troop, which was hidden from the woods by the sloping ground leading into the water. They went into the saddle at his hand signal. He turned his own troop to the right. McGruger, with Jocelyn's raw recruits, moved out to the left.

A man could not hide forever, so they breasted the rise together and drove into a gallop, riding in a huge caliper-shaped movement that would place them at right angles to the woods. Faintly came the beat of drum, the lilt of fife as the infantry surged forward in mass attack. A moment later, over the pound of racing horses, came the rattle of musketry and Emil Schwabacker knew that the Sioux had at last opened fire.

They were close in to the woods now and he unsheathed his saber, unholstered his pistol, going in with dropped reins, knees locked to the straining horse. To his right and slightly rearward, Malloy's bugle was a ringing goad, the sounds of "charge" spanging among the trees, absorbed like a bullet in cotton.

Then they were into the Sioux, suddenly, shockingly. Into the knife sticks, and the scalp-hung war lances. Guns smashed and horses collided with men. Sabers rose and fell, streaming blood and the acrid taint of powder smoke raised tears in the eyes.

Trooper Malloy's call cracked, then resumed, but pinched as he blew blood out the bell. He rode into them, a hand clutched to his stomach, his knees locked against the horse until he died there, still clinging, his horn whipping at the end of the gay yellow neck thong.

Schwabacker could hear the fierce sounds of battle where the infantry threw their weight against the Sioux, but these sounds came from a long tunnel that opened into another world. His own was death and the smells and the sounds that went with it. He jerked and nearly fell when a bullet ripped through his thigh and struck his horse a glancing blow. The horse, frightened now, plunged ahead, driving against a Sioux who appeared miraculously. Hooves smashed out, a man went down in blood, then Schwabacker checked the animal and wheeled to new attack.

He could not win this; he knew instinctively that he was beaten. "Fall back!" The power of his own voice surprised him. His troop, what remained of it, whirled and fought clear, then raced back toward the lake.

The infantry were retreating before the Sioux fire, leaving men in sprawled shapes along the way. What remained of McGruger's force fell back, and Captain Blaine threw his fire power into covering the sergeant's retreat.

Around Schwabacker were men who stared with glazed eyes, spit-froth on their lips and chins and the acid-brass taste of death in their mouths. The enemy had been met and men had stood and bled; there was something wholly numbing about combat. No words fitted it, for too many years of civilized veneer had been stripped away and the naked lust for survival exposed.

Butler was working frantically with his two enlisted

corpsmen. McGruger was helped off his horse and spread on a blanket, but he died almost immediately, the back of his head shot completely away.

Schwabacker turned to Linahan. "How many, Corporal?"

"Eleven of our troop, sor." He scrubbed a hand across his eyes, trying to get them to focus. His breathing was a loud whistle through his teeth. "I'll check McGruger's bunch, sor, but they've been thinned."

Something to do, that kept a man going when everything wanted to stop. At Captain Blaine's position, Schwabacker saw how terrible had been the toll. Twenty-five men down. Three-quarters of them dead. Blaine's face was gray in the sunlight and there was blood on his sword. His pistol was completely empty.

What could he say? Schwabacker turned his horse and rode back to his own position. He wanted to dismount, but his leg was numb and he knew he could not stand on it. Corporal Linahan came back. He merely shook his head and said, "We'll not be able to split again, sor."

"I understand," Schwabacker said. "Absorb them into the troop, Corporal."

"Aye, sor." He saw Schwabacker's blood-drenched leg. "Let me help you down, sor." He spoke to a couple of troopers who crouched nearby, staring at the ground between their legs. "Give us a hand here, buckos. Th' lieutenant's been wounded."

They lifted him from the horse and placed him on the ground, where he lay back, gasping with vast relief. By turning his head he could see the breastwork and past it

135

to the timber. Several of the Sioux came forth, intent on scalping the slain, but several of the infantrymen fired, and when the Sioux fell, no more came into sight.

Cove Butler came around later, but Schwabacker had already bandaged his thigh and would not let the doctor fuss with it. There was a burying detail to organize; he chose a spot near the water's edge. Squad fires were built and coffee made, which seemed to help some. The morning wore into afternoon.

Water had to be rationed, for the lake water was not fit to drink. Around four o'clock a hot meal was cooked, and the command ate in sections, one on guard, two eating. Lieutenant Emil Schwabacker ate by himself, for his thoughts were too bitter to tolerate company. Nearly a quarter of his command had died, and this would be difficult to explain. He knew for sure now that Wessels would never arrive. If he was to get out he would have to do it on his own.

He was still mulling this dismal thought over through the long shadows of evening. The laudanum Butler had supplied numbed the throb in his leg and he found rest possible, but the weight of his responsibilities forbade sleep.

Through the long night he waited, his eyes constantly on the dark smudge of timber several hundred yards away. Two hours before dawn he made his decision, and if it sounded insane, even to himself, he put it down to the slight fever coloring his cheeks.

10

CORPORAL LINAHAN WAS SUMMONED, AND WHEN HE knelt down in the predawn darkness by Lieutenant Schwabacker, he was made sergeant, which was a surprise to Linahan, whose drinking habits had broken him five times in nine years.

"Please summon Captain Blaine and Dr. Butler," Schwabacker said in a whisper. "Quietly now." He sat there and waited. Finally they arrived, Butler first, but Schwabacker said nothing until Blaine got there. "I think I have the way out," he said. The two men looked at each other. Butler was sure it was the fever, and Blaine was equally convinced that there was insanity in Schwabacker's family.

"We can't survive another day," Schwabacker said. "The Sioux softened us yesterday; they'll come to us at dawn and then it'll be another Fetterman affair."

"You don't expect us to attack again," Blaine said.

"No, I don't," Schwabacker said. "I'll attack with the cavalry and buy you the time to get out by the north end of the lake. Assemble your command very quietly and move them out by companies. Form at the north end of the lake, in the rocks. You will hear us attack, and then make your best march speed toward Kearny."

"Good God," Butler said. "You'll die in that woods!"

"Die?" Schwabacker shook his head. "I'll try not to, Doctor. I've no intention of waiting until dawn to charge. We'll go in dismounted until there is danger of their guards spotting us, then we'll try to catch the camp by surprise."

"I'm a doctor," Butler said, "but I've been around the army enough to blow a dozen holes in that plan."

"You're not invited," Schwabacker told him. "This is the way it'll be. This is an order." He glanced at Blaine. "I'll expect your first company to move in fifteen minutes. Leave behind every piece of equipment that will rattle."

"All right," Blaine said. "If you think there's a chance."

"Stay here and there will be no chance at all," Schwabacker said.

Captain Blaine left, but Cove Butler remained. "What was going on between you and Jocelyn yesterday?"

"A personal matter. Get him out of here, Cove. I'll have Sergeant Linahan load the wounded into the ambulance. It will be crowded, but you'll have to make do."

"We'll make do," Butler promised. "Can you make it with that leg?"

"Someone will put me on a horse. If I fall off, it won't matter." He touched Butler on the arm. "Say nothing of this to Captain Jocelyn. I mean, about my troop attacking the Sioux camp."

"Real heroic," Butler said. "In the Jocelyn manner. Are you going to turn into one of these long-suffering martyrs too?"

He left the question hanging and walked away. Sergeant Linahan knelt again. "Orders, sor? I overheard."

"Strip the troop, Sergeant. Bring the horses in off pickets and get rid of anything that will rattle. We'll carry carbines and wrap rags around the rings to keep them from jingling."

"Aye, sor." He stood up. "How much time, sor?"

Schwabacker glanced at his watch, turning it so he could vaguely see the hands. "Thirty, forty minutes on the outside. Have two troopers come around and lift me on my horse."

"Aye, sor," Linahan said and ambled off, his words quietly falling as he moved among the troop, bringing them to their feet.

Blaine's first company of infantry gathered in loose formation and shuffled past, remarkably quiet. Captain Blaine had stripped them of horsecollar blanket roll, canteen; everything but their rifles and the accouterments that served them. Even the rattly bayonets and scabbards had been abandoned.

The second company passed by a few minutes later, then the third. Schwabacker unfrogged his saber, drew it, then fought to a one-legged standing position. Trooper Haukbauer came up with his horse. Haukbauer could blow a bugle and had taken Malloy's place. With Haukbauer's help, Schwabacker mounted, but the effort left him sick and sweating. He was the only man mounted, and at his signal the troop moved toward the woods at a walk. Finnegan had taught him enough about the Sioux to know that they never camped in timber, for they possessed a deadly fear of ambush. So he went over the terrain in his mind, conjuring up a mental map, and remembered a large, cleared plain about a mile southeast of this timber.

There would be scouts in the woods, but he knew how lax Indian sentry duty could be. The Indian had little heart for regimentation, and a brave designated to guard the horse herd would most likely spend half of that time snuggled up to his squaw. Schwabacker was counting on this native slovenliness. Their fear of the timber, the triumph they had had, all led him to believe that the woods were thinly guarded.

So he moved his command to the very fringe without apparent detection. Then he held to the deepest shadows he could find, working his way around the west side. For almost an hour he moved at a slow parade walk. They made little or no noise and he was mildly surprised at how quiet a man could be when his hair hung in the balance.

An hour. Blaine would be pushing his men hard, and with no packs to slow them, they were probably four miles from the lake by now. Schwabacker's head turned as he searched the sky to the east for the first shards of the false dawn. Indians were early risers. Dawn would bring them from their lodges, ready for war. He judged he had forty minutes left. Forty minutes to live? This was a question no man liked to think about.

His knowledge of Sioux ways stood him in good stead, for on the other side of the timber lay their camp, the tall lodges built into a huge semicircle with the openings facing east, to the coming sun.

He raised his hand, halting the troop a thousand yards from the Sioux. The predawn darkness was still intense and he could barely make out the lodges. Could he close undetected to seven hundred yards? Five? Never before had he considered a man's chances for survival in so many feet, but there it was, measured out for him. The closer he got, the more damage he could do before they were completely aroused. The prize was tempting and he signaled a slow advance.

There was no change in the east. The night held, but the lodges became clearer as he narrowed the gap to dangerous proportions. At seven hundred yards he caught his breath and closed the distance to six. Behind him, Sergeant Linahan and Trooper Haukbauer were growing nervous. Each man walked beside his horse, one hand over the saddle, ready to spring up at the first hostile cry, which would betray their presence.

When he judged they were no more than five hundred yards away, the tension became too much and he hand-signaled them into the saddle. Carbines and pistols were cocked. The sound was like a bundle of small twigs being broken.

Schwabacker's nod to Haukbauer sent the troop into a wild run. The first notes of "charge" split the silence like huge rents in cloth. Haukbauer cracked on the high notes and on the trills, but the sound was "charge," in the cavalry key of "C," and the horses knew it and every man knew it.

The Indians knew it too, for a shrill yell went up as they broke through the opening of the camp. A brave made a foolish appearance out of nowhere and went down with his face shot away. Into the lodges they drove, over men, scattering the Sioux in confusion. Guns pounded and muzzles lanced flame back and forth, then in an instant they were through and into the horse herd, cutting, shooting, driving them in frantic terror out onto the rolling land beyond.

Carbines cracked, answering the dull blasts of trade rifles from the Sioux hornets' nest. Two men fell but there was no stopping now. Schwabacker held the troop into a wild race for a mile, and when the horse herd was scattered, he wheeled his horse and re-formed the command.

Four down; he knew without counting. A good officer gets that feel of his troop, knowing instinctively when there are gaps in the ranks. The Sioux camp was in an uproar and there were still sporadic shots aimed into the night.

To Linahan, Schwabacker said, "We're going back, Sergeant."

"Jasus Christ, sor! Not through 'em again?"

"Just into them, Sergeant."

"That's worse!" But Linahan was a sergeant now and the troop formed on him, pistols and carbines reloaded. Schwabacker flailed his horse into a dead run, straight for the shattered Sioux camp. Behind him a little over fifty men rode low over their horses' necks. Fifty against two hundred, and there would be no surprise this time. The Sioux were waiting.

Their fire was undisciplined, ragged, but somehow two more saddles were wiped clean. Schwabacker felt his own horse stumble, break its stride, then pick up gallantly. The angry Sioux never lacked for courage, and at the sight of the charging long knives, raced out to meet them, shooting as they ran.

Suddenly Schwabacker halted his command; this was too good to pass up. And he caught the Sioux that way, in the open, away from cover, and poured in his fire dismounted. Carbines roared in chorus, in squads, then dropped back to reload while another squad poured lead into the Sioux. Horses went down, good cavalry mounts, and men went down, then the Sioux had had enough and broke, running back toward the village.

"Cease fire!" Schwabacker shouted, and the bugle took it up. His own horse was down, thrashing, and he mercifully put a bullet into its head. Several of the troopers were pairing off, going into the saddle double. Sergeant Linahan dismounted hurriedly and boosted Schwabacker into the saddle, then mounted behind him.

"Do we git, sor?"

Schwabacker found he could smile. "We 'git,' Sergeant. Haukbauer, sound 'recall.'"

They formed on the horn and wasted little time putting distance between themselves and the infuriated Sioux. Schwabacker knew that they were a long way from being out of this, but his chances of survival now had risen to endurable heights. He watched his men, saw the change in them. Victory did that to a trooper, made him whole, gave him faith in himself. The day before they had taken a licking and hadn't liked it. Now they had handed it back, hard, and they did like that. Even Jocelyn's recruits had changed. Schwabacker could scarcely tell them from his own seasoned men.

They halted a mile and a half away to tie the wounded to the saddle. He had lost eight; two had gone down that he hadn't seen, and he felt this loss sharply.

Schwabacker stayed on Sergeant Linahan's horse; dismounting was a painful chore. He felt a sharp, stinging sensation along his ribs and for a moment thought some insect was pestering him until he touched his fingers to it. Then he recognized the stickiness as blood. God! He hadn't even been aware that he was hit!

The east was growing light and he could make out faces now, some of them smiling. There was murmured talk, and this was a good sign. He spoke to Linahan. "We're wasting time, Sergeant. You want to lose your hair?"

Linahan came into the saddle and the command turned west, toward the Bozeman Road and Fort Kearny. There was time now to think of Captain Blaine's command. The jogging horse made watch reading difficult, so Schwabacker guessed. An hour and a half? No, hardly that. The fight couldn't have lasted over fifteen minutes, but fights were deceptive, often appearing in retrospect to be distorted, with time all jumbled up, condensed, minutes into hours, even great hazy gaps of days.

Linahan said, "You think they'll pursue, sor?"

"Take a guess, Sergeant."

"Ah," Linahan said, "so th' fightin' may not be over." He paused for a moment. "You suppose them duck-footed infantry men got clear, sor?"

"They are probably double timing all the way to Kearny," Schwabacker said, finding amusement in this mental image. It was something beyond him, this natural contempt a mounted man has for the dismounted. Since the dawn of animal domestication he supposed it had been so—the mounted man was always considered the superior.

He was thinking this when he slipped forward and off the horse before Linahan could throw out an arm and stop him.

"Hold up there!" Linahan shouted. "Th' lieutenant's fell off his horse!"

He swung down and helped Schwabacker to a sitting position. Schwabacker's face was aflame with fever and Linahan discovered the gaping trough in the flesh of his side. "Jasus, he's been hit again."

With help, Linahan tied him to the saddle, then swung up behind him. "Looks like I'm in command of this here sortee," he said. Schwabacker's head bobbed like a ball on the end of a rubber string. He lacked the strength to lift his head.

Linahan said, "I guess th' lieutenant would have fought some more, but I ain't as all-fired brave as that. Let's get to Kearny an' waste no time about it."

Linahan led them across the rolling land, sometimes at a trot, sometimes at a walk to spare the hard-used horses. Lieutenant Schwabacker remained tied to the saddle, slumped forward when sickness made sitting erect impossible, but he had moments of clarity, when he knew and understood everything that was going on around him.

He meant to tell Sergeant Linahan to be on the lookout for the infantry but somehow this thought slipped away before he could put voice to it. The sergeant had a small detail riding rear guard, for the possibility was strong that the Sioux would recover some of their horses and give chase.

The jogging of the horse filled Schwabacker with a cancerous pain that seemed to grow until he felt swollen with it. Every movement pinched his breath, but an inspection with his fingers told him that he was not bleeding so badly now.

Linahan kept talking to him, a lot of softly running nonsense, yet it seemed to Schwabacker that this talk kept him from slipping off some great, undefinable edge into oblivion. Linahan seemed to know, for he kept it up until the point saw the tawny, weathered log palisade of Fort Phil Kearny.

Schwabacker found the strength to look.

The great gates yawned wide and there was music issuing forth, followed immediately by General Wessels' colors. The entire regiment marched into view, stopped, and waited in stunned silence while the battered remnants of Lieutenant Emil Schwabacker's troop approached.

General Wessels gave an order and A Company broke ranks, running forward, hands lifted to dismount the wounded tenderly. Schwabacker was lifted off his horse and borne to the general. Wessels' face was grave as he had his look. "Get him to the hospital," he said. "On the double!"

From that moment everything became a chaotic blur to Emil Schwabacker. A strange officer was giving orders to Sergeant Linahan, an ambulance came up, pulled by maniacal horses, and he was hoisted bodily into it.

He recognized one of Cove Butler's corpsmen and in

that way knew that the infantry had made the post in safety. Somehow his grievous losses did not seem so futile now; the heavy responsibility of his command decision was immeasurably lightened.

The swaying ambulance carried him across the parade to the infirmary and there he was litter-carried inside. He felt an undefined shame at being handled in this manner and tried to get up, but a corpsman with little nonsense in him pushed him back.

A regimental surgeon attached to Wessels' command was assisting Butler, who wore a haggard expression. He looked around as Schwabacker was carried inside, then he smiled and came over, his bloody hands gentle as he removed Schwabacker's shirt.

"Did . . . did you make it . . . without loss, Cove?"

"Sure," Butler said in a soothing voice. "We made it, son. We made out fine and so will you."

Ether always left him nauseated and he made a feeble objection when Butler dropped the cone over his face, but then the sick sweetness hit him and he no longer cared. Sounds faded and light dwindled to far-off dancing specks, then a sheet of darkness came down, so thick nothing could penetrate it.

He was in bed when he came out of it, but twenty minutes passed before his sickness left him. His stomach and chest felt restricted by the thick bandage. There was another around his thigh. Someone conversed outside his small room and then Cove Butler opened the door, took one look at him and beckoned General Wessels in. From the position of the sunlight entering the room, Schwabacker knew that it was late afternoon. He felt a twinge of guilt for having consumed so much time.

Wessels moved a chair close to the bed and sat down. "How are you feeling, Lieutenant?"

"Fine, sir." Schwabacker's voice sounded strange, like a rusty hinge that hadn't been moved for years. "My command, sir . . ."

"They're all right. They're being taken care of." Wessels took a cigar from his pocket. "May I smoke?"

"Of course, sir." Schwabacker was embarrassed to have a general ask such a thing. He had forgotten that special code of consideration one presented to the sick.

"I'm putting together my report," Wessels said. "I would like your account."

Schwabacker began his account at the point when he made contact with the command bivouaced on Crazy Woman's Fork. He spoke clearly, concisely, and omitted nothing, even the irregularity of relieving Captain Jocelyn of his command by force. General Wessels sat stolidly throughout the report, turning the air blue with his strong cigar. It was only when Schwabacker spoke of his decision to charge the enemy that Wessels interrupted.

"Lieutenant, it seems to me that you took quite a gamble."

"Yes, sir." Schwabacker's first thought was of the cost in men, his unforgivable tactical blunder that would remain on his record forever.

Wessels said, "My conscience has been heavy, Lieutenant. I left you out there. Refused to reinforce you and denied your sergeant permission to rejoin you or even apprise you of your precarious position." Wessels worked the cigar over to the other side of his mouth. "I didn't sleep last night."

Schwabacker stared; he could not help it. He felt an almost irresistible urge to wiggle his fingers in his ears to clear them, for surely he had heard incorrectly. The general was apologizing!

"I've talked to Captain Jocelyn," Wessels was saying, "and I'm convinced the force you engaged was commanded by Red Cloud himself; the whole thing smacks of his generalship." Wessels slid his chair back and stood up. "It may please you to know that upon Captain Jocelyn's recommendation, I am breveting you to the rank of Captain for this action."

"Sir, I . . ."

"Save your thanks," Wessels said. "Captain Jocelyn is drawing up charges against you for what he considers unauthorized action in relieving him of his command." Wessels turned to the door, his passage stirring the fog-thick smoke. His smile was genuinely paternal. "Get some rest, Captain."

He closed the door softly behind him.

Captain! Brevet Captain! The same pay, to be sure, but the rank was real. There would be no turning that back now, no taking it away, for a brevet rank was given by a general officer only for outstanding bravery. Schwabacker closed his eyes, for he felt slightly dizzy.

Cove Butler came in some time later. "There's a half-wild Irish sergeant out here to see you."

"Finnegan?"

"Aye, sor," Finnegan said, pushing past Butler. "Glory be, sor, but you can put a man through hell. It was my thinkin' that I'd never lay eyes on you again, sor."

"This was a rough one," Captain Schwabacker said regretfully. "I've lost good men, Sean. Forgive me for it; I'd bring them all back if I could."

"There'll be no apology from you, sor. I'll not be hearin' it." Finnegan sat down and wiped his nose, snuffling as he did so. "Th' troop's proud of th' fight, sor. Real proud. So's th' general. It's th' first time that heathen Red Cloud's had his horn pulled proper an' E Troop did it, sor."

"Have you seen Captain Jocelyn?" Schwabacker asked.

Finnegan nodded. "Aye, an' he's an angry man, sor. It's his feelin' that he should have commanded that troop instead of you."

"The man was in no shape to command the awkward squad!"

"Aye, sor. But th' captain's got a different opinion."

"I suppose he's included you in his charges?"

"That he has, but don't you be worryin' about it, sor. This bucko's been inside th' guardhouse before." He bent forward and touched Schwabacker lightly. "You're a blinkin' hero, sor. Th' general just dispatched a rider to Laramie with a full report of Red Cloud's lickin'." Finnegan's eyes took on a pleased shine. "Ah, it's me own pension I'd be givin' to have been in that raid through his village."

Schwabacker tried to sit up in bed, suddenly alarmed.

Hero? No! There was a terrible mistake! If this word got to the newspapers! "Sergeant! I want to see the general. Now!"

"Now you rest, sor," Finnegan said, sure that his commanding officer was out of his head. He got up and went outside, and from the speed with which Cove Butler entered the room, Schwabacker could guess the context of Finnegan's remarks.

"Want me to get you something?" Butler asked.

"Get me the general," Schwabacker said loudly. "Cove, for Christ's sake, I'm not a hero!"

"The report's gone," Butler said. "There's nothing you can do now. Try and get some sleep. You've lost a lot of blood." He patted Schwabacker's shoulder, smiled and went out. The newly promoted captain lay on his bed and fretted.

Hero? Name of a . . . He took a deep breath to clear his head. He had to think! The full story was bound to come out and where would the heroics be then? There wouldn't be any, that's what. When it was finally held up to the light and the facts aired, all you would have left was one frightened first lieutenant who but for the grace of God made a near-fatal blunder.

He closed his eyes and tried to sleep, but his uncertain future made him turn fretfully on the narrow hospital bed.

11

GENERAL WESSELS CALLED HIS STAFF MEETING AFTER
the evening mess. Major Powell was there, and Jim
Bridger, who had just come in from a brief "look-see,"
as he put it. Half a dozen officers were present and the
first arrivals took what chairs were available; the others
stood against the wall while Wessels paced back and
forth, reducing visibility in the room with his rank cigar.

Finally the orderly closed the door and Wessels
stopped pacing. "Gentlemen," he said, "I've called this
meeting because I firmly believe we're on the threshold
of something great, the turning point in our one-sided
campaign against Red Cloud's Sioux."

The murmur went around the room like a brook drop-
ping down over rocks. When Wessels took his cigar
from his mouth to speak again, the movement brought
an end to their buzzing talk; they watched their commander with the same attention that a musician gives
the symphony conductor.

"Bridger has been on a scout all afternoon." Wessels
turned to him. "Did you learn anything?"

"Red Cloud's lickin' his wounds, Gener'l. That young
lieutenant shore give him jessy!" Bridger threw his
arms out wide. "Wrecked his hull camp. You should've
seen it, Gener'l; lodges an' traps scattered over a hull
half-acre. Looks like a herd o' buff'lo went through it
lickety-split."

"You saw no sign of the Sioux?" Powell asked this.
He was a small man, moon-faced, with a neatly clipped

mustache and a manner that invited no nonsense.

"Nope," Bridger said. "Reckon Red Cloud's somewhere behind Lodge Trail Ridge, cussin' a blue streak. You can't blame him none. All along he's been makin' some powerful medicine. Got most of his bucks believin' he's th' wind and the thunder." Bridger chuckled. "That there lieutenant sorta knocked that into a cocked hat for him. Red Cloud'll be doin' his dancin' tonight; you can bet your prime beaver on that. He'll have to make some medicine again' that lieutenant. Make it or lose some face. Yessiree."

Wessels had heard enough. He put his cigar down and sat at his desk. His face was lined and haggard, for he was a troubled man, heavy with responsibility and shouldered with a campaign which had no certain happy ending. Yet there was hope in his voice as he said, "Inadvertently Captain Schwabacker has performed a miracle for us. Gentlemen, I'm violating no confidence when I say that the government, especially the military, is eager to abandon this campaign. It is my personal opinion that General Cooke and many others are now sorry it ever began. However, we have a semi-political position to consider, and that is this. A withdrawal of troops from Fort C. F. Smith and Fort Phil Kearny while Red Cloud was in a victorious military position, would leave a bad taste, so to speak, in the public's mouth. The United States Army, gentlemen, does not begin a campaign to leave it in complete rout. We are faced with the task of withdrawing only at impasse, and I believe Schwabacker's action may afford us the opportunity."

"I fail to see where our situation has been altered, General." This from Powell.

"Tactically, it hasn't," Wessels said. "But before this Red Cloud took the field upon every occasion. He has kept Kearny in veritable siege since the building of it. Fort Smith has fared little better. Red Cloud's actions have been ones of contempt for us. He shows it every time he allows a courier or a small detail to travel from here to Smith without harm. He doesn't care whether we discuss our abominable plight or not, simply because he feels that he can wipe us out when he gets good and ready." Wessels banged the flat of his hand on his desk. "But at last Red Cloud has met a force in the field, vastly inferior to his own in numbers, but he took a licking. He gave ground, gentlemen, and I imagine that was a severe blow to his pride. No, I believe a great event has occurred, and I intend to make the most of it. Gentlemen, understand that a peace commission has stood ready to make overtures to Red Cloud and bring this bloody mess to an end, but we needed a victory on our side before we could argue. Think, gentlemen! The defeated army does not dictate terms to the victor, and until this afternoon, Red Cloud has been the victor!"

"But will this be enough, General?" Captain Tenador Ten Eyck asked. He leaned against the wall, a slender man with dark, burning eyes.

"Enough to insure peace?" Wessels shook his head. "I don't know. But it can offer hope. I've finished a report that will go out by courier tonight after tattoo. In this report I've suggested that the peace commission return to Fort Laramie, and that a possible meeting be arranged. We will never have a clear-cut victory here; I'm sure of that. But I think even Red Cloud will agree that it is ridiculous to waste lives on both sides when neither can win." He looked at each of them. "That's the situation as I see it. You're excused, gentlemen."

They filed out, all but Jim Bridger, who stayed because General Wessels signaled him. Wessels touched a match to his dead cigar and puffed furiously. Bridger remained slumped in his chair, his whiskered jaws working gently on a cud of tobacco. "Somethin' under your skin, Gener'l?"

"A command decision is always a difficult one," Wessels said. "For a week now I've been kicking a prospect around in my mind, unable to reach a conclusion."

"About abandonin' Fort Smith, General?"

Wessels made no attempt to mask his surprise. He took the cigar from his mouth and said, "How did you know, Jim?"

"Warn't hard to figure," Bridger said. "Was I runnin' this shebang, I'd have done it. Fort Smith ain't big, Gener'l. You got a nigh more'n forty men there. Was there a big fight, Red Cloud'd send Crazy Horse up there with a handful of good bucks an' huff down th' walls for you."

"I know that," Wessels said. "I sent a courier there days ago with express orders to have everything ready to move on a minute's notice. At that time it was my intention to buy Red Cloud's peace with Smith."

"He might've gone for it too, Gener'l."

"That's what I thought," Wessels said, scrubbing a

155

hand across his face. "But the complexion has changed, Jim. If I abandon Smith now, the peace commission won't have a dog's chance to talk with Red Cloud. How can I take a chance? They may not even come to Laramie, and I may not be able to arrange the talks. If that happens and I leave Smith occupied, they stand a good chance of being wiped out to a man."

"Got you between two rocks, ain't they?" Bridger hoisted himself erect. "You know somethin', Gener'l? I don't envy you a damn bit fer havin' this job."

Wessels stared at the door after it closed, and had he cared to admit it, he would have agreed with Jim Bridger. He settled back with the sour stub of his cigar and let his many worries have their way with him. He began to understand Colonel Carrington a little more clearly, and with this understanding came the first shards of pity, for Carrington had faced a hopeless cause from the very beginning. Lacking combat experience, he had been the unwitting whipping boy for post-Civil War politicians and ambitious generals.

The arrival of the dispatch rider from Fort Laramie brought General Wessels to his office door. The orderly signed for the dispatch case and mail pouch, then came in with the saddlebags over his shoulder.

"Dump it on the desk," Wessels said. The orderly sorted the mail in three piles, official, enlisted men's, and officers'. Wessels took charge of the dispatches and official mail and the orderly went out with the other two piles to distribute them before tattoo.

A bulky letter drew Wessels' attention and he spread it on his desk to read:

Fort Laramie, Wyoming Territory
Office of the Commanding Officer
May 5, 1867

To: The Commanding Officer
  Fort Kearny, Dakota Terr.

Subject: Charges for courts-martial.

On or about April 20, 1867, Captain Nathan B. Kincaid, Infantry, unassigned, sustained wounds in an engagement east of this post, which resulted in his death. Mrs. Kincaid, widow of the deceased, was accompanying her husband to his new assignment when this tragedy occurred.

In a sworn deposition, Mrs. Kincaid states that it is her belief that her husband's death was the direct result of unauthorized surgery performed, without anesthetic, by Lieutenant Emil Schwabacker, temporarily commanding E Troop, 3rd United States Cavalry.

It was my sincere wish that an informal hearing be conducted to clear this matter in order that Mrs. Kincaid's pension could be probated. I personally placed a negative endorsement on the pension documents due to the unusual circumstances surrounding Captain Kincaid's conduct prior to his death. However, Mrs. Kincaid has filed formal charges with Department of Platte, removing the matter entirely from my hands.

Since Lieutenant Emil Schwabacker has been

*transferred to your command, the following
endorsements will be required on the enclosed documents: Two on the Adjutant General's copy. Three
on the Commander, Department of Platte's copies.
One on the affidavit stipulating that Lieutenant Emil
Schwabacker will be freed from all duties, at a time
to be established by higher authority, to answer
these charges.*

   *I remain your most respectful, obedient servant,
General Philip St. George Cooke,
Commanding, Dept. of Platte*

                  *(signed)   Nelson Ashford
                               Brevet Colonel,
                               Commanding,
                               Fort Laramie,
                               Wyoming Territory*

"Tattoo" was being blown when General Wessels left
his office and walked toward the infirmary. There was
lamplight streaming from Cove Butler's office window.
When the general entered, Butler was at his desk,
writing reports; he stood up as Wessels closed the door.

"Here's a letter for Captain Schwabacker," Wessels
said. "Give it to him, then come back. There's something I want to discuss with you."

Butler went out a side door that led into the few hospital rooms in the back. Emil Schwabacker was awake
and a small lamp burned low on the night table by his
bedside. "News from home," Butler said, handing him
the letter. He turned the lamp up and left immediately.

As always, the first thing Schwabacker noticed was

the faint aroma of sachet. He opened it and read, smiling, for even two thousand miles away, Henrietta Brubaker had the power to bring happiness to him. He could almost hear her chattering gaily of the small things she knew he enjoyed hearing. Her words came alive for him, bringing his home in St. Albans into close focus. He could see the cherry blossoms, just starting to break open, and the leaves, green shoots now, but carrying the promise of shady beauty.

He stopped reading and let the letter lie, content to close his eyes and feel the warm love this woman offered him. There was never a time in his life when he could remember being without her; she lived down the block from his father's house and he had carried her books to school. A letter from her brought forth a thousand memories—the sound of her laughter, or the candlelight shining in her eyes, the years with her, sharing the secrets only his heart acknowledged, sharing those long summer evenings when the very moon seemed breathless and life was as sweet as youth could make it.

He read the last of the letter and was folding it when General Wessels knocked on his door before entering. Schwabacker was surprised and tried to sit up, but Wessels waved him down and pulled a chair close.

"Captain, it seems that I have some unfortunate news," Wessels rubbed his hands together and appeared to be without words. "Mrs. Kincaid has filed formal charges against you. She feels that your amputation of her husband's arm was a direct cause of his death. I spoke to Cove Butler and he is inclined to agree. He also said that Kincaid would have died anyway."

"That . . . that looks bad for me, doesn't it, sir?"

"I'm afraid so," Wessels said solemnly. "I'll be frank with you, Captain; you've been an excellent officer and I'll not see you thrown to the dogs so that some bungler's widow can milk the government out of a pension she doesn't deserve." Wessels drummed his fingers against his thighs. "A thing like this is difficult to prove either way, but it's my opinion that Mrs. Kincaid is interested in the pension, not who she drags into the mud. Whatever happens, it'll go on your record as a charge. That's unfortunate, but I'm powerless to change it."

"I understand, sir."

Wessels stood up, a tired man who took every responsibility seriously. "Captain Jocelyn's charge can be dropped, by him. But in the event he does not drop it, I'll sit on it here as long as possible. One on top of the other will look very bad, Captain. It could guarantee a conviction before the evidence was read."

"Thank you, sir," Schwabacker said. A yawning trap door seemed to open and all his dreams slid into oblivion before he could stop even one.

Wessels felt compassion. He recalled an isolated incident at Fort Leavenworth, when a junior officer had struck a woman to keep her from spreading panic. The woman preferred charges, unjustified attack against a civilian female. Acquittal, to be sure, but the officer carried that stain on his record to this day. That was what Emil Schwabacker faced, not necessarily open condemnation, but a mark permanently placed for every commanding officer to see and wonder about.

Wessels left him alone, and when the door closed Emil Schwabacker drew paper, pen and ink from the table and began to compose a letter to his fiancée in Vermont.

When it was completed Schwabacker summoned an orderly and had it taken to headquarters, luckily in time to catch Wessels' courier before he left for Fort Laramie. After that he lay back and listened to the night sounds of the post. A sentry called out from his place on the ramp above the gate, and the call was passed along to the other posts until it made the complete round back to the guardhouse. One of Doctor Butler's orderlies walked down the hall, his boots rattling a loose board.

Schwabacker turned his lamp down, for only darkness was fit company for his thoughts. His side and thigh ached and every movement had to be made gently or the pain made him gasp. Finally he slept, a dreamless sleep, yet not a restful one.

12

WITHIN A WEEK, SCHWABACKER WAS OUT OF HIS BED and walking slowly around the post. Doctor Butler frowned on this activity, but found acquiescence an easier out than arguing against Schwabacker's almost fanatical stubbornness. On the ninth day he tried to visit Captain Temple Jocelyn, who was still bed-ridden with a slight fever, but Jocelyn refused to see him, and Schwabacker went away, a great, undefined worry fermenting in his mind.

At the end of the second week, Schwabacker ordered

his new horse saddled and rode around the remount yard, getting acquainted. Sergeant Finnegan was there, worry wrinkling his face, for if the horse threw him, unlimited damage could result. Yet Schwabacker was not thrown. He commanded the animal with a fine blend of tolerance and discipline, and after forty minutes of this, horse and rider came to a wordless understanding.

In the early afternoon a wagon train arrived from Fort Laramie. Not just any wagon train, but ordnance wagons, each bearing cases of the new breech-loading Springfield rifle.

The entire post turned out to see this new rifle.

General Wessels opened the first case and held up a rifle so all could see. The sunlight glinted on the blued length, reflected golden lights in the polished walnut stocks. The breech was hinged and, when open, allowed the shooter to feed ammunition directly into the chamber. And the ammunition was brass-cased, waterproof, a large, businesslike cartridge of fifty caliber, pushed along by seventy grains of black powder.

General Wessels spoke to Major Powell. "Have this weapon issued immediately. Sixty rounds of ammunition per man. I want a rifle butt set up immediately and the regiment fired for record before sundown."

"Yes, sir." Powell whirled to carry out this order.

Then Wessels saw Schwabacker standing there. "Captain," he said, "do you like your new horse?"

"Yes, sir."

"Then come into the office. I'm going to give you a chance to ride him." He pivoted and pushed his way through the crowd, Schwabacker following him. Once inside Wessels' office, the general indicated a vacant chair and struck a match to his cigar. "Captain, do you realize what those rifles mean?"

"I think I do, sir. More fire power. A troop could deliver the impact of a regiment."

"Yes, by God!" Wessels said, smacking the desk with his hand. "And not a .44 Henry either, with a range of only a hundred yards. Or a .56-56 Spencer, with a trajectory like a round rock. No, these are high-powered weapons, and I'd say accurate up to five hundred yards." He puffed on his cigar furiously, a habit he had when his thinking excited him. "Captain, I'll confess that I've been bearing a cross, the decision whether to abandon Smith or hang on and get the command killed. This may be my salvation, Captain, but I'll have to move fast, and damned quietly."

"Quietly, sir?"

"Yes. Don't think for a moment that Red Cloud doesn't have an intelligence system. Within three weeks, unless we're careful, he'll know about those rifles." Wessels paused to go to the door and bellow for an orderly, who appeared almost instantly. "Have Major Powell report here as soon as he is free." Then he turned back to Schwabacker. "Captain, do you feel up to a patrol?"

"I believe so, sir."

"Then I want you to sneak forty of those rifles and four thousand rounds of ammunition up the Bozeman Road to Fort C. F. Smith."

"How, sir?"

"Good God, use your originality!"

Powell entered then, out of breath from his run across the parade, and Wessels said, "Major, I want an order issued that these rifles will be fired slowly, with the usual pause between each shot. At no time will they be fired rapidly unless the detail bearing them comes under overwhelming attack."

"I'm afraid I don't understand, sir." Powell was genuinely puzzled.

Wessels' cheeks puffed in exasperation, but he let none of it come into his voice. "Major, you came here when this was soapweed and sage. You suffered through Carrington's hard winter. Surely your observations of Red Cloud in action should have taught you that he has a battle tactic which he uses to great success."

"Yes, sir, but . . ."

"But nothing! Major, our own armament has defeated us! He has always attacked in waves, the first wave drawing the bulk of the fire power because it was always the heaviest. Of course he suffered losses, but while the largest percent of troops were cramming ball and powder he would loosen a second wave, drawing the rest of available fire. Then on the heels of the second came his third wave, the finest of his warriors. And they have always caught the army with empty carbines, or not enough loaded ones to do any good. Major, the minute a trooper fires this new breech-loader rapidly, our hand is tipped. You have orders, now see that they're obeyed. I want to challenge Red Cloud on my own ground, with our new weapons, and then we'll see whether he beats us or not."

"I understand, sir." Powell saluted punctiliously and left Wessels' office.

The general turned to Emil Schwabacker. "End of the sermon, Captain. I'll expect you to vacate the post with your troop by nine tomorrow morning. There will be no wagons or pack animals. Any questions?"

"None, sir. We'll get the rifles and ammunition to Fort Smith, sir."

"I'll consider it done then," Wessels said and Emil Schwabacker went outside.

Forty rifles! Four thousand rounds of ammunition! Schwabacker stood on headquarters porch and flailed his mind for ways and means. One wagon would be enough, but the general had forbidden a vehicle or pack. *Well, now! That's an interesting word: pack. Let's see, thirty-five men; that would be all that could answer muster—yes, the thought had merit. Damned if it didn't.*

Schwabacker left the porch and limped across the parade. He figured that he would find Sergeant Finnegan near the stable. The sergeant straightened as Schwabacker approached.

"You got th' divvil in yer eye, sor."

"Patrol tomorrow," Schwabacker said. "An important detail to Fort C. F. Smith. I want the troop mustered at eight sharp."

Finnegan didn't seem to share Schwabacker's eagerness. "You'll rip open th' doctor's sewin', sor."

"Nonsense," Schwabacker said. "I'm healing nicely and I have no intention of riding faster than a walk. Well, maybe a trot now and then to prevent animal fatigue."

Finnegan shook his head. "It's a stubborn man you are, sor. What's th' detail?"

"We're taking forty rifles and four thousand rounds of ammunition to the garrison at Fort Smith."

"Then I'd best be gettin' a wagon from th' farrier."

"No wagon, no pack animals."

"How th' divvil—"

"We're going to carry them, Sergeant." There was elation in Schwabacker's voice. "Each man will carry two carbines, one across the saddle and another on the ring. Double ammunition for each man. I know that two full belts around the middle will be uncomfortable, but this has to look like any other patrol."

"By th' sainted mother, sor, I think it'll work." Finnegan smiled. "You'll be a gener'l yet, sor; you've th' imagination for it."

Schwabacker went to his quarters on the end of officers' row and the room gave out a strong musty odor when he opened the door. For a while he just sat and massaged the muscles of his thigh to ease the soreness. Walking on it was the best, but the cure caused him considerable discomfort.

Sergeant Finnegan knocked just before evening mess. He swept off his kepi and took a chair by the bed. "I made a check of th' troop, sor. We'll be able to muster thirty-six men."

"Then have Linahan and Collins draw seventy-two of the new Springfield carbines," Schwabacker said. "We'll leave forty of them at Fort Smith and remain armed with the other thirty-two."

A thought rumbled in Finnegan's mind, but it was a

166

moment before he spoke of it. "It's my thinkin' that Red Cloud'll know your guidon, sor. When he sees that, he'll surely attack." Finnegan rotated his kepi in his big hands. "He'll never forget how you stormed through his village, sor, an' a chance to get even will be too good to pass up."

"Likely you're right," Schwabacker said. He pursed his lips and his face grew studious. "Sean, how much of a march is it to Smith?"

"A day, sor. A long day."

Schwabacker got up off his bunk and limped around the room. "The general said to vacate the post *by* nine tomorrow. He didn't say *at* nine." Schwabacker snapped his fingers. "Sean, quietly alert the troop. I want troop mounting to take place in an hour." He looked at his bull's-eye watch. "A quarter to six; we'll leave the post at dusk. You attend to the troop. I'll meet Linahan and his detail at the ordnance shed."

"Aye, sor," Finnegan said and hurried out.

Schwabacker took down and buckled on his pistol belt and saber, took up his cape and hat and went outside to limp across the parade. Sergeant Linahan was counting the new carbines which Ordnance-Sergeant Collins had laid out in neat rows. Three troopers sweated over the ammunition, placing a hundred rounds with each carbine.

When Schwabacker stepped near, he said, "Thanks for the new pistol, Sergeant."

"One of my reserved stock," Collins said and offered the record for Schwabacker's signature.

An hour passes quickly when a patrol is making up,

and on the dot, Schwabacker mounted the troop and led them around the parade to the main gate. There was a light in General Wessels' office when they trooped by, but the general did not come to the headquarters porch and the gate closed behind them.

Dusk turned into night and the troopers closed the interval to a length and rode two abreast instead of a single line. To the west the Big Horn Mountains loomed darkly, jagged upthrusts whose shoulders seemed to support the sky.

Soon after leaving Fort Kearny, Brevet Captain Emil Schwabacker established the march speed, a slow walk. He selected this pace because it kept down the dust, which an Indian could smell for miles, and because there was less rattling of bit chains and equipment rings.

However, he held to no foolish illusions; he knew that the Sioux were thick about him and that he would never take an unobserved step between Fort Kearny and Fort C. F. Smith. One of Red Cloud's greatest assets was his intelligence service, his constant observation and measurement of the enemy strength.

At ten o'clock Schwabacker's command crossed Goose Creek, and he allowed a brief halt for watering the horses. Finnegan turned once and looked toward the ink-dark ridges, knowing there were Sioux eyes there, but the sergeant said nothing. None of the men spoke, not even to swear.

Mounted, they moved out and again Captain Schwabacker held the pace to a walk. Finnegan began shooting questioning glances toward his commander, but Schwabacker offered no invitation to comment; the sergeant remained quiet.

The men were adding and dividing in their minds: Ninety miles from Kearny to Smith; twelve hours to make it in. Seven and a half miles an hour and the command was making four and a half at the best.

They passed through a thickly timbered stretch, and once clear of this, Schwabacker pushed his horse into a trot. The command followed eagerly. That is, all except Finnegan, who worried about Schwabacker pulling his stitches.

The first mile was difficult, but Cove Butler's strangulating belly bandage took the strain and Schwabacker thereafter alternated his pace between a walk and a trot.

At midnight they dismounted at Pass Creek, a small trickle cutting through heavily grassed land. "Canteens and horses," Schwabacker said softly to Sergeant Finnegan. "Ten minutes."

A nervous ten minutes, with every trooper swinging his head constantly. Even the horses drank briefly, lifted their heads for a listen, then lowered them to drink again. Farther up the trail a rider crossed over, the sound of his horse a brief racket.

"Unshod," Finnegan said softly.

The troopers fingered their carbines.

"Mount at will," Schwabacker said and pulled himself into the saddle. The troop went up and he led them out, breaking into a trot as soon as the interval was established. Riding a few yards ahead of the others he caught the faint pungency of dust where the Indian had crossed, but there was no sign of anyone.

Red Cloud let them pass through unchallenged and the wondering why drew each man's nerves to screaming tightness. An hour and a half before dawn they paused at Goose Creek and, for the first time since leaving the Kearny gate, relaxed a little; this was predominantly Crow country, and the Crows were hereditary enemies of the Sioux. Red Cloud respected the Crows, for they were fierce fighters, unrelenting enemies who gave no quarter and asked for none in return. Colonel Carrington, Schwabacker decided, had used his head when he built Fort C. F. Smith in the heart of Crow country. The attacks were lessened because Red Cloud was reluctant to move around freely with an enemy behind every bush.

The sun was a golden sphere and flaming streaks of daylight shot over the high summits, moving up the sides of the surrounding hills to the west like water rising in a green bowl.

With daylight, Schwabacker could relax; the troopers could let off with their nerve-breaking vigilance. Two scouts were sent ahead of the point and the troop broke from double column, becoming a column in line.

According to Schwabacker's calculations, he was several hours from Fort C. F. Smith, and he decided not to stop for cooked rations. He instructed Sergeant Finnegan to pass the word back: cold rations in the saddle.

The first glimpse of Fort Smith was a disappointment to Emil Schwabacker. He had known beforehand that the post was small, and manned with only a handful of troops, but nothing had prepared him for that first view. The post sat on a flat stretch of ground with timber on all four sides. The walls were not high enough and there was only one blockhouse visible from the southern approach.

A sentry saw them, and when they drew near, a creaking gate opened and admitted them to the cramped parade ground. On Schwabacker's order, Finnegan dismounted the troop and dismissed them, and judging from the meager buildings, Schwabacker guessed that they would spend the night on open ground.

Lieutenant Colonel N. C. Kinney was in command, a rotund man with a bull voice and a great respect for the Sioux. He came out of the mud-and-stick headquarters building and ushered Captain Schwabacker inside.

The office was a bare room—one desk, a few scarred chairs, and a poorly fitted window that let out onto the parade. Kinney stood by this and observed Schwabacker's troop. "Damned fortunate you had a strong force, Captain. Red Cloud's killed two couriers in the last eight days." He turned to face Schwabacker. "I would hesitate to send a force south in less than company strength."

"We were under constant observation, sir," Schwabacker said, "but there was no hostile movement that we could detect."

"Ugh," Kinney said. "They're hostile as hell. Oh, not here. The Crows are too strong." Kinney laughed. "I might as well be on some damned island. The only reports I get from the outside are what my Crow scouts bring me. Something's stung Red Cloud in the behind, Captain. As I get it, his bucks took a whipping a few weeks back."

"Well, yes, sir," Schwabacker said. "I have the honor to have been the officer in command, sir."

Kinney's plump face bloomed in a wide smile. He shook Schwabacker's hand. "Congratulations, Captain. A job well done."

"Thank you, sir. I've brought you some new tools, Colonel. The new Springfield breech-loading carbine. Forty of them and four thousand rounds of ammunition."

This unexpected blessing seemed to stun Colonel Kinney. He made the door in three jumps and bellowed for his orderly. "Fetch me one of those new rifles on the double!" He turned back to Schwabacker, massaging his hands together. "Captain, you've given me a new lease on life. I don't imagine any man can visualize the powder keg I've been sitting on these last five months. Two bare companies and the whole Sioux nation in my back yard." He cracked his knuckles. "Captain, I don't even have a 'critter' troop to my name."

"I understand, sir," Schwabacker said. "And General Wessels is fully apprised of your circumstances. The general will never fail you, sir. Only yesterday afternoon these new weapons arrived. The general thought of you first and dispatched my troop."

"God bless you, sir," Kinney said.

The orderly came across the porch and burst into the room with a huge grin and a Springfield carbine. Colonel Kinney took it, opened the breech, then studied it tenderly.

"A magnificent weapon," he said softly. "Captain, it is truly magnificent."

"Yes, sir. The fire power will be tremendous." Standing made Schwabacker's leg throb and he shifted awkwardly. Colonel Kinney noticed immediately.

"What's this? By George, man, you've been wounded!" He hastened to offer one of the hardbacked chairs and Schwabacker sat down with a good deal of relief. He straightened his leg and rested his hand on his wound. Kinney was saying, "You've endured a hard ride, Captain; we'll find you suitable quarters, although your troop presents a housing problem."

"They'll be quite comfortable in the stable, sir, and Sergeant Finnegan will make certain that smoking is done outside."

"I wouldn't want us burned out from within," Kinney said. "When do you plan to depart for Fort Kearny, Captain?"

"Tomorrow," Schwabacker said.

"Then I'll have a detailed report for General Wessels," Colonel Kinney said. "If you have his ear, Captain, plead my cause and give us some cavalry support. I couldn't attack a platoon of old squaws with my infantry."

"I'll relay your message, sir," Schwabacker said. He took his leave quickly and went across the short parade ground to the officers' quarters. None were vacant and he was to share a room with two lieutenants of Infantry.

They were waiting, both young men, and hiding their curiosity poorly. The introductions were somewhat formal; protocol demanded it: "Captain Schwabacker, may I present Lieutenant Regan." ". . . Captain

Schwabacker . . ." "Lieutenant Stone" ". . . Captain Schwabacker . . ."

A bottle of brandy was produced and water tumblers clinked, and when the second drink was a thing of the past, talk came more freely.

Lieutenant Regan was a tall man with a long face that reminded Schwabacker of a basset hound; the eyes carried a wrenching sadness. Stone was the opposite, a man of exuberant spirits, especially since the bottle was his and his glass was always a little fuller than the other two.

"Those carbines created a bit of excitement, Captain. It's been the general opinion that Kearny'd forgotten us." He laughed and set the brandy on a side table. "Help yourself to it; a gift from the officers of Fort Smith." He rose, touched Regan lightly and they went out.

The brandy filled Emil Schwabacker with an unaccustomed warmth as he undressed and crawled between the rough blankets. The bunk was lumpy and the ropes serving as springs needed tightening, but he could not recall when anything had felt so restful. He could even forget the aches and itchiness caused by healing wounds. He could forget everything now and sleep.

And he did, through a day and a night.

Sergeant Finnegan woke him before dawn and only then did Schwabacker realize that he had slept the clock around. Dressing, he was conscious of a ravenous appetite.

He found the mess opening. Three cups of scalding coffee preceded the meal, and he was finishing his last stack of wheat cakes when Finnegan appeared.

"Th' troop's ready to move, sor."

Schwabacker turned a surprised expression on his sergeant. "Do you read minds, Sean?"

"Ah, sor, a man gets to know his commander. You're not a man for sittin' when there's somethin' to be doin'."

"I take that as a compliment," Schwabacker said and got up from the table. "We'll leave in a half-hour."

"Very well, sor." Finnegan went out and Schwabacker crossed to headquarters to pick up Colonel Kinney's dispatch. Kinney was on the headquarters porch, a cigar jutting from his lips, a heavy dispatch case under his arm. He surrendered the case, then offered Captain Schwabacker his hand.

"A daytime march will be risky, Captain." He smiled. "But then you're an Indian fighter; you don't need my advice."

"I thank you for it, sir. We'll be alert."

Finnegan was forming the troop and Schwabacker went to his horse, swinging up. The sentries cracked the gates and he rode from the post with the entire personnel of Fort C. F. Smith watching, as though he were some celebrity.

Once the gates were behind them, Captain Schwabacker signaled Sergeant Finnegan forward. "Scouts out, Sergeant. I think fifty yards will do. Column of two's, carbines at the ready. We'll go straight through with a minimum of stops."

"Aye, sor. Is that all, sor?"

"One more thing," Schwabacker said. "Do you know a Crow Indian when you see one, Sergeant?"

"It's a fact, sor, that I don't."

"Neither do I," Schwabacker said. "If we are challenged in any way, Sergeant, I want the men to fight mounted, on command of the horn."

Finnegan nodded and rode back to detail scouts. Schwabacker settled in the saddle, canted slightly sideways to ease his bad leg. He wondered how a man could tell a Crow Indian from a Sioux. Probably because a Sioux would attack without parley, yet he couldn't be sure of that. Well, he knew what the Sioux looked like, and if he saw any Indians who were different, he would assume they were friendly Crows. Yet that seemed a little foolish; with hostile land surrounding him, and ninety miles of it to travel through, he could find merit in the assumption that it was better to shoot first and talk later.

13

THE ARRIVAL OF A PASSENGER STAGE FROM FORT LARAMIE was an event that drew nearly every free trooper and officer to the palisade ramp, for nearly a year had gone by since the last stage had made a successful, uncontested journey along the bitterly fought-over road.

At the officer of the day's command, the gates yawned and the stage teetered through, the driver slacking the horses from a dead run. Dust boiled up from the wheels. With a flourish, the driver braked to a halt by regimental headquarters, then dismounted insolently while the coach still rocked back and forth on its fore and aft springs.

The door opened and a man with gold-rimmed glasses and a yellow linen duster stepped down. He turned and offered a hand to a woman, who looked around the post quickly, as though she expected to meet someone. A boy, big for his seven years, jumped down and fell to his hands and knees. He stood erect quickly, uncertain whether to cry or not, then brushed himself off. The man in the duster spoke a few softly murmured words to the woman, touched the brim of his bowler respectfully, then hurried onto the headquarters porch, there meeting General Wessels, who came to the door.

The officer of the day hurried up, presented himself smartly to the woman, then said, "Delighted as we are to have you honor us, madam, General Wessels does not permit women . . ."

"I quite understand," she said, "but I have General Cooke's written permission." She regarded him levelly, almost haughtily. She was still young, in her late twenties, and hard work had never reddened her hands. She was slender, but well formed, and her hair was a bright salmon-red.

"Very well, madam," the O.D. was saying. "Your name, please?"

"Mrs. Temple Jocelyn."

Then the O.D. understood what had been bothering him—that touch of the South in her voice, the soft slur that brought to mind the fragrance of oleander and night-blooming jasmine and his brief stay in Richmond. The officer of the day said, "Perhaps you would like to go to your quarters and . . ."

"I'd like to see my husband," she said in a voice that

177

closed out all avenues of argument.

The O.D. made a slight bow. "As you wish, madam." He offered her his arm, and the boy his hand, and conducted them around the parade to the infirmary.

Cove Butler looked up from his writing when the door opened. He had never seen her before, not even the daguerreotype Temple Jocelyn guarded so closely, but he knew instinctively who she was. "Madam," he said, "if you'll follow me."

He led the way down a short hall and opened a door. When Evangeline Jocelyn and her son went in, he closed the door and motioned the O.D. back to his office.

Jocelyn lay with his eyes closed, his thin face now gaunt and waxen. He had one hand outside the cover, a bony hand with the sinews standing out clearly through the skin. The hand stirred restlessly, like a bird's claw. "Reilly?" he said. "Bring me some more water, Reilly."

When there was no answer he turned his head and opened his eyes. For a moment he stared, and then the skin went slack and his expression sagged like slowly melting wax. "I'm dreaming," he said, convinced of it.

"I'm very real, Temple," Evangeline said. She gave the boy a slight push so that he stood before her. It was almost as if she were afraid to approach this man who was her husband, and wanted the child to make the first overture. "This is your father, Stuart, whom you've never seen, and who has never seen you."

The boy studied Jocelyn with wide-innocent eyes. He was going to have Jocelyn's height and lean ranginess in the cheeks. Slowly, with a strength and determination

178

agonizing to see, Jocelyn raised himself to his elbows, and then to a sitting position with his arms out-braced. This required several minutes and the effort brought sweat to his face. His breathing was loud and labored.

He was a magnificent man, a determined man, and if he had to crawl those last few feet separating them, then he would. But he could go no farther. He sat in bed, braced on stiffened arms, then his head tipped forward and began to bob rhythmically and tears of defeat dropped to the covers, making small dark spots.

Evangeline Jocelyn broke past her son and went to her knees beside his bed. She touched him, encircled him with her arms, and the strength seemed to leave him, for she was now his strength, and she held him, rocking back and forth, whispering to him.

The boy began to cry, partly because he was frightened and partly because he was suddenly alone, on the outside of love, looking in. He came forward timidly and Jocelyn's hand came out, touching him lightly on the head. Silent understanding passed from one to the other in that touch, for they were father and son. The boy climbed up on Jocelyn's bed and kissed him.

The man in the yellow duster accepted one of General Wessels' fine cigars and a chair. Between puffs, he said, "You have no idea . . . General, how pleased I am . . . with this assignment. It isn't often that a newspaperman gets an exclusive."

"Since Ridgeway Grover of *Frank Leslie's Illustrated Weekly* was killed less than a mile from the main gate," replied Wessels, "both General Cooke and I have taken a dim view of noncombatant civilians on the post. However, the situation has changed, Mr. Davis."

"Indeed it has," Davis said. "General, the dispatch you released two weeks ago has been reprinted in every major newspaper in the United States. Public reaction was immediate and definite, sir. A peace commission is coming west to make a new treaty with the Sioux and their allies. Reinforcements are on their way as soon as Jefferson Barracks can muster two regiments."

"Two regiments!" Wessels rubbed his hands. "Fantastic." He turned to the window overlooking the parade. "And I can thank Captain Schwabacker for this, Davis. He's a most capable officer."

"My newspaper seems to think so," Allistair Davis said. "They sent me all the way from Chicago to interview him. With your permission, of course, sir."

"Permission?" Wessels thought of the charges hanging over Captain Emil Schwabacker. Good publicity would have tremendous weight. Enough of it could tie a board's hands, make punishment impossible because of public opinion regarding a popular hero. "Yes," Wessels said, "I grant permission. Please clear the copy through my office. I'll dispatch it with my courier; you'll get faster results that way."

Allistair Davis rose. "Thank you, General. I've a story here; I can feel it." He thumped his chest to point out the place. He shook hands with Wessels and went out with his cigar streaming pale smoke behind him.

Brevet Captain Schwabacker's return to Fort Kearny aroused no excitement, for the hour was late, and since he bore only Colonel Kinney's written report, he sent this to General Wessels by messenger, then went to his quarters and poured water for a bath.

He had just dried off and was slipping into his underwear when Cove Butler knocked, entering on the heels of it. Schwabacker smiled and said, "Doctor, you could be damned embarrassed doing that some day."

"Nothing embarrasses a doctor," Butler said. "You ought to know that; you're a better one than I am. Let me look at that side."

"It's healing fine."

"Never mind; I'll look at it." Butler moved the lamp around and turned Schwabacker so that the healing wound was exposed to the light. Butler grunted in satisfaction, then indicated that Schwabacker could finish dressing. "How was the ride to Smith, Captain?"

"Not dull," Schwabacker said. "They were glad to get the carbines. Forty men, Cove; that's all they have. And Fort Smith is the last white settlement until you reach Bozeman City."

"This is Indian country," Butler said dryly. "We should have stayed home in the first place." He paused to pack and fire his pipe. "A stage arrived this afternoon. Jocelyn's wife and son were on it."

"The hell! She didn't waste any time, did she?"

"Seems like it," Butler admitted. "She left word with the O.D. Wants to see you. Quarter H near the end."

"Now?" Schwabacker stuffed his shirt tail in his waistband and pulled up his suspenders. "It's nearly eleven, Cove."

"The O.D. was in my office when she told him,"

181

Butler said. "And she said as soon as you returned."

Schwabacker slipped into a blouse, not bothering with his sidearms. "Are you going to wait?"

"No," Butler said. "I have a dressing or two to change. I turned five of your men back to duty today."

"I can use them," Schwabacker said and went out. He found Quarter H with little difficulty, and rapped softly. The door opened almost immediately and he snapped his heels together. "Captain Schwabacker, madam. I just received your message."

Evangeline Jocelyn stepped back. "Won't you come in, Captain. It was good of you to come." She shut the door and smiled. "You must excuse me, Captain, but this is the first time I've been surrounded by Yankees; it's an odd feeling."

She crossed the room and closed a connecting door. "My son's asleep. We'll have to talk softly."

"Have you seen Captain Jocelyn, ma'am?"

"Yes, for over an hour." She gave him a direct glance. "Doctor Butler assures me that you're a capable medical man, Captain. Is he dying?"

Schwabacker wondered what a man said at a time like this. He tried an evasive answer. "Dr. Butler is doing everything in his power to heal Captain Jocelyn's wound. If he is dying, it is because he refuses to respond to medical treatment."

"That's not what I asked," Evangeline Jocelyn said.

"Perhaps it isn't," Schwabacker said. "But let's be honest with each other, madam. Had I not written and spoke of his serious condition, would you ever have communicated with him again?"

"Yes," she said. "The hate died years ago, and left nothing but emptiness behind. You know him, sir, his pride, his aloofness. I have that too. It's a heritage, or a curse. Any excuse would have brought me to him. You gave me that excuse and I'll always be in your debt."

"You intend to stay?"

"I think that is militarily impossible," she said. "But I'll be waiting for him, in St. Louis; wherever he wants me to be."

"Captain Jocelyn is a military man. The army is his life. The 'blue-bellied Yankee' army, ma'am."

She turned her back to him then. "The war was terrible, Captain. Neither side will forget, but I was wrong in thinking we had to go on spitting on each other." She faced Schwabacker then. "And you, sir, are you going to make your peace with my husband? Or are you two going to repeat a mistake and spit on each other."

"You make it sound very simple," Schwabacker said.

"I'm not trying to," Evangeline said. "He has preferred charges against you; he knows that he is wrong. You spoke in an angry manner against him. You know that you were wrong."

"Who told you of this?"

"Lieutenant Butler, the surgeon," Evangeline said.

Damn Butler and his nosy . . . Schwabacker glanced at his watch. "It's quite late," he said, "and you must be very tired." He turned to the door. "Good night, and I wish you the best."

"But not my husband."

"I'm sorry," Schwabacker said. "I never wanted to

183

compete with him. It was something beyond my control."

He left her then and returned to his quarters to find Sergeant Finnegan stretched out on his bunk, asleep. Schwabacker shook him awake and the sergeant sat up, rubbing his eyes. He took a letter from his pocket and handed it to Schwabacker. "Found this with th' troop mail, sor."

"Thank you," Schwabacker said and turned to the light. The scent of satchet was absent and he frowned. Then he recognized the writing and stood motionless.

"Somethin' wrong, sor?"

"Uh? No! No, nothing's wrong, Sergeant."

Finnegan could take a hint. He got up and went to the door. "Good night, sor."

"Yes. Good night, Sean."

When the door closed, Emil Schwabacker sat down and carefully opened the flap with his thumbnail. He turned so the lamplight fell over his shoulder and read:

St. Albans, Vermont

Dear Son:

Since our parting was unpleasant, and since neither of us has altered his opinion of the other, I have refrained from corresponding these past six years. When you entered the military academy at West Point, I prophesied a dismal future; you are not military minded, my boy. However, certain newspaper accounts of your exploits have been made public, exaggerated to be sure, and I thought it my duty to warn you of the danger of public parading, regard-

less of your innocence or good intention. These exploits are best kept to one's self, or confined to the limits of yellowback novels. Already, numerous people of St. Albans have approached me and spoken of these accounts with a great deal of excitement and enthusiasm. Should this continue, a good man's reputation could be reduced to that of a medicine-show performer.

As always, it is my desire to advise you and guide you so that you might profit from my experience, although for some reason beyond my understanding, you seem loath to do this.

Your mother is well, as are your sisters. . . . Marriage would be good for you at this time, as it has a settling influence. Henrietta has remained true, which surprises me, as I always considered her a light-headed person. It is my suggestion that you resign your commission before you become too deeply involved, and return to St. Albans. With your education you could open a pharmacy. I'll speak to Lige Higgins and make all the arrangements.

Your father,
Gustave Schwabacker

Angrily Schwabacker ripped the letter into four parts and flung them across the room, where they floated down like autumn leaves. Then he rocked forward and sat with his face in his hands, shaking.

The kerosene lamp sputtered and he filled the glass base from a small can he kept under his bunk. He glanced at his watch: quarter to twelve. Opening the door, he stepped out to the edge of the duck walk and stood there, looking at the dark parade. A man came along the walk, his shoes lightly rattling the boards. When he passed Schwabacker, he turned and came back.

"Captain Schwabacker?"

"Yes?"

The man offered his hand. "I'm Allistair Davis, a newspaper man. Care for a cigar?"

"No, thanks."

Davis lighted one for himself, and in the brief match flare, Schwabacker studied his face. Davis whipped the match out and said, "I've come from Chicago for an interview with you, Captain. You're big news. Two weeks ago you crowded the proposed transcontinental railroad off of page one."

"That's very flattering," Schwabacker said, "but what is it you want?"

"A story," Davis said. He nodded toward the open door of Schwabacker's quarters. "May I come in?"

"Certainly," Schwabacker said and followed him inside. He closed the door, indicated a chair, then sat on the bed while Davis got out paper and pencil.

"A few unofficial opinions, Captain," Davis said. "You engaged Red Cloud; isn't that right?"

"I engaged a small portion of his forces," Schwabacker said. "I don't believe we have enough troops on the frontier to survive a mass attack."

". . . survive mass attack . . ." Davis stopped writing. "Captain, I understand that a new rifle has been issued to the troops. Do you feel that this will provide an advantage over the hostiles?"

"As long as we can keep it quiet," Schwabacker said. He lifted his head quickly. "Mr. Davis, this *will* be cleared with General Wessels, will it not?"

"Certainly," Davis said and went on writing. "Now, Captain, you say, as long as the issue can be kept quiet. What do you mean?"

"Well, we are aware of the fact that Red Cloud usually employs one method of attack when engaging our troops. It's the general's opinion that this method is successful because of our muzzle-loading weapons. However, if we can dupe Red Cloud into attacking in his usual manner, we can surprise him greatly by presenting a rapid-fire breech-loader in defense."

Davis' pencil scratched on. "You've just returned from Fort Smith. What is your opinion of the post and its defenses?"

"Barely minimum," Schwabacker said. "You can spread men just so thin, Mr. Davis. General Wessels has just so many to spread."

"I see. Do you feel that Department of Platte has been negligent in supplying troops and material?"

"That's not for me to say, sir."

"There's a peace commission preparing to journey west to Laramie, Captain. Do you think the Sioux are ready to talk peace?"

"Not at this time," Schwabacker said. "Mr. Davis, Red Cloud will have to be drastically reduced in fighting strength before peace terms can be presented. The Cheyennes may react quite differently. It's been my honor to have drubbed them thoroughly on two separate occasions. They're good fighters, but they lack the Sioux heart. Mr. Davis, the Sioux Indian is quite possibly the finest light cavalry in the world. The warriors are fanatically brave, their leaders intelligent, and they go into battle with prearranged tactics, like any other army. They deploy, flank, circle, attack in waves. All they lack is artillery and a quartermaster corps."

Davis laughed at this, but took care to write every word of it down. When he was finished, he said, "It seems to me that the peace commission will have difficulty arranging a meeting between the warring Indians and the government."

"That will be the most difficult," Schwabacker said, "the initial contact. Timing is of the essence where the Indian is concerned. If they believe their medicine has been turned against them, they will listen to talk. If they feel that the medicine is right, the man who enters their camp will probably never come out."

"That's an unpleasant thought," Davis said and flipped a page. "During your patrol to Smith and back, did you observe hostile activity?"

"Mr. Davis, you can't step off the post without being among them. However, the bulk of the hostile forces seems to be shifting. They've abandoned harassment of the road between here and Laramie, and are concentrating forces between here and Fort Smith."

"For war?"

Schwabacker smiled. "Mr. Davis, they've been making war ever since Colonel Carrington built Kearny and Smith."

"Of course," Davis said hastily. He closed his book

and stood up, putting pencil and book in his inner coat pocket. "Thank you for the interview, Captain. The readers back East like to know what's going on out here. After all, it's the taxpayers' money that's being spent." He smiled and went to the door.

"You will clear this with the general?" Schwabacker reminded him.

"Of course," Davis said. "I have other material to gather. Good night, Captain."

"Good night," Schwabacker said and stood in the doorway while Allistair Davis walked away.

Schwabacker wrestled off his boots and lay down on his bunk, his hands behind his head. He couldn't help thinking of Davis, coming all that way for a story. Must have taken him a week of day-and-night riding in dirty trains and dusty stages. He went over in his mind the many things Davis had asked, and wondered if he hadn't said too much.

The sentry at the main gate called for the sergeant of the guard and Schwabacker listened to the sounds. A pair of horsemen rode across the parade, then the gate squeaked and they were let out. The gate closed and the post fell silent.

Finally he got up, pulled on his boots and went out. At the guardhouse he spoke to the officer of the day, who was brewing a fresh pot of coffee to push back his sleepiness. He offered Schwabacker a cup, along with the remark: "This is the dullest damn duty. Red Cloud's nightly snipings of the guards along the wall was bad enough, but it at least broke the monotony."

Schwabacker leaned against the rough wall and

offered no comment. The coffee was strong and scalding. Finally he asked, "Which quarters are occupied by Allistair Davis?"

"A, with Lieutenant Eastwood, but Davis is not on the post."

"That's ridiculous! He left me not over fifteen minutes ago."

"I won't dispute that," the O.D. said, "but he's gone. He checked a horse out of the remount stables and left with the late courier. Davis is on his way to Laramie right now. Said he had an important telegram to get off to his paper."

"You fool!" Schwabacker snapped. "Did you check his pass? Did he have a clearance from General Wessels?"

"Well," the O.D. said, suddenly realizing that a captain was speaking to him, and that he was in trouble, "No, I didn't, sir. I supposed that he had cleared with headquarters. Hell, sir, he came up with the courier. I thought . . ."

"You thought! Mister, you're bragging!"

"I'm sorry, sir. I could send out a detail . . ."

"They'd never catch them," Schwabacker snapped. "Phillips was riding courier tonight and there isn't a mount in the regiment that can catch his roan." He set the cup down, spilling some on the table. "Mister, you're on report!"

Captain Schwabacker stormed out, then stopped on the dark walk. What could he do now? Hold his breath until the newspapers started hitting the streets? God damn Allistair Davis anyway!

190

. . . I'm in hot water now. Schwabacker could feel it eddying up around his feet while his impetuous remarks about the military situation clanged in his head like a bell.

14

THE FIFTEENTH DAY OF JULY TURNED OUT TO BE A scorcher, but Captain Schwabacker suspected that it would be when he came from his quarters shortly after dawn and saw the flaming sun climbing over the east palisade wall. The sky was like blue ice, nearly white, and it seemed that a man could see into infinity, for there was not the slightest wisp of cloud or dust to obstruct the vision.

He had his breakfast in the troop mess, then reported to headquarters when an orderly said that General Wessels wanted to see him. Walking across the parade, Schwabacker wondered if Wessels had received word from eastern headquarters. A week had gone by since Allistair Davis rode from the post with his story. Undoubtedly the story was in the papers, but with mail stages running few and far between, another two weeks could go by before a paper reached the frontier. Dispatch riders carried only letters. Papers and packages were too bulky for saddle handling.

The regimental clerk ushered him into Wessels' office. The general was crouched behind his desk, half hidden by a haze of cigar smoke, half surrounded by a blizzard of papers.

"Take a chair," Wessels said and went on writing for

another ten nerve-breaking minutes. He finished at last, blotted the paper and stuffed it carelessly in a desk drawer. "Captain Jocelyn is being released from the infirmary today," Wessels said. "I could give him his own troop back."

"He has the seniority, sir," Schwabacker's heart fell. He was surprised Wessels didn't hear it.

"I could make him post adjutant too," Wessels said. "Which is what I think I'll do." He rustled papers. "I'm sending out a mail stage next week. His wife and son will be on it." He found the paper he was looking for and handed it to Schwabacker. "Communication from Colonel Ashford at Laramie. Mrs. Kincaid is growing impatient and wants me to send you back to answer charges. I've ignored this for a week, Captain, but I can't sit on it forever."

"I understand, sir." He read the request for immediate return, and noted that Lieutenant Eastwood had been named officer of the court. Schwabacker handed the letter back. "Am I relieved of my command, sir?"

"You'll be relieved when I tell you," Wessels said, "and I haven't told you. However, I don't want to be a sneak about this, Captain, or lie to Colonel Ashford. So I can't send you back if you're not here, can I?"

"No, sir."

"I'm sending you back to Fort Smith, Captain, but without your troop."

"I don't understand, sir."

Wessels glanced at the sour stub of his cigar and stripped the wrapper off a fresh one. "A cigar is a comfort," he said. "Are you addicted to them, Captain?"

Schwabacker shook his head. "Filthy habit," Wessels admitted. "I'm not human until I have my fourth cigar. Nearly lost a battle once because I ran out of cigars. Couldn't think to save my soul." He got it going and leaned back in his chair. "Jim Bridger came back last night. Woke me out of a sound sleep. He's been living with the Crows, and according to them, Red Cloud's massing men for a big push."

"Is Bridger on the post now, sir?"

"No," Wessels said. "I sent him to Laramie before dawn with a complete summation of the campaign to date. He's to remain there until the peace commission arrives, then present the situation for their recommendation. Meanwhile, I've decided to withdraw the troops from Fort Smith before Red Cloud wipes them out. You're going to carry that order for me, Captain."

"Yes, sir."

"Don't say it so casually," Wessels said flatly. "The situation's changed since you made that night march. No one has been able to get through for ten days. Bridger did, but he traveled alone. You'll travel alone. Colonel Kinney has to be advised of the peril and vacate without delay."

"When do I leave, sir?"

"Tonight," Wessels said. "The farrier sergeant will have an unshod horse for you. I'd advise pistol and carbine. Leave anything that will rattle behind. Any questions?"

"No, sir." Schwabacker turned to the door. "Sir, there's one more thing. Have you heard from Mr. Allistair Davis?"

"Not a damned word," Wessels snapped. "He left this post without authority and I've registered a complaint with his paper about it, but a lot of damn good that will do." He drew deeply on his cigar. "I trust that you were discreet during the interview. It'll play hell if you weren't. The damned politicians are hollering now about military feet-dragging. Some innocent remark thoughtlessly given could tip the scale irreparably and we'd leave here with a stain on us that would never come off."

"Yes, sir," Schwabacker said and hurried out. He stood on the porch and tried to compose himself. Phrases of Wessels' conversation kept running through his mind. . . . Thoughtlessly given . . . tip the scale irreparably . . . stain . . . *God! What have I done? . . .*

And the whole horrible answer became numbingly clear. Schwabacker wondered how blunderingly stupid and self-effacing a man could be. He had sat there like some damned sage spouting opinions when he had never actually been a part of anything. Hell! He hadn't even seen Jim Bridger, who knew more about the Indians than anyone! And yet he had had the audacity to act like he knew everything, shooting his mouth off about strategy like some retired general sitting under a park elm ten years after the war was over. He remembered what he had told Allistair Davis and could foresee the disastrous results. If there was anyone who could fulfill General Wessels' fears, Emil Schwabacker decided that he was the man to do it. As far as he was concerned, his mouth had all but ruined the campaign politically. It was merely a matter of time now. Thundering repercussions would arrive on the next mail stage.

He spent a miserable day in his quarters. During the afternoon he tried to sleep, but found it impossible. He felt like a man waiting for the execution date to be set. The court-martial charges faded to pale insignificance when compared to his damning statements.

Night finally came and he got up and washed his face. The evening mess was nearly empty when he went in, ate his meal in silence and went out, leaving a few remaining officers wondering. Sergeant Finnegan came around while Schwabacker was at the stable, saddling the unshod horse. The sergeant stomped around and fretted like a mother allowing her only daughter to take her first buggy ride alone with a handsome man.

Schwabacker said, "Can't you stand still? You're making the horse nervous."

"Ah, sor, take me along."

"Can't," Schwabacker said, stepping into the saddle. "Keep the troop from fighting with the infantry. I don't want to get half of you from the guardhouse when I come back."

"Be sure an' come back, sor," Finnegan said and gave the horse a slap. At headquarters, Schwabacker stopped long enough to pick up the small packet of orders from Major Powell, then the gates opened and let him out into the hostile land.

He drove the horse into a gallop, splashed across Piney Creek and entered the fringed cottonwoods along the bank a mile and a half away from the fort. A half-hour later he came onto the road north of Lodge Trail

Ridge, paused for a quick look that told him nothing, then gigged the horse with his heels.

A cavalryman's caution told him to save the horse, spread the animal's strength over the ninety-mile distance, but some inner wisdom told him that this was impossible; the Sioux would contest his passage before he rode a quarter of the distance.

So he drove the horse until he was forced to slow his pace, then he dismounted and led the horse for nearly a mile before vaulting into the saddle again. Twice, mounted warriors crossed the trail ahead of him; he caught a whiff of their dust, and once saw a shadow enter the trees to the right. There was no way to check his back trail, but he suspected that Sioux braves pressed him close.

Pressed him, yet never closed, and this was enough to worry Emil Schwabacker. The unshod horse helped, for there was a different tenor to the hoofbeats. And he did not have the usual rattling cavalry equipment. He had left his hat behind to avoid a give-away silhouette, and strips of cloth muffled every equipment ring, even the one on the side of the carbine.

By the time he reached Goose Creek, his horse was well lathered. He splashed across the creek, then wheeled into the brush on the other side and waited.

A minute passed, then stretched into three. Then he heard the slight sound, not a horse, not a man, but an alien sound. A rider hove into view, bent over to peer up the trail. Schwabacker saw the bare upper body and the scalp-decorated lance.

When the Sioux entered the creek he stopped and the

horse lowered his head and drank for a moment, making blowing sounds. Schwabacker held his breath. No more than fifteen feet separated them, too close for comfort, and yet not close enough to jump the Sioux. One yell and he'd have a swarm bearing down on him.

The horse stopped drinking and the Indian left the creek. He turned and looked back, and leaned forward again to peer up the road. When he drew parallel with Schwabacker's concealment, the young officer jabbed spurs to his horse and rode full tilt into the Indian, carbine swinging.

In spite of the suddenness of the attack, the Sioux whirled and made a thrust with his lance. Schwabacker felt it pass beneath his arm, go through the shirt and rip out, then the carbine caught the Sioux on the back of the neck and he left his horse in a sprawl.

Schwabacker left the saddle and grabbed the looped reins of the Indian pony. He went up bareback, kicked the horse with his spurs and was rewarded with a burst of speed. He had a fresh horse now, one that with luck would take him into the Crow country near Grass Creek.

Provided he could get through the Sioux. The thought was alarming. He supposed that not more than a half-hour would go by before the Indians found their fallen comrade and then the deadly chase would be on in earnest. They would find the jaded cavalry horse and know.

Schwabacker measured his chances and found them distressingly slim. For a moment he thought of making a stand, then dismissed it as pure suicide. Ride! That was all he could do, and he settled down to the grim business.

Well after midnight he knew that the Sioux pony was nearly exhausted, but he told himself that he had set a blistering pace and there had been no sign of pursuit. Yet he was being pursued.

He dismounted from the foaming horse and wiped him down with grass. Twenty minutes of this was all Schwabacker could take, for his nerves were getting so tight that he saw an Indian lurking in every shadow. He mounted again and went on at a walk. An hour later he crossed the lower fork of Grass Lodge Creek without incident.

Quite beyond his understanding, he felt that there were no hostile Sioux in the vicinity. Night animals prowled, and in the timber owls fluttered on silent wings after mice. The land seemed normal, with all the normal sounds and smells. He seemed absolutely alone in it and this he could not understand. It seemed to him that the Indians had come to an invisible boundary and had stopped. He wasn't in Crow country, and that wouldn't stop them anyway, if they wanted to come after him; these thoughts ran through his mind.

The horse needed rest if he ever intended to ride him into Smith, which was, by his calculations, better than five hours away. Schwabacker chose a thicket a hundred yards away from the trail, picketed the horse and settled down on the grass, his carbine across his lap. Behind him a bear snorted in a berry thicket, caught the man scent and ambled off with a great crashing of brush. Farther away, where the hills began to deepen, a bull elk trumpeted briefly, then fell silent. Sound was all around him, the sounds that spelled safety, and Emil Schwabacker could not make sense of it.

He let an hour go by, a dragging hour, then got his pony off the picket and went onto his back. At the road he paused, looking both ways, but he saw nothing, heard nothing. Turning the horse, he struck out at a trot.

Alternating between the trot and the walk, Schwabacker reached the southern limits of Crow country around dawn, and wasted a bleary-eyed moment studying the graying ridges. He saw nothing but sharp rock and irregular timber. Uneasy and greatly disturbed, he moved on toward Fort C. F. Smith.

Twice he stopped at small creeks to water the pony and refresh himself. The sun was up now, bright early heat. He recognized his position. Smith lay over the next rise, three and a half miles at the outside.

Breaking out into a wide clearing, Schwabacker yanked the pony to a halt and stared blank-faced. Before him lay a battleground, dotted here and there with huddled shapes, half-naked bodies postured ungracefully by death. Soldiers moved around; it seemed that the entire command of Fort Smith was there. Soldiers lay on the ground, blanket covered; he could count six. Nearly twice that many were being tended on blankets.

There was the smell of death in the air, and no sounds, save what came from the clearing. He could hear those sounds, voices, clearly in the cathedral quiet. Automatically he nudged the horse and rode forward.

Instantly the tenor of the soldiers changed. A few rifles came up, pointing his way, but before he could call out and identify himself, Colonel Kinney's command held their fire.

Around Emil Schwabacker now were the sprawled shapes of dead Indians. He recognized them as Cheyennes, nearly a hundred at a quick guess. Then he was riding among the soldiers, the men who had killed and stood to be killed. He saw the raw shock on their faces, the round eyes, the blank way they had of looking at a man, for the mind became numb from the sounds and the smells, the adjectives of death.

He approached Colonel Kinney and dismounted. Disjointed fragments of the fight fell into place for Schwabacker: The trapped soldiers—from appearances they must have been gathering wood. Two half-filled wagons stood nearby, the horses dead in harness. Everywhere he walked he stepped on empty brass cartridge cases, .50-70 cartridge cases. Army brass and army death.

Schwabacker saluted. "Dispatch from General Wessels, sir."

"How did you get through?" Kinney's voice was raspy. Around them swirled the cleaning detail, the surgeon, the troopers trying to find some semblance of order when none could prevail.

"I really don't know, sir. My horse gave out and I got this one from a Sioux."

"This day will live forever in my mind," Kinney said. "They caught my wood-gathering party at dawn. The Cheyennes. Lieutenant Bristol says there must have been three hundred of them." Kinney wiped his face and looked around. "God, I can't bear to think what would have happened if we hadn't had those rifles, Captain." He took Schwabacker's arm and shook him. "Nineteen men against three hundred, Captain, and we whipped them. Sent them running like dogs with their tails between their legs. We've made history, Captain. Wherever men gather from this day forward, they will speak of this fight. The Cheyennes will speak of it too, Captain, but with awe and fear."

"My dispatch, sir," Schwabacker said and handed him Wessels' leather case.

Colonel Kinney read the orders and his face colored. He looked at Schwabacker like a man ready to fight. "I disregard this order, sir! Our battle has already taken place. Fort Smith still stands against the enemy, by God!" He folded the orders and handed them back. "Return this to the general with your report, sir. You have eyes; I need not tell you the details."

"Yes, sir."

"You've made a gallant ride, Captain, but in vain. Now make a better one and pray that Fort Phil Kearny is not ashes when you get there."

Kinney's words were a bell-toll of doom to Schwabacker. For the first time he considered the Indian strategy and knew then that this was not a hit-or-miss attack, but a carefully timed effort to knock out the army's northernmost post. Red Cloud! The name was a shout in his mind. Red Cloud had split his forces at last, the Cheyennes to the north, the Sioux to the south. Now all the small things fell into place, why the Sioux had broken off and turned back. None of the braves wanted to be left out of the dawn attack on Fort Phil Kearny!

"Can you spare a fresh horse, sir?"

"Captain Lovering!" Kinney signaled an officer who supervised the wounded. Lovering came up on the double. "Find Captain Schwabacker a good horse." When the officer trotted away, Kinney said, "Can you hold up under another ninety miles of it, Captain?"

"It isn't a question of can I, sir. I must return to Kearny, sir. If General Wessels has succeeded in repulsing an attack, he will want to know your status here."

Lovering came up with a superb mount, the private property of a newly deceased officer. Schwabacker stripped the saddle off and mounted bareback. He whipped the horse into a run toward the south and, when he topped the rise to leave the clearing, did not look back. There was no need to. He knew all there was to know about dying. He had had his own victories, his own defeats, and yet he regretted deeply the time he had wasted along the road. An hour and a half would have made the difference between participating and looking on after glory had been won.

To Schwabacker's way of thinking, special gods saw to it that he looked through the window at life, instead of allowing him to come to grips with it. No one had to tell him what awaited him at the end of this ride. Whether Wessels achieved victory or ended in defeat, the battle would surely be over, and Captain Emil Schwabacker would be denied participation. One of these days he would return home and someone would ask him about the fight at Fort C. F. Smith. He could patiently explain that he had been an hour and a half late. Someone would ask about Jim Bridger, and Schwabacker would have to say that, although he was stationed on the same post, he had never seen Bridger. Now he wondered how late he would be at Fort Phil Kearny.

15

Major J. W. Powell was not an impressive man, and there was little in his past to mark him as a strategist, but he had been at Fort Phil Kearny since Colonel Henry B. Carrington first paced off the parade ground, and thereafter had learned a great deal about Sioux strategy.

In command of the wood-cutting detail, Powell took his small force of thirty-two men to the Piney, a few miles from the fort, and there established a camp. The woodcutters moved into the timber while Major Powell had the wagon boxes dismounted from the wagons and placed in a rectangle. Within this enclosure he stationed his soldiers. Through the afternoon the ring of the ax was spaced by falling timber. That evening the civilian woodcutters walked the few miles back to the fort, but Major Powell remained camped within the enclosure of the wagon boxes, much to the disgust of his men.

Powell was never a talkative man, and whatever thoughts he had, he kept to himself. Most of Powell's command were seasoned infantrymen, good shots, and well aware of their dangerous position. All of them remembered Captain Fetterman and his ill-fated command, which by all rights should have been Powell's.

But Fetterman had outranked Powell by a former brevet and so led the luckless eighty. Yet each man knew that if Powell had been in command, the massacre might never have taken place, for behind Powell's placid, moon-shaped face, a brain functioned ceaselessly; here was an officer who rarely made a mistake.

Such a thing can give an enlisted man confidence when there is every reason not to have it.

There were guards, a quarter of the men at a time, and during the night a careful alertness was maintained, but Powell slept without stirring. He did not believe the Sioux would attack at night, even to pluck such a defenseless plum.

Before the first streaks of dawn brightened the sky to the east, Major Powell was awake and making sure every man was awake, although he kept them well down beneath the wagon boxes. Almost deliberately, it seemed, he allowed the horse herd to stray until it was dangerously far away. Powell's sergeant, a grizzled man with a lifetime of service, thought about mentioning this, but Powell was not the kind of an officer who needed advice.

Private Lippincot saw them first and turned to Powell, his face gray, his mouth wide open. Powell smiled and spoke softly, "Thank you, Lippincot. I see them."

Every man saw them and every man recognized the leader as the Sioux poured off the rim of a nearby hill. They had all seen this Indian before, the one they called Crazy Horse. He had led the decoy party that had duped Fetterman to the top of Lodge Trail Ridge.

On he came, leading a hundred warriors in screaming

fury, bearing down on the small nest of wagon boxes drawn together on open ground. Powell spoke to his men and let the Sioux come on. From the fort, a sentry fired into the air, alarming the garrison to the coming fight.

Then the Sioux were upon Powell's command and he gave the command to fire as Crazy Horse began to circle. Carbines boomed in unison and a number of the Sioux stumbled, but they were strong and the ring tightened.

From every ridge they poured, in painted, howling waves that all but drowned out the rhythmic firing of Powell's command. Crazy Horse was fanatically brave and he brought his force in close, believing that the carbines would soon cease firing while the troop reloaded; but there was no let up. Sioux went down in alarming numbers. Then as quickly as he had attacked, Crazy Horse withdrew, for Red Cloud and his five hundred were entering the fight, drawing a noose about the wagons.

The troopers' fire did not slacken and the great Sioux leader threw an unexpected mass attack toward the besieged, but before they could reach the wagons the unrelenting fire broke them, caused them to split and retreat into a circling movement.

Nearly a hundred of Red Cloud's finest braves were down, and yet he had not breached the never-ending carbine fire. Even the courageous Crazy Horse knew better than to crowd another attack; already half of his first wave were dead.

With a shout of rage, Red Cloud broke away, his warriors following him to the higher timbered ground. He could look back and see his people's blood on the ground, and their bodies surrounding the fanatical men in the wagon boxes.

As suddenly as it began, the fight died. From the post, Wessels and his command streamed forth, lugging several ungainly howitzers. But they were not needed. Powell had made his gamble, baited his trap and landed his game. The ground surrounding his fort of wagon boxes was proof enough.

The United States Army had at last achieved victory over the Sioux.

This was the fight and this was what Emil Schwabacker heard that night when he returned to Fort Phil Kearny on a badly jaded horse.

He went to headquarters and entered General Wessels' office. The general was not there and an orderly went after him. There was a celebration in the officers' mess, with Major Powell the hero of the hour. When Wessels arrived, he found Schwabacker slumped down in a chair.

"Good God," Wessels said, "I didn't mean for you to turn around and come right back!" Schwabacker tried to stand, but the general pushed him back in the chair and poured a stout shot of brandy for him.

After Schwabacker tossed it down and set the glass on the desk, he said, "It's my pleasure to report, sir, that approximately nineteen men of Colonel Kinney's command met and defeated over a hundred Cheyennes several miles from Fort Smith."

Wessels' mouth dropped open. "What?" He shouted it.

"Yes, sir. Colonel Kinney respectfully requests permission to hold at Fort Smith, sir."

"My God, what a glorious day for the military!" Wessels began to pace back and forth. "Can it be that we've given the devils a licking? I must get a dispatch off immediately." He went to the door and shouted for the orderly, who proved he had been listening by entering with Wessels' dispatch case. The general let this slide because he had more important things on his mind.

Schwabacker said, "May I be excused, sir?"

"Of course," Wessels said. He was in an expansive mood. "You're relieved of duty for the rest of the week, Captain. And thank you."

Schwabacker was too tired to light the lamp in his quarters. He unbuckled his pistol belt and tossed it on the floor, then tugged off his boots and stretched out, fully clothed. He could hear singing from the officers' mess, but the celebration meant nothing to him. Once again he had been somewhere else, doing some mundane service while history was being made.

This was his thought when he fell asleep.

Streaming sunlight woke him, and when he got out of bed, his back was one solid ache. It was moments before he could trust his legs to support his weight. He washed at the basin, then shaved carefully before changing into a clean uniform. He was knotting his neckerchief when General Wessels' orderly knocked.

"Up, sir? The general would like to see you right away."

Schwabacker frowned, but the orderly was hurrying along the duck boards. He put on his pistol belt, settled his hat and stepped out into the hot midday sun. A small headache pestered him, but he supposed that was from lack of sleep.

As he approached headquarters he saw the dispatch rider leading his horse toward the stable area, and a warning gong sounded in his mind. Wessels was in his office and his jocularity of the night before had completely vanished.

He was reading a newspaper and not liking it.

"Sit down, Captain," Wessels said and gnawed on a cold cigar. "I've been reading your statements. Somehow I get the impression that you are better informed on strategy than I am." Wessels sat down and slapped the desk with the paper. "Captain, allow me to inform you that a peace commission is at Fort Laramie. Within a week or ten days, they will dispatch a representative to meet with the Sioux and Cheyenne leaders, provided Jim Bridger can find them, and hold a preliminary peace parley. Provided of course that your insane comments fail to arouse the politicians!" Wessels spread the paper and read a few passages. "By God, I've been crying my head off for replacements and you sound as if we had the situation well in hand!" He blew through his nose and shook his head. "I can think of a dozen politicians who will take this as gospel. I can already hear them making speeches about how the army is wasting the taxpayers' money. Good God, how can the peace commission hope to arrive at any sort of conclusion with the army pulling one way and the politicians pulling the other?"

"What can I say, sir?"

"I'll say it for you," Wessels snapped. "Captain Schwabacker, you are as of this moment relieved of your command and placed on inactive status pending transportation to Fort Laramie, where equally grave charges await you."

"Yes, sir."

Wessels drummed his fingers on his desk. "Captain, try and understand me. I'm a general officer; I can't stand for any mistakes. Your comments seem innocent enough, but I can't risk them. Try and appreciate my position. We have achieved a victory over Red Cloud, but by the time the peace commission acts upon it, the tables may be turned around. He can make medicine, do a hundred different things between now and parley time."

"Send out an envoy of your own, sir."

Wessels laughed hollowly. "I have no authority, Captain. They'd dishonor it and throw it back in my teeth." He sighed. "Now get out of here and let me think."

Leaving General Wessels' office, Schwabacker decided that the weight of command was not nearly as heavy as the weight of dishonor, and that was what he now faced. Gone were all his dreams; marriage to anyone was now impossible.

Alone in his own quarters he tried to hate Allistair Davis, but could not. The man was doing a job any way he could, and if he had been gullible enough to provide the story, then Davis was not to blame.

Where did it all come from? This sense of eagerness, the sharp disappointments? Why did he have to be the best? Because his father made him feel disgraced if he wasn't the best? He supposed so, but how easy it was to lay one's troubles at another man's feet. No, this was his own doing and whatever came of it he would have to accept like a man, without whining or casting blame.

He answered mess call in the evening, then went back to his quarters. When Finnegan came in after dark, Schwabacker was asleep, but woke when the sergeant stumbled over a chair.

"Light the lamp," Schwabacker said, and Finnegan struck a match.

"Heard th' news, sor," Finnegan said. "It's all over th' post."

Schwabacker sat up and rubbed his eyes. "Jocelyn must be pleased. He has his troop back now."

"Na, sor, I'd say he wasn't pleased."

Schwabacker looked sharply at Finnegan. "I don't get that."

"It don't matter, sor." The sergeant toed a chair around and sat down. "What's th' way out, sor?"

"No way out," Schwabacker said. "Have you got a bottle, Sean?"

"Aye," Finnegan said, producing one. "You're not goin' to start on that stuff, are you, sor?"

Schwabacker shook his head and upended the bottle. He pulled it away, gasping, his eyes watering. "Maybe it'll give me the guts I lack," he said.

"That day'll never come, sor, when you need guts."

"I've been thinking," Schwabacker said softly. "I'm through in the army, Sean. It's just a matter of time. But there's one thing I'd like to do before it's all over. Yet I'm scared; the thought alone is frightening enough."

"What's that, sor?"

Schwabacker looked at him intently. "Find Red Cloud and his Cheyenne friends and sue for peace." He set each word out quietly, like a man handling fragile eggs. Finnegan stared.

"God, sor . . ."

"Don't say it; you'll talk me out of it," Schwabacker said. "Sean, understand that there's a time for everything, a moment that makes an eternal difference. A moment that comes and goes, and if a man's not there at the right time, he'll never get another chance. That moment has come and gone for me all my life, but this time I can't let it pass. Red Cloud's hurt, his medicine's backfired into his face. Someone could get away with a peace parley now. Arrange a meeting for a month hence. Get his word. He's an honorable man. Once he gave it, he'd die before he went back on it."

"Aye, sor. I agree, but . . ."

"No but's, Sean. I know, I wouldn't have authority, but how would they know? It wouldn't matter what I did, as long as I arranged the talks. Don't you understand? If the peace commission waits a couple of weeks, it will be too late!"

"Aye. What is it you want me to be doin', sor?"

"I've got to have a horse by the water gates. I can sneak out there and cross Piney Creek. After that, it doesn't matter whether the post is aroused or not; they won't come after me."

The seriousness of this plan made Finnegan's voice hoarse. "When, sor?"

"An hour at the outside," Schwabacker said. "Will

you do it, Sean? I have no right to ask."

"You've every right," Finnegan said, "but there's one catch, sor; I go with you."

"No!"

"Why not, sor? Jocelyn's goin' to chunk me in th' stockade as soon as he can git a court-martial to sit still. Besides, sor, this is a two-man job."

"All right," Schwabacker said. "But no firearms, Sean. Bareback and unarmed."

Finnegan nodded. "What time is it, sor?"

Schwabacker looked at his watch. "Quarter after seven."

"In an hour then," Finnegan said and went out.

There was little to do but wait and think. Another foolish move? Emil Schwabacker decided not. If he won, then his defeat would not be pointless; his shame would have some meaning, if only to himself. He thought about writing a farewell letter to Henrietta Brubaker, then decided against it because it was melo-dramatic. His father would laugh at such a gesture, for it was what he had learned to expect from his only son, ridiculous, irresponsible acts.

The hour passed slowly, and in the last remaining minutes Schwabacker straightened his room. He wanted everything to be convenient for the officer who would have to box his belongings and ship them back to St. Albans, Vermont.

Figuring two minutes to walk to the stables, Schwabacker blew out the lamp and stepped outside into the darkness. From that moment, there was no turning back, yet the thought did not unnerve him.

16

SCHWABACKER'S TIMING WAS IN ERROR. WHEN HE arrived at the water gate, Finnegan had not yet appeared. Schwabacker stepped into the inky shadows and became almost invisible. From his position he could see the huge L-shaped stables and the hay shed. On the other side of the compound, the stable guard walked his measured patrol, carbine at the trail.

The cavalry yard was in the main post compound, and Schwabacker looked to his left, past the wagon sheds and farrier's shop. Near the hay scales a gate opened up into the main yard, and through this Sergeant Finnegan led two unsaddled mounts. The guard had passed the wagonmaster's office and was approaching the teamsters' mess when he saw Finnegan.

"Halt there!"

"Sure now," Finnegan said. His voice came softly, unhurried, across the brief distance. The guard trotted up, very curious. He recognized Finnegan, and his rank, and was very careful of his inquiries.

"What ya doin' with them horses, Sergeant?"

"Exercise," Finnegan said. "Bullets here's got a stiff leg, Peterson. A man's got a right to care for his mount, ain't he?"

"I . . . I guess so, Sergeant."

Finnegan smiled disarmingly. "Go on about your business, lad. It's a good word I'll be puttin' in for you, stickin' to yer duty this way." He slapped Trooper Peterson on the shoulder. "You're a good lad an' a credit to th' troop. That you are."

This unexpected praise from a sergeant who habitually snapped was enough to convince Trooper Peterson that he was indeed lucky to be pulling a tour of the guard this night. He walked away with a lightened step, the vision of corporal's stripe in three or four years not too remote a possibility.

Finnegan waited a moment, then came on, whistling softly. He approached the water gates and Schwabacker stepped from the shadows, slid the oak bar and opened one. Finnegan passed through with the horses and Schwabacker stepped outside, closing the gate softly behind him. He took the reins from the sergeant and was ready to swing up, then stopped when Finnegan said, "Sor."

Schwabacker flipped his head around, thinking someone had exited behind him, but there was no one. Then he followed Finnegan's stare and saw Captain Temple Jocelyn walking slowly toward them from Piney Creek.

Jocelyn leaned heavily on a cane and his pace was geared to his weakened condition. He stopped a few feet from them, his glance going from one to the other. It steadied on Schwabacker.

"Going for a ride, Captain?" The ice-eyes slid on to the horses. "Without saddles?"

"I'm vacating the post," Schwabacker said. "Are you going to stop me, Captain?"

Jocelyn shook his head. "Not here. However, as soon as I walk to headquarters, I will report your absence to the officer of the day."

"Of course," Schwabacker said. "I expected that."

"And I shall have to testify to this conversation at your court-martial, Captain. Bear that in mind and say nothing you don't want used to convict you." He looked at Sergeant Finnegan. "You *were* an able non-com, Sean, but you allowed yourself to be swayed by corrupting influences. Return to the post now and I'll say nothing of this, for old time's sake."

"No, sor," Finnegan said. "I want to go with th' capt'n. I guess that's somethin' about you I never knew before, sor; that you'd do a thing fer old time's sake. Capt'n Schwabacker he don't rate that, 'cause there's no old ties. Well, sor, I don't either. Fer years I stuck with you 'cause I wanted to, but I was wrong, Capt'n. I'm with Capt'n Schwabacker now 'cause he's right, not fer old time's sake."

"I see," Jocelyn said. "I don't suppose there's anything else to say, is there?"

"There is," Finnegan said flatly, "but you ain't man enough to say it."

For a second Schwabacker thought Jocelyn was going to strike Finnegan; he lifted his cane in a threatening manner, then the anger drained from him and his square shoulders rounded imperceptibly.

"You're right, Sergeant." To Schwabacker he said, "I am in your debt, Captain. Your letter to my wife angered me once, but I'm eternally grateful. Remember that I bear you no personal malice, but the warmest regard, as both an officer and a gentleman." He turned toward the gate. "Good evening. If you're going to desert, I don't want to assume the unpleasant task of reporting that I was a witness."

He parted the gate and entered the post. Schwabacker waited a moment, then vaulted onto the horse's back. Finnegan went up and a moment later they entered Piney Creek, splashed across, and began a large circle designed to take them away from the post and to pick up the Bozeman Road to the north.

The large, unanswered problem in Schwabacker's mind was where to locate the Indians. Since Lodge Trail Ridge was their picket post, he led the way around Sullivant's Hill, a bare, treeless knob of earth and rock, then entered Big Piney, swimming his horse across. Finnegan stayed a length behind and they paused on the northeast bank, water streaming from their clothes.

The country here was choked with cottonwood trees. Less than a half a mile east, the Bozeman Road cut north, toward Fort Smith.

Schwabacker said, "I don't know whether to hunt for the Sioux or just move around and let them find us." He shifted on the horse and had a look around.

"This is where Fetterman started to chase th' Injuns," Finnegan said. "Gives a man a creepy feelin', don't it, sor?"

"It gives a man ideas," Schwabacker said quickly. "Which route did Crazy Horse take when he decoyed Fetterman away from the Fort?"

Finnegan pointed to the northwest. "Toward Peno Creek, sor. There's some open country back there."

"Let's look at it," Schwabacker said and wheeled the horse around. Lodge Trail Ridge was on their right, a looming shape in the darkness. A ten-minute ride took them far enough away from Big Piney to bring them out of the cottonwoods and brush. Hills surrounded them on all sides and Schwabacker walked the horse, his head swinging constantly, searching out the pine-blanketed slopes.

Nearly three hours later they were near Peno Creek and the inner reaches of the long valley. Suddenly Schwabacker said, "We'll cut southwest, Sean." He offered no explanation and Finnegan did not question the decision.

Peno Head was a low mountain, too big to be called a hill, heavily furred with pine and hemlock. It took another hour and a half to navigate the upper slopes, and when they were in the thickest timber, Schwabacker dismounted and let the horse graze. Finnegan flipped off and stood near Schwabacker, his heavy face weighted by worry.

"What's on the other side of this?" Schwabacker asked.

"Another small ridge, sor."

"There's too much timber up here," Schwabacker said. "If we're going to find a Sioux camp, we'll have to find open ground, or where the timber is less thick."

"Looks like a long hunt, sor."

"Then let's get at it," Schwabacker said and mounted.

They left the timbered closeness of Peno Head, cutting southwest across a steep-sided valley. There the timber thinned slightly and they traversed a rocky ridge to drop over the other side into a timbered valley. Cleared patches stood out against the darkness of pine, and as they worked their way through, Schwabacker saw that the trees grew in orchards, with long, grassy meadows between.

This was the kind of country the Sioux liked, with water and wood nearby, but not so close as to constitute a threat. Schwabacker stopped and checked his watch, squinting to make out the hands. Nearly two. He turned slightly to the left until he came to a small creek, then walked the horse along the bank where the thick grass muffled all sounds.

A few minutes later he saw a mounted man cross the creek a hundred and fifty yards ahead. An Indian. Schwabacker looked at Finnegan, then they both gigged their horses into a trot to follow. The pine orchards kept interfering with Schwabacker's observations and he pressed dangerously close. Too close, for the Indian suddenly wheeled his horse, shouted once and fired his rifle at them.

The boom of the gun was a thunderclap which reverberated through the hills. Finnegan swore in a dull voice and Schwabacker said, "After him!"

The race began, with the Indian striking out across an open patch of ground. When the Indian entered an elongated patch of timber, Schwabacker lost him completely. Finnegan was for pulling up, but the rash captain charged into the dark woods and complete darkness forced him to slow, finally to dismount.

Twenty minutes later they emerged on the other side and stopped. The thirty-odd armed warriors blocking their path were reason enough. Beyond the warriors lay the Cheyenne-Sioux camp, big beyond imagining, at least a thousand lodges, hundreds of fires, a regular community.

Faced with a ring of rifles and steel-tipped lances, Schwabacker dropped the reins of his horse and stepped away, both hands held high. Because he didn't know what else to do, Finnegan imitated the captain.

One of the Indians spoke: *"Ma-twau! Nut-tinne um-mis-sin-oh-ko-nuh! Kish-pissu wun-nene-heau!"*

"What's he sayin', sor?"

"I don't know," Schwabacker said. Four of the Cheyenne braves slid off their horses and bound both men with hair ropes. There was little gentleness in this treatment.

The Cheyenne spoke again: *"Pey-ay!"*

One of the Indians whirled his horse and raced toward the camp, sending his shouts on ahead. A vast clamor rose then, and the Cheyenne leader, who now held both rope ends, turned his horse and started off at a walk. Schwabacker and Finnegan trotted to keep up. The other braves who had participated in the capture made up the rear guard, and Schwabacker felt certain that any of that dozen would have been only too happy to put a bullet in his back.

Approaching the village, Schwabacker saw that the crier's advance news had brought everyone from their lodges. A wall of screaming Indians confronted the approaching party, but the Cheyenne who claimed these prisoners waved his lance and a lane of spitting women opened up. The children ran alongside Schwabacker and Finnegan, pelting them with stones, bombarding them with willow switches. The men seemed completely absent until they entered the vast circle of this camp.

Then they were led before a huge fire, behind which sat a row of angry, bronze-faced men. Their eyes were as emotionless as glass beads. The Cheyenne dismounted and went into a long harangue about his capture of the long knives. Neither Schwabacker nor Finnegan understood a word of it, but they knew who was the object in point, for the Cheyenne waved his arms at them and twice turned to spit.

Finally the talk ended and a tall man stood up. He was a Cheyenne; Schwabacker could tell by his dress, and the earring. His face was old beyond imagining and his dark eyes contained the wisdom of the world. He had a noble face, seamed by the years of trouble through which he had lived. His hair was parted in the center of his head and hung past each shoulder, bound in muskrat furs. One feather was worn, thrust into the hair at the back of his head. The feather did not sit straight up, but sideways, the tip colored a bright vermilion.

He spoke to Schwabacker. "You do not understand the words of the Cheyenne, pony soldier?" His voice was a bass rumble.

"They are strange to me," Schwabacker said evenly.

"Why is this, pony soldier? We have fought." He held up two fingers. "We have given blood, yet we can not speak except in your tongue."

"You are Spotted Tail?"

"That is what they call me," Spotted Tail said. "You have a Cheyenne name, pony soldier. It was given to you by my people."

"I would like to hear it," Schwabacker said.

"*Met-ah Wabe-gushau.* Who-Fears-His-Heart." Spotted Tail's marble eyes never left Emil Schwabacker's face. "The name is true, pony soldier. You come to this camp without arms. Is the brave one tired of war?"

"Yes," Schwabacker said. "All pony soldiers are tired of war. We wish to speak of peace."

Finnegan muttered: "Somethin' wrong here, sor. This is too easy."

The sergeant was right, for another Indian stood up, and every eye turned to him. He was a Sioux, a large man with a broad, powerful face and the most commanding eyes Emil Schwabacker had ever seen. He wore one feather in his hair, the only decoration about him, and Schwabacker knew that he needed none, for this was Red Cloud himself.

"I will speak," he said and Spotted Tail sat down.

"You speak of peace, pony soldier? Then you lie! The long knives have spoken of peace before, but there has been no peace, only lies. Twice I have put my mark upon the paper, but there was no honor in the long knives' mark. Each time there was another paper to change the paper signed before."

Schwabacker didn't need an adviser to tell him the temper of these people, for an angry muttering went up among the packed thousand. Suddenly Schwabacker felt a raw shock of fear. He was like a man who swims to the middle of the lake, then finds that he is in danger of drowning because he can't swim back. Until now he had been confident of himself, but his confidence fled silently, leaving him on a lonely island surrounded by anger. He looked at Sergeant Finnegan and found him white-faced, lines of strain pulling at his cheeks.

Red Cloud was speaking again. "You have come into my camp without arms, pony soldier. Do you wish to die?"

"I came to speak," Schwabacker said, surprised that he had a voice. But once he had spoken, control returned and he let no fear show on his face. "Must my hands be tied while I speak?"

A nod from the Sioux chief removed the ropes and Schwabacker had to stifle an overpowering impulse to rub his wrists, for the ropes left grooves in the flesh. Yet he did not, understanding without thought that a show of weakness would be fatal.

"My sergeant," he said, "must be released too."

Red Cloud wouldn't go for this; it was in his eyes.

Schwabacker said, "Does the great Sioux leader fear we will escape? Do two pony soldiers frighten five hundred braves?"

When Red Cloud nodded, Schwabacker offered himself silent congratulations. Pride; that was the key to doing business. Throw them on their pride. When the ropes were removed from Finnegan, Schwabacker said, "The pony soldier has lost many men, Red Cloud. Last year you won a great victory on Lodge Trail Ridge."

"Red Cloud has many victories," the Sioux said. "There will be many more before the winter sun shines."

"And many dead braves," Schwabacker told him. "How many braves died at Fort Smith, where the

222

Cheyennes were defeated by twenty men?"

He was touching the dynamite fuse and knew it when Red Cloud's eyes narrowed and several of the Cheyenne chiefs reared to their feet. A wave of Red Cloud's arm was enough to make them sit down again, but the anger stayed in their eyes. . . . *They don't like to have their nose rubbed in it, either.* . . . But he knew that this was the answer.

Red Cloud said, "A few braves were lost."

"Red Cloud lies!" Schwabacker snapped. "Over a hundred Cheyennes were killed!" He held Spotted Tail with his eyes. "Do you lie too, Spotted Tail, who fights with honor? Do you lie to a warrior who has fought you twice?"

"Who-Fears-His-Heart speaks the truth. Many death songs were sung. The day was dark for my people."

Red Cloud did not like this admission, for it weakened his position. Schwabacker watched the Sioux and hoped strongly that Red Cloud would upbraid the Cheyennes as cowards, but this was diplomatically impossible, unless he wanted a civil war started in his own camp.

. . . *Play both ends against the middle.* . . . Pretty poor strategy, but he had little choice.

Schwabacker spoke to Red Cloud. "I saw the battle with these eyes, Red Cloud. I saw too the defeat you suffered at the wagon boxes. Over a hundred of your warriors were lost, Red Cloud. Do I speak the truth?"

For a full minute, Red Cloud refused to speak. Then he said, "You speak the truth, pony soldier."

"Then who has lost?" Schwabacker asked. "Who has

lost the most men, Red Cloud? Is not the way of peace better?"

"There will never be peace with the long knives," Red Cloud said. "To mark the paper means nothing. I have spoken before that I will never sign again."

There was no changing this man; Schwabacker realized it and gave it up. He turned to Spotted Tail. "Do you wish to lose your braves? How many braves can you spare, Spotted Tail? Two hundred? Five hundred? The defeat at Fort Smith was only the beginning. There will be others, whenever you meet the soldiers, until there are no more Cheyenne."

This was something to think about, and Schwabacker suspected that Spotted Tail *had* thought about it. A man could get tired of another man's rule, could grow weary of spending his strength for a cause in which he did not completely believe. Schwabacker figured it was that way with the Cheyennes. They had been reluctant from the beginning to join Red Cloud, and now after several sound defeats they were primed for peace. The only question that remained large in his mind was, could he get out of the camp alive. His only hope lay in Cheyenne protection.

Spotted Tail rose to speak. "What you say is true. My lodges are empty. Children cry for their fathers, who will never hunt for them again. Women sing the death song. This is not good."

"Then I offer you peace," Schwabacker said. "In the name of the United States Government, I offer you a chance to meet with men who want peace. They wait now at Fort Laramie for you. I will take you there,

Spotted Tail. You and your chiefs."

Red Cloud was on his feet, shouting. "He lies! You will die there! Once away from your warriors and he will kill you!"

Schwabacker challenged that cold glance. "I am without weapons, Red Cloud. We are alone and Spotted Tail may take as many braves as he wishes, all armed. You are the one who lies, Red Cloud. Your heart is dark and filled with war. I will speak to you no more of peace, for you do not understand."

Schwabacker deliberately turned away from the great Sioux chief and a roar of disapproval went up at this unforgivable insult. Finnegan was sweating. "Jasus . . ." He let it trail off into nothing.

Red Cloud was surrounded by his bravest. The fanatical Crazy Horse leaped to his feet, ready to kill for Sioux honor, but Spotted Tail shouted one word and a deep silence fell over the camp.

Schwabacker looked around. Everywhere Cheyenne warriors stood, armed, ready for the one word that would turn this camp into death. The Sioux waited for Red Cloud's signal, but none came. When a full minute passed, Schwabacker knew there would be none.

"I will speak," Spotted Tail said. "Red Cloud, you spoke many times of driving the long knives from our land, but this has never come to pass. They are as many as the stars in the heavens and they have great medicine. Who-Fears-His-Heart comes unarmed to the enemy, not to make war, but to speak peace. My heart is heavy with death. I will go with him, as will my chiefs. Who-Fears-His-Heart entered this camp with a Cheyenne rope on him. He is mine to deal with, and he shall ride at my side when I go to speak with the long-knife chiefs at the fort." He spread his arms wide. "We can leave this camp in peace, Red Cloud. Or we can leave with war between us. Speak now."

Schwabacker could have cheered, but he kept all emotion from showing on his face. Red Cloud's brow was a mass of unpleasant wrinkles. Finally he said, "Go in peace, Cheyenne brothers."

There was the camp-breaking to attend to. Emil Schwabacker and Sergeant Finnegan stood to one side with the imperturbable Spotted Tail while others did the work. Spotted Tail was being polite, but Schwabacker knew that eyes were always upon him and one wrong move now could spin them both into tragedy.

Spotted Tail said, "The long knives have great medicine, Who-Fears-His-Heart. Two sons have I lost to this medicine. My daughter-in-law still sings the death song and throws ashes on her hair." He bared his arms, displaying hundreds of knife slashes, each a mark of grief. "Peace will be good. I will try once more."

Try once more . . . One chance only. Schwabacker knew this was true. There would never be another, regardless of who spoke for the peace commission. Spotted Tail was ready now. Ten days from now he would be less a victim of his grief.

Suddenly Emil Schwabacker was eager to get out of this camp, out of the noise and the stink and the barking dogs. Time was of a sudden a very precious thing; he had so little of it to waste.

Then the rosy picture faded; a practical side of his

mind made him think of General Wessels, and what he would say when he learned that an officer who had been relieved of his command had the temerity to sue for an unauthorized peace.

Since the Indians' possessions were few, and what they had was highly portable, they departed from the Sioux camp within an hour. The horses were returned to Schwabacker and Finnegan, and, accompanied by Spotted Tail, Man-Afraid-of-His-Horses, Little Wound and Pawnee Killer, they rode out. Behind them were over a hundred armed Cheyenne braves; the women and children trailed behind, bearing the burdens.

Finnegan spoke softly. "I'm alive, but I don't believe it."

"I wonder who will end up shooting us?" Schwabacker said, half to himself. "Spotted Tail or General Wessels' firing squad?"

17

AT DAWN, A VERY SURPRISED SENTRY STARED OUT OVER the palisade wall at the huge gathering of Indians camped less than two hundred yards away. He called for the sergeant of the guard, who took one look and decided this was a problem for an officer. The officer of the day was summoned on the double and, after a quick study through his field glasses, said, "Rouse General Wessels and be damned quick about it. Those are Cheyennes and they have Captain Schwabacker and Sergeant Finnegan with them."

Wessels stormed from his quarters a few minutes

later, still sleep-rumpled and made irritable by his responsibilities, now aggravated beyond human endurance by the escapades of Brevet Captain Emil Schwabacker. He climbed the ladder and looked out through the O.D.'s field glasses as Sergeant Finnegan rode forward, backed by two dozen armed Cheyenne warriors. The meaning of this irregularity was beyond General Wessels and he waited, angry-eyed, until Finnegan stopped, twenty yards out.

Finnegan said, "Mornin', Gener'l."

"God damn the pleasantries," Wessels snapped. "Who in the blue blazes is that out there with Schwabacker?"

"Spotted Tail, sor," Finnegan said. "Th' whole Cheyenne nation, sor. Wimmen, lodges an' all."

"In the name of sanity, how . . ."

"Well, sor, Captain Schwabacker figured he'd find Red Cloud's camp an' sue fer peace, sor."

"Pea . . . ! He went into Red Cloud's camp?" Wessels acted like a man who had just been told he had won a thousand dollars, then before he could exclaim his surprise, more money was added, and faster, until he was faced with incalculable good fortune.

"Aye, sor. In an' out, but he brought th' Cheyennes. He's goin' to take 'em on to Laramie fer peace talks, sor."

"Good God, this is unauthorized . . ."

"That sure is true, sor," Finnegan said, not losing his point. "But if th' peace commission wants to talk peace, here's someone to talk to."

"By all that's holy!" Wessels turned to the O.D. "Saddle my horse and be damned quick about it. I'm

228

going to Laramie with this unprecedented upstart of a captain."

"We'll just go on ahead, sor," Finnegan said. "Capt'n Schwabacker don't want to be clapped in th' stockade before he's done his job, sor."

"Now you wait!" Wessels shouted. But he was shouting to Finnegan's back, for he was riding back to join the main party. Wessels swore beneath his breath and left the palisade ramp with long steps.

Schwabacker searched Finnegan's face for some clue as to what had transpired between this sergeant and a general. But Finnegan only said, "Th' gener'l's comin' to Laramie, sor."

"He's mad?"

"Hoppin', sor. But he ain't a man to pass up a good hand when it's given to him."

Spotted Tail said, "We go now?"

"Yes," Schwabacker said. "To Fort Laramie."

With this word he led the Cheyennes toward peace, and for himself an undetermined future.

General William T. Sherman was the ranking member of the peace commission, which was composed of three other generals—William S. Harney, Alfred H. Terry, and C. C. Augur—and four civilians, who were there to see that the army didn't get all the gravy from this forthcoming feast of peace.

Sherman occupied the best quarters on the post, and in the afternoons Generals Harney, Terry and Augur joined him for small talk, a game or two of cards, and a sample of Sherman's fine wines. Sherman was an impressive man, severe-faced, but a sound military commander with a long record of victories behind him. General Harney was the oldest; white-haired, white-bearded, he looked more like a senior partner in the retail hardware business than a competent general. Terry was a flamboyant man, with a full beard luxuriously curled. He had dark eyes and a strong voice for command, which he did quite well.

These generals were sitting on the shady side of the veranda that ran around Sherman's quarters, when a crisp-looking orderly came up, saluted and said, "General Sherman, there is a large party of Cheyennes approaching the post, sir. They are in the company of two soldiers, sir, a captain of cavalry and a sergeant major, same unit."

"You're sure of this?" Sherman set his port aside carefully.

"Yes, sir. A patrol sighted them through glasses not ten minutes ago. We got the message from the signal picket on Laramie Peak."

"Very well," Sherman said. "See if you can ascertain whether these Cheyennes are hostile in intent."

"I believe that has already been done, sir. When the picket signaled the officer with the Indians, he received this answer, flashed on a piece of polished silver." He handed General Sherman the message and Generals Harney, Terry and Augur crowded around to read.

Advise C. O. Cheyenne party approaching Laramie to discuss peace terms.
                    Schwabacker, Captain of Cavalry

Sherman pocketed the note. "This is amazing, gentlemen. We haven't even selected an envoy yet, but here they are. Does this captain read minds?" He finished his port hurriedly. "I believe I'll observe this approach from the blockhouse. Will you join me?"

The news went around the post like a rumor of payday, and within fifteen minutes, everyone knew who was approaching and what for. Colonel Nelson Ashford violated a long-established habit of not rubbing elbows with high brass unless necessary and joined the four generals on the blockhouse platform. The four civilian members of the commission went to the palisade wall for their front-row-center seat.

On the veranda of the guest quarters, a portly man came out, his face lifted to the palisade walls. A moment later a woman joined him, a young woman with large shining eyes and an air of breathless expectancy about her.

The man took out a huge watch and popped the lids. "Late," he said. "Emil will be late for his funeral." The man put his watch away as though he had reached an indisputable verdict, then stood there, rocking back and forth on his heels.

The young woman watched everything that went on within the range of her vision, not with wide-eyed innocence, but with a genuine interest. She spoke to the portly man with the unforgiving manner. "I'm glad I came, Doctor. I don't think I'll go back."

"Romantic nonsense," the man said, and in his mind that put an end to it.

Near the main gate a sentry called out, then all who

had this high vantage position looked in one direction, along the westward reaches of the road. The post adjutant, acting upon Colonel Ashford's orders, wheeled out the regimental band and they stood in disciplined rows, their instruments brightly playing the "Garryowen."

Outside the post, commotion rose in sheets of sound as the Cheyennes pitched a camp near the main gate, much to the disgust of the officer of the day, who foolishly rode forth, hoping to instill some semblance of military order in a race of people who did not know what the word meant.

Captain Emil Schwabacker rode into the post with Sergeant Finnegan while the band played brightly and regimental colors fluttered in the breeze. Behind him rode five armed Cheyenne chiefs, apparently unaffected by this folderol; they acted as if they did this every day of the week and four times on Sundays.

The music broke off and the bugler played "the general" while the sergeant of the guard hoisted the general's flags beneath the regimental colors. In a line, like toy soldiers on parade, Generals Sherman, Harney, Terry and Augur left the blockhouse and solemnly greeted each of the Cheyenne chiefs.

Schwabacker stood to one side with Sergeant Finnegan. Turning to the O.D., Schwabacker spoke softly. "Lieutenant, I'm Brevet Captain Emil Schwabacker, absent from my command without leave. Please place me under official arrest."

The lieutenant looked at the prize, then at Schwabacker, then back to the Cheyennes. Here was an officer who had delivered the military prize of the year, yet asked to be arrested. He said, "Captain, I don't think I'd . . ."

"If you don't," Schwabacker said, "you may deeply regret it. Will you assign quarters to me and see that Sergeant Finnegan is in the stockade." He glanced at the sergeant. "You understand, Sergeant. This is something we can't duck."

"Yes, sor. I understand."

The generals were talking eagerly with the Cheyennes, and amid this disciplined activity, Schwabacker turned with the officer of the day, leaving this chatting group. Sergeant Finnegan was remanded to the custody of the sergeant of the guard, who did not have the heart to march him prisonerlike to the guardhouse. Instead they walked side by side, talking like old bunkies returning from the sutler's with a thirty-day thirst slaked.

Schwabacker followed the officer of the day around the parade perimeter, and when they approached the guest quarters, Schwabacker stopped like a man stricken. The young woman smiled, and her eyes sparkled with the shine of tears. Then she lifted her skirts to run off the porch. The portly man grabbed to hold her back, then stood stupidly regarding her shawl, which was all he managed to retain.

She went into Emil Schwabacker's arms and he kissed her like a man starved and facing a feast. He spoke her name over and over until embarrassment made him release her.

The portly man came off the porch then and shook hands solemnly, like some businessman completing a deal that involved only the minimum profit for himself.

Emil Schwabacker said, "It's good to see you, Father." He stood with his arm around Henrietta Brubaker, then he remembered the O.D. and what he was waiting for. He dropped his arm away from her waist. "I'm sorry for the unfortunate circumstances, Father, Henrietta, but I'm under arrest of quarters. I'll ask the mess sergeant to serve three meals. Perhaps we can talk then."

Henrietta Brubaker would have spoken, but he shook his head. Doctor Gustave Schwabacker wouldn't have spoken if commanded to do so. He turned and went back to the porch while Schwabacker kissed Henrietta again.

"Seeing you again is worth anything," he said, then he joined the O.D., who saw that he was properly billeted in one of the better officers' picket quarters.

The room was a captain's room; there was more furniture and the rug was not so threadbare. With the window open, Emil Schwabacker could hear the band blaring on the parade, and the regimental drill team issued forth from a long barracks, their shining bayonets like a living machine as they performed their intricate maneuvers.

Finally the post grew quiet. The O.D. appeared again, stating briefly that meals would be brought to the quarters and that Schwabacker was not permitted to leave, except by written permission of the commanding officer.

Schwabacker knew the routine and was glad when the O.D. went away. Now that his career was drawing to an end, everything seemed anticlimactic, even the shocking appearance of his father and Henrietta. At one time he had wanted her here, to lend him strength, but suddenly he discovered that he needed none. He was the strongest man on earth, and he wished now that she was not here so she would not have to share his disgrace. He had never seen an officer drummed from the corps, but he knew the routine, the command appearance of every man, from the general to the newest recruit, the reading of the charges and the verdict, the standing in full dress before the world while epaulets and buttons were ripped off, the dress sword broken. . . .

He turned away from the window, his own thoughts intolerable.

Before the bugler sounded evening mess call, his father appeared with Henrietta. Schwabacker ushered them into the room and watched his father look around. He had seen that look before, whenever he walked into a poor man's house; there was condemnation in the glance, and very little understanding.

Schwabacker handed Henrietta into a chair, then took one across from her. Doctor Gustave Schwabacker declined to sit, preferring to stand with his cigar eddying smoke around his face.

"Perhaps you would care to explain this hideous affair," he said. "Emil, an explanation is due me."

"I suppose it is," Schwabacker said, but suddenly wondered, as he had always wondered, how to explain the obvious, the small things that always guided a man in making the ultimate decision. He looked at Henrietta. "Do you want an explanation too?"

"No," she said. "Emil, dishonor isn't in you."

"Thank you. That's all that really matters." He looked then at his father. "Why did you come, sir?"

"Because it isn't fitting for an unmarried woman to travel alone. She has no father or brothers."

This angered Emil Schwabacker beyond reason. Slowly he stood erect and in the calmest of voices said, "Please get out, sir."

Doctor Gustave Schwabacker took the cigar from his mouth. "What did you say to me?"

"I said get out, sir! Get out now and leave me alone."

"Wh . . . why, I want to help you!"

Schwabacker pushed past him and went to the door. A sentry walked his post across the compound and Schwabacker called to him. "Sentry! On the double here!"

His father stared unbelievingly, then angrily pushed him aside and stomped out, his patent-leather shoes rapping the duck boards. The sentry was approaching on the run and Schwabacker waved him back before turning inside.

Henrietta Brubaker sat with her hands folded in her lap, her heart-shaped face serious and somewhat worried. Concern pulled the bow of her mouth down. "Why did you do that, Emil? Because of what he said?"

"Because I've had enough," he said. He took her hands and brought her to her feet, and he kissed her gently. "Sweetheart, I've just found out that I can't talk to him. What can I explain that he'll listen to?"

"He's your father, Emil."

"I know." He released her hands and went to the

236

window. The mess boy was coming toward the quarters with a towel-covered tray. Schwabacker opened the door, took it from him and placed it on the writing desk. The meal was meat and potatoes, with greens and a pudding dessert. Schwabacker could have apologized for the service, and perhaps the quality of the meal itself, which was issue and fell far short of Delmonico's, but he did none of these things.

After his appetite was blunted, he put his fork aside and said, "Once I ran from him; that might have been a mistake. I don't think it was, Henrietta."

"But you're a doctor, Emil."

"And not a soldier?" He smiled and shook his head. "There you are honestly mistaken. I can soldier, perhaps even better than I can doctor." His smile faded. "At least I believe I can. My position now is hardly a recommendation, is it?" He poured a cup of coffee, then sat with it cradled between his hands. "It's funny, but the more I think of it, the more I realize that Father's right; there's very little I do that is correct."

"I don't like to hear you talk like that." There was alarm in her voice.

"You want the truth, don't you?"

"We don't know the truth!" She moved her hand impatiently. "Do you think your father knows the truth about himself? Have you ever been able to make him see himself? Emil, someone else always has to judge us. I think that's because we always judge ourselves too harshly."

"I've bungled my military career miserably," he said. "It began the moment I took command of my troop,

237

Henrietta. My victories were petty, and my conceit great. I might have been lucky and escaped all this, but it ran out. I don't know when."

"But I love you," she said and cupped his hands in hers. "I came because I wanted to be with you, Emil; we've been apart too long." She regarded him thoughtfully, a small smile tilting up the ends of her lips. "Darling, I don't think you need me if things turn out badly. You've changed and you don't need anyone's strength; you have your own."

"I feel that way," he said, "but I didn't want to say it."

"Darling, we've never had to explain to each other," she said. "Let's not start now."

"With you," he said, "I've never had to explain because you understood instinctively. But with my father, I never could get him to understand how important it is for a man to make his own mistakes." He got up from the table, taking his coffee cup with him. "Captain Jocelyn isn't like my father; I thought for a long time that he was. When I took command, he never once corrected me. He'd let me go, make my own mistakes. And I never thanked him for that."

"That's strange," Henrietta said. "I never thought much about it before, but it doesn't matter where a man's mistakes lead him, as long as they are his own." She shook her head. "I'm sorry for your father because he always took matters away from you at the moment when you were ready to make your decisions. It's a shame because he never saw you grow, and I imagine it's a father's finest reward, to see his son grow into a man. Jocelyn must have watched you,

Emil. You say he let you make your own decisions."

"There's greatness in Jocelyn," Schwabacker said. "My mistake was trying to copy him. I'm not heavy enough."

"But he preferred charges against you," she reminded him. "Was he right, Emil? Search yourself for a true answer."

"No," he said. "He was wrong; I'm positive of it."

"Then he's not as great as you think," she said, rising. "He can't be until he admits he was wrong." Her dress rustled as she moved near him. Then she cupped his face in her hands and kissed him. "That's your greatest flaw, Emil, this acknowledgment of imagined greatness in others, at the expense of yourself."

"Like my father?"

"Perhaps. If so, you'll have to see for yourself, Emil."

He smiled. "Are you letting me make my own mistakes?"

"I'll always let you do that," she said, "and I'll love you more for every one of them. It will be my constant assurance that you're still human."

He stood in the doorway while she walked away, and some of the weight lifted from his shoulders. He felt like a free man and he had no right to feel that way.

18

THE PRELIMINARY TALKS WITH THE CHEYENNE CHIEFS ended at sundown, and the eight-man peace commission went to their quarters, where supper was served with all the pomposity at the command of the Fort

Laramie mess sergeant. After the meal, when the dishes had been removed and cigars ignited, the four civilians excused themselves, leaving the four generals alone with one other man, Jim Bridger.

Somewhere a new suit of clothes had been dredged up, and now Bridger sat in unaccustomed style, vastly uncomfortable in starched collar and ascot tie. General Sherman sat in a stuffed chair across from Bridger. Harney leaned against the mantel, drawing gently on his cigar. Generals Terry and Augur occupied two deep chairs and maintained a thoughtful silence.

"I'm pleased," Sherman said, "with the preliminary talks. Spotted Tail and his sub-chiefs are indeed tired of war." He glanced at the others. "Almost as tired as I am."

"He'd have never come in, Gener'l," Bridger said, "if Schwabacker hadn't got him."

"How's that?" There was curiosity in Sherman's voice. Harney ceased puffing his cigar and Terry and Augur became more attentive.

"Injuns is funny people," Bridger explained. "Th' capt'n give Spotted Tail a good lickin', not once, but twice. Seems like an Injun's respect is only got by a man who can give 'em jessy. When th' capt'n talked, they listened, 'cause they knew it was no chicken talkin'." Bridger shook his grizzled head. "Nosiree, if it'd been anyone else, Spotted Tail'd had his fun, then shipped you th' remains."

"It seems," Sherman said, "that Captain Schwabacker has been quite active during the campaign. I have in my brief case several dispatches bearing accounts of his

240

activities, plus several newspapers carrying his interview with that Chicago reporter." He studied the fine
gray ash on his cigar. "Yes, the captain has been quite
busy."

"How long you goin' to let th' capt'n stay in arrest,
Gener'l?" There was more than curiosity behind
Bridger's remark; there was concern.

Harney asked, "A friend of yours, Mr. Bridger?"

"Friend? I never met him, that's a fact; but he don't
deserve bein' arrested."

"Very peculiar," Sherman said softly. He got up, summoned an orderly and had him dispatched for Colonel
Nelson Ashford. Then he turned to Jim Bridger. "It's not
like you, Jim, to be so concerned. May I ask why?"

"Well," Bridger said, scratching his head, "there ain't
no real reason, I guess, 'ceptin' that what he's goin' to
get ain't justice."

"We're not aware of the charges," Augur said quickly.
"Mr. Bridger, the man hasn't been tried yet; how can we
say what he'll get?"

"Because you go by that little book of rules!" Bridger
said. "Ain't sayin' they're wrong, but there's times
when a man's got to bend th' rules a little to fit the case."

"The army is not conducted along such flexible lines,"
General Terry said flatly. "Captain Schwabacker will be
tried and if found guilty of the charges, whatever they
are, will be punished according to regulations."

Bridger looked at General William T. Sherman. "You
go along with that?"

"I'm afraid I must, Jim. If we start changing the rules
in the middle of the game . . ."

241

Colonel Ashford's arrival prevented the completion of Sherman's comment. The colonel came to attention, then was waved to "at ease." Sherman said, "Draw up a chair, Colonel. There's a matter that needs discussion."

"Yes, sir." Ashford sat down stiffly. Generals, at least so many of them in one room, seemed to make him slightly nervous.

Sherman swiveled around a little so he faced Ashford. "Colonel, the arrival of the Indians was a great surprise to me, but I was even more surprised when I asked to meet and congratulate the officer and sergeant who had performed this magnificent job, and had the officer of the day inform me that one was in the guardhouse and the other in arrest of quarters. Colonel, I would like an explanation of this."

"Sir, the matter is relatively simple, at least on the surface." Ashford licked his lips, then went on to explain the circumstances surrounding Captain Nathan Kincaid's death, and his widow's subsequent charges.

When he finished, Sherman sat frowning. Harney laughed once, then puffed his cigar while Terry and Augur exchanged glances. Finally Sherman said, "Colonel, is Mrs. Kincaid on the post?"

"No, sir. She left two weeks ago. We have her deposition."

"Ah," Sherman said. "Always detested those things. Cross-examination of a piece of paper is difficult." He glanced at Harney, Terry and Augur. "Gentlemen, are we agreed that Captain Schwabacker should be released from arrest?"

They nodded. Ashford said, "I'll issue the order, sir."

"One moment," Sherman said. "The sergeant—why is he confined?"

"I . . . I don't know," Ashford said. "The O.D. said he was confined on Captain Schwabacker's orders."

"Confusing to say the least," Sherman said with a touch of humor in his voice. "Lucky there was not a corporal among them. The sergeant would have arrested him for something, no doubt."

The sentry at the main gate alarmed the guard with his call and General Sherman turned his head toward the sound. Into the room came the sounds of activity, a horse entering, faint voices, then one of the guards dashed across the parade and knocked on the door of Sherman's quarters. He was admitted and came to a rifle-straight attention.

"Colonel Ashford, sir, General H. W. Wessels has arrived on the post and requests an immediate audience, sir."

Before Ashford could speak, Sherman said, "Ask the general to step in, please."

The guard saluted and left. Almost immediately Wessels' boots trounced the porch planks. Sherman rose when Wessels entered the room, dusty and unshaven. "Well," Sherman said, "you've made a ride of it, sir."

"How are you, sir?" Wessels nodded at the others. "Do you know, I left Kearny an hour after Schwabacker and the Cheyennes. Look at the lead they stretched. It's no damned wonder we never were able to chase the Indians and catch them."

"Sit down," Sherman said. "Ashford, pour General Wessels some brandy." With Wessels lifting a loaded glass, Sherman added, "We've had our preliminary talks, General, and I must say the results are gratifying."

"I rode through the Cheyenne camp on the way in," Wessels said. "The devilish feeling it puts in a man."

"Then imagine the courage of Captain Schwabacker and his sergeant," Harney said. "Alone and unarmed."

"We were just discussing Captain Schwabacker's arrest," Sherman said. "And we all agreed that he is to be released immediately."

Wessels was immeasurably shocked. "Gentlemen, you condone his actions?"

"I haven't read Mrs. Kincaid's deposition," Sherman said, "but I believe that it is within my power to release Captain Schwabacker."

Wessels put aside his brandy; more serious business was at hand. "General, may I inform you that Mrs. Kincaid's charge has now paled to insignificance. Captain Schwabacker is charged with relieving a superior officer of his command, by force, and I have charges of my own to present: the unauthorized suing for peace in the name of the United States Government."

Four generals stared. Colonel Ashford sat dumbly; this was not his problem and he was glad of it.

General Terry found voice first, and it thundered. "Do you mean to sit there, General, and tell me that Captain Schwabacker, on his own initiative, and without authority, went to the hostile camp and sued for peace?"

"I do, sir."

"God, what a man," Harney said. "Brevet him!"

Sherman waved his hand impatiently. His long face grew thoughtful and he got up to walk back and forth.

"There can be no snap judgment here," he said at last. "Gentlemen, have Captain Schwabacker summoned in the morning for a general court-martial." He turned to Colonel Ashford. "Is there an officer assigned to prosecute for Mrs. Kincaid?"

"Yes, sir. Lieutenant Eastwood, who was in Kincaid's command at the time of the tragedy."

"We'll get an unbiased presentation there," Sherman said sarcastically.

"Lieutenant Eastwood rode in with me," Wessels said.

"An officer must be selected for the defense," Harney said.

"Yes," Sherman said. "We'll appoint one in the morning." He lifted his glass. "A toast, gentlemen: To a very confused but exceedingly interesting series of peace talks."

19

BREVET CAPTAIN EMIL SCHWABACKER DRESSED CAREfully in a new full-dress uniform thoughtfully provided by the regimental adjutant, but when he stepped outside into the early-morning sunlight, he was without sidearms, as befitted an officer under arrest.

The officer of the day waited with indifferent courtesy and together they walked toward headquarters, where General Sherman had appropriated a room for the hearing. A sentry stood on each side of the door, presenting arms smartly for the O.D., who opened the door, then stepped aside and waved Emil Schwabacker inside.

A long table stood at the extreme end of the room, and behind this was arrayed the most magnificent aggregation of rank Emil Schwabacker had ever seen. Colonel Ashford was there, seated to one side. Lieutenant Eastwood occupied a chair at the prosecuting counsel's table. Schwabacker came to attention, saluting.

General Sherman said, "Take a seat, Captain."

Schwabacker lowered himself into a chair and only then did he see the few chairs at the back of the room. His father sat there, stony-faced. Henrietta Brubaker occupied another, between his father and a heavily whiskered man uneasy in a suit of clothes. Schwabacker had never seen Jim Bridger before, but he recognized him immediately.

General William T. Sherman rapped with the gavel. "This military court will now come to order."

The first charge, that of Lydia Kincaid, was presented. Colonel Ashford read the charges, and the deposition, which was entered on the record by two industriously writing clerks.

"May it please the court," Ashford said, after surrendering the documents, "Captain Schwabacker is not represented by counsel."

"I'm aware of that, Colonel," Sherman said. "However, the matter has been taken care of. Orderly, will you summon the counsel for defense to this court."

There was a long period of silence, of waiting, while the orderly was out of the room. A large clock on the wall ticked with maddening regularity, then the door opened and Captain Temple Jocelyn entered the room, his cane thumping solidly on the floor at each step. He took a seat at Schwabacker's table and this brought Lieutenant Eastwood to his feet.

"General, I protest this irregularity!" He waved a hand at Jocelyn, who mopped perspiration from his brow. His long siege of illness had sapped his strength, left him alarmingly thin. "General," Eastwood was saying. "Captain Jocelyn has preferred separate charges against Captain Schwabacker. This is disqualifying!"

Jocelyn rose slowly, with the aid of his cane, and stood like a tall pine, swaying slightly. "May it please the court," he said, "but I have no charges to press against Captain Schwabacker, or Sergeant Major Finnegan."

"He relieved you of your command!" Eastwood shouted. "Damn it all, I was there!"

Sherman's gavel was a solid thumping. He hooked Lieutenant Eastwood with his eyes and said, "Lieutenant, may I remind you now that another irregular outburst will be grounds for your removal from this court. Sit down!" When this order had been obeyed, he spoke to Jocelyn. "Captain, will you be good enough to explain this withdrawal of charges?"

"Yes, sir. It's true that Captain Schwabacker relieved me of my command, and at the time I objected in the most strenuous manner, but I was motivated by a severe wound, aggravated by a fever condition. The regimental surgeon at Fort Philip Kearny will testify, if need be, to the truth of that statement."

"We're not doubting your word, Captain," Sherman said. "You admit now, before this court, that you mischarged Captain Schwabacker?"

"I do, sir." Jocelyn's voice was firm. "He did me a great service, and for any unpleasantness I have cost him, I offer my most humble apologies." He looked down at Schwabacker, and the ice in his eyes melted. A smile lifted his lips. "I'm sorry, Emil. Somehow, I could never say it before."

"I understand, sir." Schwabacker tipped his head down and studied his hands, warmth filling him, crowding out every other feeling. He knew that he never again would compete with this man, would never need to, for they were equals.

"Very well, Captain," Sherman said sternly. "The charge against Captain Schwabacker is dropped."

"My charges against Sergeant Major Finnegan are also dropped," Jocelyn said. "Sergeant Finnegan prevented me from committing murder." Sherman's eyes opened a bit wider; the other generals sat a bit straighter. "I was ready to shoot Captain Schwabacker when Sergeant Finnegan disarmed me. He performed a soldier's duty, and I'm sorry for mistaking his intent."

"This leaves me no alternative," Sherman said. "Colonel Ashford, you will secure the immediate release of Sergeant Finnegan from the post stockade." He looked at the two busy clerks. "So ordered in the records."

Eastwood stood erect. "May I speak, sir?"

"If you think you can sift the profanity from your remarks," Sherman said. He was a deceptive man, until aroused, then his eyes left little doubt in a man's mind as to his character.

Color invaded Eastwood's cheeks. He said, "Since

Captain Jocelyn's largesse has dispensed with one set of charges, may I present Mrs. Kincaid's?"

"Proceed," Sherman said.

"I intend to prove," Eastwood said, "that Captain Schwabacker acted without authority and indirectly caused the death of an army officer."

"Grave charges if you can prove them," Sherman said.

"May it please the court," Jocelyn said, rising, "Captain Kincaid's wound was received under the most peculiar circumstances, and Lieutenant Eastwood's action during the engagement leaves much to be desired in the way of military conduct."

Sherman's gavel banged. "Captain, neither Captain Kincaid nor Lieutenant Eastwood is on trial at this time. Clerks, the captain's remarks will be omitted from the records." This was done immediately while Sherman watched. Then he said, "Lieutenant Eastwood, I have before me the entire bulk of correspondence between Mrs. Kincaid and Colonel Ashford, which concerns, in the main, the pension a widow receives upon her husband's death while on active duty. I am not saying that Captain Kincaid was guilty of unseemly conduct, which would undoubtedly cloud the claim for pension, although his actions have been severely criticized in writing. Lieutenant, may I assure you that this relatively simple matter of Captain Schwabacker's unauthorized surgery, is not as simple as it sounds."

"I'm aware of that, sir."

"Excellent." Sherman said. "Are you also aware that to properly clear this matter, the conduct of Captain

Kincaid would have to be investigated? I've been in the army a number of years, Lieutenant, and the matter before us is not Captain Schwabacker, but whether an officer's widow is going to receive a government pension. Do you deny that the obvious reason behind these charges is to insure that pension?"

"No— No, sir. I don't deny it. Neither do I blame Mrs. Kincaid."

Sherman looked at Harney and Terry. General Augur was studying the hair follicles on the back of his hands. "Then I think I can dispose of this matter expediently," Sherman said. "Lieutenant, I have no intention of instigating an investigation of Captain Kincaid. The man is dead and beyond punishment. And I am not so heartless as to deprive a widow of her pension, however questionable it may be. Before me is the form, which requires my signature. Next to it is a letter of formal charges against Captain Schwabacker. If I affix my signature to the pension document, the charges must be dropped."

Eastwood breathed with difficulty. Finally he said, "I—I agree to drop the charges, General."

Sherman handed the document to Harney. "Destroy this. It will be so entered in the record." He then placed his signature on the pension papers and Eastwood came forward for them. "Lieutenant, bear something in mind: I dislike pressure methods, and I dislike any officer who condones that type of action. That is why I've disposed of this case as I have. This is a small army, Mister. Your shirt tail is not without stain. We'll be watching you." He rapped with his gavel. "Now get the devil out of my courtroom."

Emil Schwabacker sat with his face slickened by sweat. Seemingly two miracles had taken place in a row, an unprecedented thing in his life, but this kind of luck would never hold. There was another to be called.

And Sheridan called him. "Have Brevet General H. W. Wessels called to the court."

The orderly departed and Wessels entered, performed the usual military protocol, then sat down.

"General Wessels," Sherman said, "you have made no formal charge against Captain Schwabacker, and before you do I would like to address a few remarks to the assembly." He cleared his throat. "In a campaign, it is rare that one officer contributes largely to the success of the engagement. When praise is distributed, one finds that many step forward to receive the accolade, and all deserve such recognition. However, it seems here that when success is viewed as a whole, fate has chosen Captain Schwabacker as a private instrument. General Harney and I discussed this last night until a late hour. This morning, before court convened, I discussed it with General Terry and General Augur. We have analyzed the record thoroughly, the engagements fought and won, or lost, and we have come to some conclusions.

"Captain Schwabacker, while a second lieutenant, successfully engaged the Cheyenne forces in an action at Ryndlee's road ranch. This engagement was not singular in itself, and did not assume importance until much later. Looking back, it is obvious that this was the Cheyennes' first baptism of fire from the army, and the defeat they suffered weakened their confidence. Such belief was substantiated in our talks with Spotted Tail yesterday. He said that the Sioux leader, Red Cloud, had assured the Cheyennes of his strong medicine, and that the army was weak. He also stated that this defeat, at the hands of an officer without previous combat experience, caused dissension among his men, and when he again attacked the army, he suffered additional losses at the hands of the same officer." Sherman paused to look at everyone present. "Gentlemen, and ladies, we also agree that if Captain Schwabacker had not ridden into the Cheyenne camp when he did, the Cheyennes would not be camped in peace at our gates today. Spotted Tail and Little Wound both have stated that Red Cloud was talking medicine and that many of their people were inclined to go along with him."

Sherman smiled and it was fine to see. "However," he continued, "it seems that Captain Schwabacker's talents are not confined to the military, but embrace the political field as well. For nearly a year, we have been trying to enlist the press and public sympathy to our cause, and a just treatment of the Indians. Without shame I can say that we have failed, but Captain Schwabacker has not. His interview was printed in many newspapers, and because of the attention aroused, we now have the authority to abandon Fort Philip Kearny and Fort C. F. Smith if necessary to bring a just peace in this land."

Jim Bridger cheered and General Sherman tolerated the outburst. Schwabacker sat like a man belly-kicked, unable to believe his ears. He looked at the four generals and saw four dedicated men, kind men who spoke of peace and meant it. This time, he knew, their names on the peace treaty would carry weight. He knew Spotted Tail would believe it too.

"And so," General Sherman was saying, "I believe this court can adjourn with the recommendation that Captain Schwabacker be breveted at the earliest possible convenience of his commanding officer, and extended our heartfelt thanks for service well rendered." Sherman's gavel rapped once. "This court is adjourned. I could use a cup of coffee."

Schwabacker turned to Temple Jocelyn, but Jocelyn smiled and pushed him toward Henrietta, who nearly knocked over a chair in her eagerness to embrace him. Jim Bridger came up while he still held her, a smile behind his thick whiskers. He offered a gnarled hand.

"Been wantin' to make your acquaintance, Capt'n, but it seems that every time some dolgoned business come up an' I never got th' chance."

"You're a living legend," Schwabacker said softly. "It's an honor."

"Figured it th' other way," Bridger said. "You done made a few legends of your own."

The four dignified generals filed past, each offering Captain Schwabacker a brief handshake. The room emptied like a slowly draining bowl. Through the open door Schwabacker could see Sergeant Sean Finnegan, waiting with an enlisted man's courtesy. Doctor Gustave Schwabacker came up then, hesitatingly. He said, "All your life I've given you advice, son. But I can see now that you were better off without it. Can you advise *me* now? Can you show me the way to say . . ."

"There's nothing to say," Schwabacker cut in. He didn't want his father to apologize. And he didn't want to explain either; he didn't think he had to. He saw his father in a completely different light—not a big man, not God, but just another man, a little confused, a little uncertain now that he was removed from the accustomed security of his narrow treadmill. And with this shrinking stature came a deep affection. He put his arm around his father's shoulders—a thing he had never done before—and found that he was taller than his father. Schwabacker said, "It's all right, sir." His smile was an added assurance.

"What are you going to do now?" Henrietta said. "If you return to Kearny, I'm coming with you. Emil, we'll never be apart again."

"I don't think I'll return to Kearny," he said. "I'm going to request a year's leave of absence and go back East. It'll take me three months to bone up on my medical studies, then seven more months and I'll graduate. I want to be a doctor, Henrietta. I'll make a good doctor."

A frown crossed her forehead. "You're giving up the army?"

"No," he said. "I love the army. But I want to be a military surgeon. There's work here, my kind of work. It's where I belong, with men like Jocelyn and Finnegan." He looked at her. "Do you mind? The army is dull; you saw what the frontier can be like."

"I'll never complain," she said. "Never, Emil."

Impatience was upon him then. "I'll have to tell Jocelyn, and thank him for letting me command his troop." He stepped away from her but she took his arm and pulled him back.

"He won't want you to thank him," Henrietta said softly. "Emil, you're the equal to any man on earth. From this day on every man in that troop will look around when Jocelyn gives a command and wonder if that's the way you would have given it. There are no more ghosts to fight, Emil. The battle's over."

"Yes," he said. "I guess it is."

Then he took his father's arm, and his fiancée's, and together they walked out into the drenching sunlight.

Center Point Publishing
600 Brooks Road ● PO Box 1
Thorndike ME 04986-0001 USA

(207) 568-3717

US & Canada:
1 800 929-9108